Impostor

A Genealogical Mystery

by

Richard Davidson

Imp Mysteries Volume 3

Books by Richard Davidson:

Self-help:
DECISION TIME! Better Decisions for a Better Life

Mysteries:
The Lord's Prayer Mystery Series
Lead Us Not into Temptation
Give Us this Day Our Daily Bread
Forgive Us Our Trespasses
Thy Will Be Done
Deliver Us from Evil

Imp Mysteries:
Implications
Impulses
Impostor

Anthology: (Editor)
Overcoming: An Anthology by the Writers of OCWW

"Impostor," by Richard Davidson
ISBN 978-0-9829160-9-4
A Genealogical Mystery

Manufactured in the United States of America

*This book is dedicated to Robert Audstut Dairdsa,
born, baptized, and deceased 20 July 1896.*

CHAPTER 1 – SURPRISE

He slammed his fist against the top of the kitchen table, splashing overflows from both of their coffees. "That's impossible!"

The furor of Jeremy's reaction shocked Debbie, requiring her to refocus mentally before beginning her explanation. She knew that the endurance of their current live-in long-term relationship might depend on this discussion. "I'm as surprised as you are, Jeremy, but I checked my findings through four different document sources."

"You'd better check three more sources, before you tell me that I don't exist."

"Of course you exist, and you're the center of my existence too, but you're not the Jeremy Hadley you thought you were." She walked behind his chair and started to massage his shoulders.

A slight smile flickered across his lips as he patted her hand and then swiveled his chair to face her. "This has to be the most ridiculous conversation I ever heard. I'll try to be patient, but you'll have to tell me the whole story."

"Just so you don't take out your anger on me. Meditate on that old quotation about not shooting the messenger while I fill you in."

"You have my complete attention. I hope your story makes sense."

Debbie Danforth pushed her hair back from her face and took a deep breath before she started. "This year, we'll celebrate our second Christmas together, and I wanted to have a special present for you. Given my background in academic library research, I decided to track down both of our family trees. I thought they'd look great as a piece of graphic art over our fireplace after we get married."

"A bit presumptuous, but please continue."

"For your family's tree, I asked your mother for data. She gave me info and leads for her side, but said that she didn't know much about your dad's parents. She said that your dad's father passed away when you were quite young, and your dad's mother left home when your father was a young child. After searching through some old papers, she found that your dad's father's name was Stephen Albert Hadley."

"That's right, and Grandma's name was Celia. I knew their names even though I never met them. I don't see anything unusual so far."

"I'm glad you're calmer now. Your mother found an old sheet of paper that said your great-grandfather's name was Michael Farrell Hadley, and that he was born on 17 April 1914 in London, England."

"I'm with you so far. Where's the problem?"

"The problem is that Michael Farrell Hadley was born on that April date in London and died the same day. The baby didn't survive. Your great-grandfather came along later and assumed the name of a stillborn infant. I was a bit clumsy with my words before. Your family obviously exists, but you're real name is not Hadley."

CHAPTER 2 – FAMILY FABRIC

The Hadleys considered themselves a typical Midwestern American family. Jeremy's father, Walter, a small businessman, had started Hadley's Bakery and Catering Company with funds raised by selling the family's second car. Jeremy's mother, Shirley, was the secretary at Parkville United Methodist Church, Parkville being a far northwestern exurb of Chicago, Illinois. Jeremy and Debbie, not officially engaged, lived and worked together as private detectives, operating out of their apartment as the Sandley Agency. They formed this company to assist Pastor Arthur Blake and his wife Irma during their complex investigations, but now it appeared that Jeremy and Debbie had their own mystery to solve, with or without assistance from the Blakes.

The degree of difficulty of the family background investigation would depend on how much Walter Hadley knew about his ancestry. Given that his father had died almost twenty years ago, and that his mother left home when he was still a young child without siblings, Walter was the only known living person who had a direct connection to earlier Hadley generations. Debbie's disruptively seismic genealogical findings would produce an aftershock when Walter returned home after work.

CHAPTER 3 – WALTER HADLEY

Walter felt that his workday had lasted forever. The early morning visit by Mrs. Olson to pick up her husband's retirement cake had been a disaster. Walter's assistant had inadvertently decorated the cake with her husband's name misspelled as *Ocsar* instead of *Oscar*. Mrs. Olson would not settle for their reworking the frosting and decorative words. Per her insistence, they rushed to bake, decorate, and deliver a second cake in time for the noon luncheon. Later, just as they had started to get back on schedule, a contractor crashed his pickup truck into a neighborhood utility pole at twenty-three minutes before three o'clock, stopping all electrical devices. They had to close until electricity returned shortly after four-thirty. Walter worked beyond his normal quitting time to compensate for time lost during the outage, and as he arrived home, he promised himself he would start heating the ovens extra early in the morning to be sure he'd have enough pastry for the breakfast rush.

He had just placed his jacket on the hook inside the front closet door when Shirley intercepted him.

"We've been waiting for you. Debbie and Jeremy are here, and they say we need to have a family meeting. They're in the living room. I made you sandwiches to eat in there."

"What's this meeting about? I've had a terrible day; can it wait?"

"They haven't given me any details, but Jeremy says it's urgent. My guess is that they're either engaged or breaking up. We have to support them, whatever's happening."

Walter agreed, noting that Shirley's graying hair had halfway unraveled from her normal tightly wound top-knot hairstyle. Her willingness to disregard repair of her hairdo before gathering with others emphasized the importance of this meeting to her.

They entered the living room, greeted Debbie and Jeremy, and retreated to the couch to await the urgent announcements. Shirley sat on the forward edge of her cushion, anticipating either the best or worst of news. Walter tried to look dignified while shoving chicken salad sandwiches into his mouth. In between bites he asked, "What's happening?"

Jeremy took the lead because they would be talking about his family. "Mom, Dad, we have a bit of a crisis, and we'll need your assistance to try to resolve it. It has to do with information Debbie discovered when she was researching our family tree for a Christmas artwork she planned to give me."

Shirley breathed an audible sigh of relief. "Then this isn't about your relationship. You two are still doing well together?"

Jeremy smiled. "The two of us are still very much in tune with each other, Mom. This meeting is about Debbie's genealogy findings."

Walter smiled as much as he could while finishing his second sandwich. "Does it turn out that we have a skeleton in our family closet?"

"That's a partially correct guess, Dad. According to Debbie's results, we may not even own that family closet you mentioned. Tell me what you know about your father's father, my great-grandfather Hadley."

Walter took a long drink of iced tea before responding. "I know next to nothing about him. My dad would discuss almost anything with me, but he avoided any revelations about his parents. I guessed that they had been a couple of drunks and that he had grown up with little or no assistance from them. Dad told me that he ran away from home at the age of sixteen, as soon as he could get a work permit and a job. He never tried to reconnect with his parents, and he changed the subject whenever we discussed them. I couldn't turn to my mother as an alternate source for family information because she left home when I was only two years old. She gave birth to me before she was mature enough to handle the responsibility of raising a child. Why do you care about Dad's parents now, and what's the nature of that crisis you mentioned?"

Jeremy nodded to Debbie, indicating he wanted her to answer the question. "I discovered while doing my genealogy research that your father's father, Michael Farrell Hadley, was someone from a different family who assumed that identity. The original Michael Farrell Hadley didn't survive childbirth. He was born and died on the same day, April 17, 1914."

Shirley looked shocked. "Are you sure that there weren't two people with the same name born on that date?"

"There was only one Michael Farrell Hadley born in London, England on April 17, 1914, and he did not survive."

Walter leaned against the back of the sofa. "You're saying that my father wouldn't discuss his parents because they were impostors, not because they were abusive toward him."

Jeremy said, "They may have been both impostors and abusive, Dad."

Walter set aside the remains of his rushed supper. "Let me play the Devil's Advocate for a moment. The year 1914 was more than a century ago. Why should his identity affect our family now?"

Shirley said, "You can play at being philosophical all you want, Walter, but I know you're proud of the family name. You made me take a picture of you next to the town sign in Hadley, Massachusetts when we were on vacation. You wouldn't be happy if it turned out that your grandfather was a criminal."

"We don't know that's the case, Shirley. There could be some other reason for this apparent disruption to our family line. Maybe it was a simple clerical mistake. In those days, they didn't have computers. Handwritten records could have been difficult to read, or someone may have entered correct information on the wrong form line. I'm still the same person I was an hour ago."

Debbie fished a notebook out of her shoulder bag. She leafed through the pages until she found the one she wanted. "I agree that handwritten records are not always accurate. However, I found four separate sources that cited the birth and death of Michael Farrell Hadley on 17 April 1914. They can't all be incorrect."

Jeremy raised his hand in a traffic cop's stop signal. "We don't know that Great-grandfather Hadley was a criminal. There are other possible explanations for this side-branching of the Hadley family tree. I accept Debbie's documentation that it did occur, and I intend to discover what happened. I call myself a private detective, so now I'm going to learn whether I'm good at my occupation."

Debbie hugged him. "Correction – we're going to find out how good we are at this detecting business."

CHAPTER 4 – TIME LAPSE

By nine o'clock the next morning, Jeremy and Debbie were prepared to begin their new quest. They sat side-by-side at the dining room table, each facing a laptop computer.

Debbie placed a pad of paper on the table between them. She divided the top sheet into three columns: *date*, *event*, and *source*. "I think the first thing we have to discover about your mysterious great-grandfather is when he first assumed the Michael Farrell Hadley name. I presume there will be a significant gap between the real baby's birth/death date and later uses of his name. That timing might give us a clue as to the event or events that triggered his identity change."

"That sounds reasonable to me. I looked up and printed a list of databases that are widely used in genealogical research. Let's each search one, checking it off, and then we'll repeat with different sources until we've studied them all or until we've reached a conclusion about the timing of the first uses of the name after the death of the infant. Will that procedure work for you, Debbie?"

"That's a reasonable approach. I'll start with naturalization records, looking for when the family came over to the United States. I'm assuming that our culprit became Michael Farrell Hadley in England and came to America later. If I don't find anything, we'll have to assume that he was American from birth."

Jeremy stared at her. "I'm not sure I can agree with you on that one. He could have been an illegal immigrant or a refugee after the Second World War. So many people without official papers came in then, that paper trails became difficult to follow."

"If you think that's difficult, Jeremy, consider our being faced with hundreds or thousands of records for Michael Hadley without inclusion of his unusual middle name. I just searched on Google for the simplified version, Michael Hadley, and received more than fourteen million results. The name is quite common."

"We'll have to try to narrow down the results by looking in restricted time periods. Your results on Google are starting to make me feel pessimistic about our chances for success. How many Michael Farrell Hadley's did you find?"

"A big zero – Google doesn't look at old records the way genealogical sources do."

"Go ahead and start your search, Debbie. I have an idea that may lead us to a shortcut. Give me a little while to test my theory."

The room quieted except for keyboard clicks as they began to attack their challenging puzzle. Thirty minutes into their quest, their faces still displayed tight-lipped expressions.

An undetermined number of minutes later, Jeremy raised his head and looked at Debbie. "I think I've found something."

CHAPTER 5 – ARTHUR AND IRMA

Pastor Arthur Blake and his wife Irma, a semi-retired forensic pathologist, had solved many mysteries working both as a two-person team and in conjunction with their associates in local police and federal agencies. Arthur had recently embarked on a leave of absence from the Northern Illinois Conference of the United Methodist Church. He hoped that this unstructured period would serve to clarify his thinking regarding the degree to which he wanted to maintain his church pastoral ties in the future.

He hadn't always been a clergyman. He started his career as an aerospace engineer for NASA. Having made one mid-course correction to his career, Arthur knew that he could successfully maneuver his way through a second transition. The truth was that his involvement in several investigations of crimes and criminal conspiracies while serving as pastor of Parkville United Methodist Church in Parkville, Illinois had already convinced him that his future calling was that of consulting criminologist. Up to this point, he had suppressed that conclusion by publically claiming that he preferred his investigative interests to be a part-time avocation.

Arthur didn't fool Irma. She knew from the moment she resigned as County Medical Examiner that they would eventually marry and share their investigative pursuits as they moved forward into an unknown but exciting future. Guiding Arthur away from the restrictions of church discipline and hierarchy had required deftness and subtlety, but Irma now saw freedom and a common purpose on their joint horizon.

Their future would begin with a true vacation. They would grow still closer through sharing some time apart from their friends and colleagues. Only the selection of their destination stood in their way.

Irma tacked a map of the United States of America onto a bulletin board and placed it on an artist's easel in the front parlor of their century-old Queen Anne style home. When Arthur returned from his Saturday morning errands, she would insist that they choose their vacation location.

An hour later, the two of them stood in front of the map display as Irma explained their need to make a prompt destination decision.

Arthur smiled at the display. "I'll be back in three minutes, prepared to make a decision."

When Arthur returned, he was holding something behind his back.

"What are you up to? No more delays; we have to decide where we're going."

"I agree." Arthur pulled his left hand from behind his back, revealing the two darts he held in his hand. "I like your setup of the map spread over a bulletin board. We can make a prompt decision by throwing darts at the map, and they'll stick into the bulletin board."

"Is this your idea of a joke?"

"Nope, I'm serious. Shall we each throw one and then negotiate between the two locations selected?"

"No way, Arthur – if you want to have your fun, go right ahead. I'll live with your dart-throwing result. Let's see what the fates have in store for us."

Arthur lined up his dart stance with the map. Then he covered his eyes with his left hand and launched the dart in a soft arc toward the map. After hearing it strike the map, he opened his eyes and stared at the point where the dart protruded from the map.

CHAPTER 6 – PROGRESS

"What did you find, Jeremy?"

"I decided to approach the great-grandfather issue through his son, my grandfather, Stephen Albert Hadley."

"And what did you learn about Stephen?"

"I learned that he was born in 1938 in Bridgeport, Connecticut. He was born in the USA and, consequently, was a citizen from birth."

Debbie wrote that information into her notebook. "That doesn't tell us anything about Stephen's father, Michael Farrell Hadley, the man who stole the identity of that infant."

"It says that since my great-grandfather assumed the identity of a British person, while my grandfather was born American, Great-grandpa would likely have become a naturalized citizen after arriving in the US. His naturalization record would likely be in a year close to 1938, when his son was born."

"Following your logic, we have also learned that Michael Farrell Hadley would have also become an American citizen before his son, Stephen, was born."

"Sorry, Debbie, that assumption isn't valid. A person born in the USA is a citizen even if his parents aren't. That brings me to observing that we have absolutely no information on Stephen's mother. Her nationality is unknown."

"You're right, Jeremy. I'll look for Michael's naturalization record, while you try to find something about his wife. You might locate some family documents beyond what your mother gave me."

"I'll call Dad and ask about that, but he said that his father, Stephen, refused to talk about his parents."

Jeremy went into the kitchen to place his call while Debbie turned to the naturalization records. *At least this process is simpler than it was before the coming of personal computers.* Thirty minutes later, she thought, *but not much simpler. Almost all the records of that period were handwritten. I can find the batch of records by computer, but I still have to examine each individual line the old-fashioned way.*

CHAPTER 7 – DARTPOINT

Irma stared at the entry point of the dart into the map. "Did you have your eyes open and aim for that point? I can't believe this is your randomly selected destination?"

"I swear, my eyes were closed and covered. Are you willing to go there?"

"Of course I am. Who doesn't like Miami Beach? The holy pastor may run into a few sinful folks there. How do you feel about that?"

"That's what pastors like most. It's more fun than preaching to the choir. When would you like to leave?"

Irma teased Arthur by holding her long hair across the lower portion of her face like a mysterious veil. "Give me a day to pack and to find a sitter for Rex. Then we'll be off to adventures beyond our wildest dreams. You haven't seen my new bikini."

"I feel dazzled already. You'll fit right in with all of those young bodies on South Beach. I'll make the plane and hotel reservations."

CHAPTER 8 – ARRANGEMENTS

When Irma visited Penny Gonzalez, her close friend who, with her husband Joe, ran a small, unpublicized federal investigative agency, she received the pleasant news that they were currently between major cases. Penny said that she and Joe would be at home in Parkville, Illinois for at least the next month and would be happy to care for Rex, the Blakes' golden retriever. They considered Rex both an old friend and a fellow investigator who had helped solve a major mystery before he joined the Blake household.

After receiving this welcome news, Irma said, "You sound as though you know the nature of your next assignment, Penny. Is it something that might justify an assist from us? Arthur's leave of absence allows us to take this vacation, but it's also aimed at allowing us to spend more time on casework."

"We'll have more than enough on our plates for you to work with us, Irma. We're in the early research phase of trying to put some identity fraud people out of business. The problem of identity theft is much too big for any one agency to handle, so the FBI is subcontracting one thorny batch of cases to us. There are enough similarities between the victims' situations to suggest that a single group is behind them all."

"We'll look forward to that challenge. In the meantime, I have to tackle our travel arrangements and drive over to Sycamore to practice my swimming at the YMCA pool. Arthur and I have never gone swimming together, and I want to be sure he doesn't make me look bad when we get to Florida."

Penny patted her friend on the shoulder. "Don't sweat it too much, Irma. Most of the ocean beaches are so crowded that you'll mostly wade and watch other people."

"That's my concern. I want him to look at me, and not a lot of younger females."

"If he looks but doesn't touch, you'll be fine. You may not be as young, but you're still sleek. Arthur will only have eyes for you."

"I'll keep telling myself that. Thanks for the vote of confidence. I'll bring Rex and his supplies over here this evening."

CHAPTER 9 – STEP TWO

Debbie looked up from her computer as Jeremy entered the room. "What did you find?"

"I called Dad and asked him whether he had any memories about my Great-grandmother, especially her name."

"And did he?"

"He stared off into space for a while and then suggested that it might have been Annemarie or Annie but he said that those names came to him out of thin air, and he wasn't sure why. He did say that he thought A was the initial letter of her name."

"So you worked with those possibilities and found what?"

"As might be expected, I found that there were a large number of Hadleys with these names, Annemarie being less popular than Annie. Some of them had interesting stories, but I wasn't able to identify which one, if any, was my great-grandmother. I learned about some interesting people, but I'll call that effort a strikeout. Are you making any better progress?"

"You might say that. Our goal has been to find why and when your great-grandfather took the place of a stillborn infant named Michael Farrell Hadley who was born and died on 17 April 1914 in London, England."

"That's a fair statement. Why are you smiling like the Cheshire Cat?"

"I didn't get answers to the why and when of the substitution, but I did learn something interesting, assuming your great-grandfather came to America to live and work at some time. I'm smiling because I checked the

Social Security Death Index, and it does not include an entry for Michael Farrell Hadley. That suggests that either someone has manipulated his data to keep people from finding it, or that he is still alive somewhere."

Jeremy stared at her. "If he were still alive and was born in 1914, he would be a hundred and two years old."

"That's possible, except he could be a few years younger if he took the place of someone who was several years older than him. No one would have caught that minor difference in age if he took the Hadley name when he was an adult."

"We'll worry about his age later. Our next challenge will be to find out whether he's dead but undocumented or still among the living. Debbie, I feel energized by your discovery. I might actually meet him."

CHAPTER 10 – PENNY AND JOE

The federal agency that Penny and Joe Gonzalez led did not appear on any official government organization charts. The sign on the door of their Washington offices identified their group as the publishers of the *Trading Trends Newsletter*. Two women in the front office actually distributed that monthly periodical in between their classified data analysis activities. The small and invisible group offered consulting services to assist larger agencies during overload periods. However, its primary function was to handle sensitive cases requiring undocumented investigations that would evade the regulations of the Freedom of Information Act. Certain high-ranking members of the government's Executive Branch also referred special covert assignments to this agency that they swore did not exist.

During earlier cases when Pastor Arthur Blake and forensic pathologist Irma Custis assisted Penny and Joe under the guise of ABC Consultants, the pair had suggested that Penny and Joe could trade their Washington apartment for a home anywhere in the country. The Gonzalezes eventually took that step, opting to live near Arthur and Irma in the village of Parkville, Illinois, due to the several cases that had originated in Arthur's church activities. The Blakes and the Gonzalezes drew on this geographical proximity to continue building a close personal relationship that enhanced their professional ties. The closeness of the two couples made it completely natural for Penny to offer to care for Rex while the Blakes were on vacation and for Joe to drive Irma and

Arthur to Chicago for their departure at O'Hare International Airport.

As they approached the terminals and drove toward the departure entry for their airline, Joe said, "Remember, Arthur, when you return, just phone or text ahead, and I'll meet you down on the arrivals level."

"You don't have to disrupt your schedule, Joe. We can rent a car and drop it off at Hertz in Parkville after we get home."

"I insist on giving you the full blue ribbon service. By the time you return, we may have started on a new case that you'll want to hear about. My driving will allow me to update you on everything that happened during your absence. I know the two of you well enough to predict you'll want to get a running start toward re-entering the world of investigations."

Irma said, "Don't object, Arthur. He's right. We'll have a better vacation if we clear our minds of casework and then let Joe bring us up to date when we return. I accept your offer on behalf of both of us, Joe. If the timing is at all convenient, we'll call you."

When they parked at the curb and opened the trunk to retrieve their luggage, Arthur whispered to Joe, "Thanks for everything. I'm going to let Irma take the lead on arrangements and I'll be the obedient pack mule with the luggage. She's looking forward to this bit of carefree adventure, and I don't want to cloud her expectations in any way. We'll bring you folks some souvenirs when we return."

CHAPTER 11 – HELP WANTED

Joe walked into the house through the kitchen after parking his car in the garage. He was about to shout out to Penny that he was back from the airport, when the telephone rang. Joe waited to see whether Penny would answer it and relaxed when the ringing stopped. Then he walked into the front hallway, where he petted Rex who jumped up from his cushion bed to greet him. He played with the golden retriever until Penny finished her phone conversation and joined them.

"You two look as though you're having fun. Keep this up, and we'll be discussing the prospect of a dog of our own."

"That thought crossed my mind, Penny. Who was on the telephone?"

"That was Jeremy Hadley calling. We haven't seen much of him since ABC Consultants days when he worked with the Blakes. He and his girlfriend Debbie Danforth are private detectives now, operating as the Sandley Agency. They have a case that might benefit from our input, so I invited them to come over and discuss it with us."

"Shades of Arthur and Irma Blake ... No sooner do we send one pair of our cohorts off on vacation, than they're replaced by their younger protégées."

"That's an interesting point, Joe. We'll have to see how similar the two couples are in the way they attack a case."

About an hour later, the front doorbell rang. Joe opened the door and greeted Jeremy, who introduced him to Debbie. Joe made a mental note that beyond her physical attractiveness, this young woman's penetrating gaze seemed to strip a person of defensive guile and perform an instant diagnosis of his or her capabilities. He would not want the assignment of deceiving her.

"Welcome to both of you. We'll head for our family room for an informal conversation instead of sitting around a table. Penny has some pastry, coffee, and soft drinks in there to keep us well-nourished while we talk."

They walked through the dining room and kitchen to reach the family room and found Penny already sitting there with a cup of coffee. She rose to meet the newcomers. "Hi, Jeremy, it's good to see you again. You must be Debbie; I'm looking forward to getting to know you too. Arthur mentioned your new detective agency, but I hadn't realized how soon we would have the opportunity to learn more about it."

They all grabbed drinks and pastry before settling down. Then Debbie gave a brief nod to Jeremy, and he led off the discussion.

"This may be a little unusual, but our new Sandley Agency is here to ask for your assistance in investigating me, or at least my family. It appears that we aren't really Hadleys at all. Debbie will summarize what we've discovered up to this point."

Debbie proceeded to go over their sequence of discoveries, covering everything from the stillborn ancestor to the possibility that Jeremy's great-grandfather might still be alive, although possibly more than one hundred years old.

Penny and Joe listened intently and made a few notes. Then Penny asked, "Are you looking for guidance, for our unofficial support, or are you here to convince us that your investigation justifies official federal assistance?"

Jeremy leaned forward on his chair. "I hadn't thought about your latter option, but this might indeed fall within federal jurisdiction. We're talking about a person of unknown origin, who assumed the identity of a British citizen, and then used that identity to come over here and presumably qualify to be naturalized as a citizen of the United States. We don't yet know whether he fraudulently claimed benefits, such as social security, but that question would be a federal matter. I suspect that there would have been a perjury, fraud, or criminal aspect to the original identity change."

Debbie squeezed Jeremy's shoulder. "I appreciate your trying to justify jurisdiction for Penny and Joe, but you might want to refrain from pegging your great-grandfather as a criminal."

Penny laughed. "Everyone relax. This is just an informal session. Nothing anyone says here will be on the record. Jeremy, your great-grandfather has an interesting personal history. There could be any number of reasons for someone to want to assume a new identity and steal an available one from a stillborn infant. What do you think about this genealogical discovery, Joe?"

"The switch must have occurred sometime between the arrival of that baby in 1914 and the birth of Walter's father, Stephen in 1938. That's essentially the interval between the beginnings of the First and Second World Wars. I wonder whether it had anything to do with either of them."

Debbie said, "What about the fact that I couldn't find Michael Farrell Hadley in the Social Security Death Index? Does that mean that he's still alive?"

Joe said, "It might, but it also might mean that he never registered for Social Security, or that he left the country at some point and didn't claim eligibility."

Jeremy stood and stared out the window. "You raise a complicating point, Joe. The last contact the family had with him was when my grandfather Stephen left home in 1954. He may have decided to go to another country. That would really make tracking him difficult."

"I was just speculating when I said that, Jeremy. If Penny doesn't object, I believe we could at least get involved to the extent of checking a few government databases, such as Social Security and immigration records to see whether your great-grandfather legally entered this country and remained here during his senior years."

Penny said, "That's a reasonable approach, Joe. We'll look in a few of the obvious places for his paper trail. That may be all that's required. If we aren't able to track him in that way, we'll have to decide whether to get more sophisticated in our attempts to discover details about him. Give us a week for the preliminary inquiries, and then we'll meet with you again to give you our findings."

Jeremy shook hands with Penny and Joe. "I appreciate your help. This business of not being the person I thought I was has me on edge. I don't even know what I have to offer Debbie with this confused family background."

Debbie said, "You're still the same lout I fell for. Don't think you're going to wriggle out of our relationship on a technicality. We'll see this investigation through to the end, but even if we learn nothing, you're stuck with me."

CHAPTER 12 – PRELIMINARY RESULTS

Four days after the meeting at Penny and Joe's house, Debbie answered the telephone and heard Penny's voice. "I don't know whether I should feel disappointed about the lack of difficulty, but we have some results for you way ahead of schedule. We'll come over to your apartment with them in an hour, if that's convenient."

"That's great news. We'll be ready for you."

Debbie ran down the stairs to the parking lot, where Jeremy was washing their cars. She waved to him, and gestured for him to come to her.

"Is there a problem, Debbie? I'm almost done."

"You'll have to finish later. Penny and Joe are coming over with some preliminary results regarding your great-grandfather. Penny sounded as though we should expect a surprise."

"What do you mean by that?"

"She sounded like a poker player who wanted you to believe she had a mediocre hand but couldn't keep from showing her excitement."

They went upstairs to their apartment and did a quick cleanup of the living room. Debbie took out two platters. On the smaller one, she arranged the remaining half of a box of chocolate chip cookies. On the larger one, she spread some cut raw vegetables: celery, red peppers, and green onions. It wasn't fancy, but it would be enough. She had made a pot of coffee just before Penny called, and she had a few soft drinks and beers in the refrigerator. They were ready for company.

Ten minutes later, the doorbell rang. Jeremy buzzed his guests through the downstairs security door and waited for them in the hallway. Following greetings all around, they gathered in the living room.

Jeremy said, "Debbie tells me that you found information about my great-grandfather ahead of schedule. That's impressive. Your request for a special early meeting suggests that your findings are important. Are you about to tell me whether he was a criminal or a saint?"

Joe removed a small notebook from his pocket. "Before I touch on the question of conclusions, let me tell you what we found. First, Michael Farrell Hadley became a citizen of the United States in early 1938, about one and one half years after coming here from England. He had dual citizenship, carrying both British and American passports. Although the British went to war with Germany in 1939, the government there never called him up for military service. He never registered for the draft with Selective Service in the United States. We have no record of him having been in either the British or the American military services during World War II. We also found no records of his having used his passports during that war." Joe stopped speaking and looked at Jeremy as though he was expecting him to comment.

When Jeremy didn't react to Joe's cue, Debbie said, "I conclude from Joe's findings that Michel Farrell Hadley either remained a civilian living in the United States for the duration of the war, or he was an intelligence operative working for both Britain and the United States. I suspect the latter possibility is most likely."

Jeremy scanned his eyes from Debbie to Joe and back again. "I'm beginning to understand. The fact that neither country called him up for military service suggests that they didn't want him in the military because they had other work for him."

Penny contributed, "Add to that his having required a shorter than two year waiting period for naturalization to

US citizenship, and I see the hand of the federal government manipulating his course."

Joe looked at Debbie. "Do you want to draw the next linked conclusion in this chain of events, or should I?"

"I'll take it, Joe. Thanks for your vote of confidence. "Michael's arrival in the US in 1936, three years before Britain went to war with Germany, suggests to me that his assignment here was planned by the man in Parliament without an official government office, who was invisibly and unofficially preparing for war and who, while pushing for Britain to have increased military capabilities, was developing his own network of agents. I suggest that Michael Farrell Hadley worked for Winston Churchill."

Penny, Joe, and Jeremy all stared at her as if shocked by her words. Then Joe said, "That was a long leap of faith. I expected you to say that the next logical conclusion was that since Michael didn't use his passports during the war, he carried out his assignments under a different name. I never saw the possibility of a Churchill connection."

Penny said, "It's more than a possibility, Joe. It's quite likely. Churchill wanted his country to be ready when the inevitable war came. He had no official power, but he had friends in high places in the governments of both countries. By sending Michael to the US and arranging for him to be fast-tracked for citizenship there, Churchill started an active project that the British governments of Prime Minister Stanley Baldwin and his successor, Neville Chamberlain, couldn't stop. It would have been so small and hidden that the American isolationists wouldn't have had any reason to interfere with it either. Thanks for your insight, Debbie. The Churchill connection makes a lot of sense; right, Jeremy?"

"The Churchill connection means that whatever assignment my great-grandfather had, it was important."

CHAPTER 13 – POSTWAR QUESTIONS

Jeremy looked over the notes he had taken. "Joe, you said that Michael never used his Hadley passports during World War II. How soon after the war did he go back to using them?"

"He used his British passport once in November of 1945, for a trip from England to France and back again. He used his US passport in November of 1946 to travel from England to America and for a round trip between the USA and Argentina in 1953. After that, he used his American passport only three times, but he kept it renewed, presumably because he thought he might do unexpected international traveling."

Debbie raised her index finger as if to add one more thing to the conversation. "Passport use wouldn't be significant if he had a third passport under a different identity or was involved with the military. I don't think that troops landing in other countries worried about passports."

Jeremy said, "I thought we concluded that he probably wasn't in the military."

"Civilian officials traveling with the military would not need official permissions for cross-border travel either. During the war, everything was done differently. Penny, did you run across anything that indicated his occupation?"

"I did, Debbie. According to the 1940 Census, Michael Farrell Hadley was a writer, and he lived with his wife, Stephanie, and his son, Stephen, at 88 Manhattan Avenue, Bridgeport, Connecticut."

"That suggests that Jeremy's grandfather, Stephen, was named after his mother, Stephanie. That's interesting, because Stephen grew up wanting nothing to do with his parents. Penny, why do you think they decided to live in Bridgeport?"

"That's an easy one, Debbie. They were living in the house that had been home to Stephanie all her life. She moved in with her parents while Michael was in England, presumably doing journalistic work. Early in 1940, her mother died from pneumonia, and later that year Stephanie's father decided he missed his wife too much to keep living without her. He rowed a mile out into the Atlantic Ocean and jumped overboard. According to the newspaper article I found, he wanted to be far enough out that he couldn't change his mind and swim to shore. Stephanie inherited the family's house."

Jeremy stood and started to pace back and forth. "Don't mind my moving around while I talk, but it helps my nerves. You guys mentioned my great-grandfather's return to America after the war using his American passport. I have to question where he had been. You already indicated he wasn't in the military."

Penny said, "He definitely didn't serve in the military for either England or the United States, but he may have used military service as a cover story for being away so long. One possibility is that he arranged for the family to receive periodic letters from an Army unit to which he supposedly belonged. Soldiers weren't allowed to write home about where they were or their battles, so he could have easily prepared letters in advance to be occasionally posted on his behalf by someone else. Michael may have been in England, or may have traveled to any number of other locations from England."

"In other words, you're suggesting that my great-grandfather was a spy and that some hireling in a government agency had the assignment of convincing his family that Michael Farrell Hadley was overseas in the Army or Navy. The U.S. didn't have a separate Air Force until after the war ended. Did you find out where he actually was and what he was doing there?"

Joe said, "Be a little more diplomatic about the value of hirelings in government agencies, Jeremy. In response to your question, we have no idea what Michael did during the war. The records may be in British classified libraries to which we don't have access. All I can say is that it must have been important. They've declassified all of the documents about mundane missions. I'll guess that he did something that should make your family proud."

CHAPTER 14 – A LONG TIME AGO

The driver of the long black Jaguar would not respond to his questions about their destination or the identity of the person who had requested a meeting with him. When they exited his flat, they encountered an excited mob of neighbors surrounding the new 1936 limousine. The crowd circulated around the vehicle examining the large headlights and wing-mounted spare tires, while peering through the windscreen to see the interior. The chauffeur's authoritative bearing parted the onlookers, as he guided his passenger to the rear door. Upon entering the vehicle, the passenger admitted to himself that the car equally impressed him. This whole scene was out of kilter.

Why would anyone with a limousine and a uniformed chauffeur even know about him? He was nothing but a smooth-talking orphan who had run into trouble with the law. It happened when he tried to impress a slightly older woman at a party by pretending to be an Oxford graduate. Everything went smoothly between them until she introduced him to her brother, a real Oxford scholar who asked detailed questions about the university that he couldn't answer. He hadn't expected any legal consequences from his deception, but it turned out that the brother had a relative at the party who was a police superintendant. Said relative decided to teach him a lesson by means of several days in jail.

After traveling nearly two hours, first on wide carriageways and then on narrow byways, the driver turned the Jaguar into a long tree-lined private lane as the sun began to set. When they emerged from the trees, he saw that the car was approaching an imposing country house of traditional design and obvious age. They followed a circular drive to the massive front entrance and parked. The chauffeur opened the rear door and escorted him to the building entry, where a butler awaited them. Then the driver departed. He was uncertain about what awaited him inside the building, but was determined to carry off this encounter as though he really were someone of substance.

The butler ushered him into the library and requested that he remain there, awaiting his host. The butler also stated that he would return shortly with tea.

As he waited, he studied the books on the shelves. *This person must be serious about life. Most of these volumes deal with history, philosophy, warfare, and politics. I'll have to avoid making jokes and defer to his leading the conversation.* He heard voices, apparently two men, approaching the room. The door opened. He was surprised that one of the newcomers bore a familiar face. That individual approached and shook his hand.

"Good afternoon, young man. I hope that we haven't kept you waiting too long."

The butler returned carrying a tray with an antique silver teapot and three cups. He placed his offering on a side table and left, closing the door behind him.

"No sir, I barely had time to scan the books in your library."

"Are you a reader?"

"I am, but my tastes are not as scholarly as yours, Mr. Churchill."

"So, you recognize me. Good, that indicates that you're aware of what goes on in public life. That will be valuable. With regard to my library, I do have to plod through some tiresome stuff at times. My associate is Thomas Hadley. I requested your presence here today because I think you might be suitable to take on an assignment for me, and if so, Hadley will be your mentor in preparing for it."

"I beg your pardon, Mr. Churchill, but how would you know whether I am suitable for anything. Do you know anything about me?"

"I know that you're an orphan without any family responsibilities that might bar you from taking on a special assignment. I know that you can take in stride imprisonment for at least several days without emotional reaction. I also know that you are convincing enough while assuming a false identity to fool my daughter, who is not easily tricked."

"She was your daughter ... I apologize; I had no way of knowing."

"There's no problem. She enjoyed the novelty of it and raved about your ability to deceive her. I have two questions for you. Had you rehearsed your Oxford impersonation or planned to use it at the party, and how did you develop your apparent qualifications for the part?"

"As I responded before, I am a reader, and I enjoy studying a wide variety of subjects. With regard to the character I assumed, I plead guilty to being somewhat manipulative. I became an Oxford scholar because I judged that such a person would be attractive to your daughter, although I did not know her identity at the time. Had I met a lady of letters, I would have been an author or perhaps a librarian."

Thomas Hadley gestured to Churchill that he would like to speak, and he received a nod in response. "Tell me; are you fluent in any languages other than English?"

"I have read books in French, Italian, and Spanish, but I am not fluent in any of those tongues. I could probably communicate well enough to survive if abandoned in any European country, but I would be an obvious foreigner. Why do you ask?"

Churchill responded, "You know who I am. I will assume that you also know something about my self-appointed unofficial mission to have our country prepared when war breaks out, as it almost certainly will. Others hold the major portfolios in our government, but I have hidden allies who are helping me to monitor the plans and strategies of this man, Hitler, who is and will be our enemy, no matter what Baldwin and Chamberlain say. I would like you to become one of my hidden people."

"But, why select me? I am no one. You have learnt things about me, but you haven't even used my name during our conversation."

Hadley said, "Please forgive me. Omitting your name was my suggestion. It does not appear in any of our notes in order to protect you. If you choose to refuse our invitation to become part of the effort, there will not be a record of our ever having approached you or even studied your background. Should you choose to join with us, we will give you a new identity that will serve you during the period of your education, training, and initial assignment. Once your mission becomes active, your identity may change again, to one of several for which we have people, even now, preparing documented histories."

"So, I'm to be a spy, and one who is not directly supported by the official intelligence agencies. Aren't you taking a great risk by selecting someone of my young age?"

Churchill laughed. "I told you he would be perceptive." He turned to the candidate. "You won't be the only arrow of this type in our quiver, but the connections among our people will be as invisible as possible. May we count on your participation in our mission?"

"I'd enroll, but from what you've said, I don't even know what name to sign."

Thomas Hadley said, "Welcome aboard, Michael Farrell Hadley. We're now kin, with you having assumed the identity of a stillborn baby in my family."

CHAPTER 15 – WALTER AND SHIRLEY

Walter Hadley sat in front of the fireplace studying, or at least contemplating, its flames. *How much should the details of your ancestry affect your outlook on life? Did he believe that someone descended from royalty could bake a cake any better than he could? That would be illogical, but he still had trouble accepting the fact that he wasn't a true Hadley.*

Shirley watched him from the doorway for several minutes before she made him aware of her presence. "Do you know that you're twitching periodically? Is something bothering you so much that it physically affects you?"

"It's that business about our family not being a branch of the Hadley family tree. It's hard to live most of your life with an outlook based on your assumed roots, only to find that you actually come from a different family, about which you know nothing."

"That is, but isn't true, Walter."

"What do you mean by that?"

"You and we are exactly the same people we were prior to learning about the dislocation in your ancestry. You never met your grandparents, so why should anything that happened to them bother you?"

"It does, and it should, because my sense of self worth would vary, depending on whether my grandfather turned out to have been a scoundrel or a hero. I also have spent my entire life with the self-image of being a Hadley, and now I know that I belong to a different, unknown family."

"You see something sinister in all of this because the news came so abruptly, but is it any different from the way you would feel upon learning that your father or grandfather had been adopted?"

"That's a valid line of thought, Shirley, but the difference is that people seek to adopt children and usually welcome them. It appears that my grandfather took the name of a stillborn baby without getting the family's permission. That's stealing for lack of a better word."

"I agree that we'd probably feel better about it if we knew the circumstances behind Grandfather's identity change. Is there any chance that you could come up with a time machine, so that we could go back to the key date and check the facts?"

"Thanks, Shirley that outrageous question makes me feel better. I might have to go and invent that time machine you mentioned. You also made me realize that I am indeed in the same position as a descendant of an adopted child. My situation isn't as unique as I originally thought. Until recently, laws kept adopted children and their families from ever learning the identities of the birth parents who gave the child away. Would you have married me if my family background had been less stable?"

"I decided to marry you long before I knew anything about your relatives. An alternate family background might have made the process more complex, but I was going to get you, no matter what. You had no choice, but you didn't realize it. These recent events change nothing. You're stuck with me. If you feel lost without a continuous family tree, we can use my maiden name and be Shirley and Walter Schmeddling."

He got up and hugged her tightly. "Thanks for the offer, but Hadley is our surname now and in the future, no matter what it was in the distant past."

CHAPTER 16 – THOMAS HADLEY

Thomas and the newly christened Michael Farrell Hadley toasted their future relationship over pints of Boddington's ale in the subdued back corner light of McReady's Iron Horse Pub across the street from the railway station. The clock above the dart board displayed three o'clock in the afternoon, a slack period between the more popular gathering times. The two Hadleys attracted little interest from either the few patrons in the front of the establishment or the proprietor. It took two rounds of libations and introductory conversation for them to loosen up with each other, but the inevitable transition occurred, facilitated by their mutual enjoyment of ale.

Thomas, being the appointed mentor, initiated the more serious discussion. "Michael, you've turned a corner in your life's journey, and you'll have to leave most of your past behind. You must always think of yourself as Michael and be ready to respond when someone unexpectedly calls you by that name or by Hadley. I'm your cousin, and I'm twenty-nine years of age to your twenty-two. Your parents are Gerald and Annie Hadley while mine are Rodney and Julia. Your mother, Annie, moved to Ireland after your father, Gerald, left home and went to Australia. You will not have to interact with your parents in person, but we'll expect you to maintain semi-regular correspondence with them to maintain the image of a dutiful son. I'll give you the addresses."

"How will my parents react to letters from a son they've never known?"

"The correspondents on the other ends will be members of the diplomatic community, proper indoctrinated, who will be acting unofficially based on personal connections to the old man."

"You mean Churchill."

Thomas laid his right hand on Michael's left wrist. "That will be the last time you refer to him by name. We have no official or unofficial connection in that quarter."

"In other words, anything I have to say or report stays within the family. I inform you and don't have to know about any other links in the communication chain. I assume that the sprinkling of correspondence with parents who never receive my letters serves as window dressing so that I'm more complex than a stick figure chess piece."

"Good; you learn fast."

"One thing bothers me, Thomas. We've protected my family by keeping them entirely out of the picture with my new identity. How will we protect the Hadleys if something goes wrong when I'm on assignment? As a new member of the family, I wouldn't want to create problems for you or the others."

"We'll protect the Hadley family the same way we're protecting your family."

"What do you mean?"

"You won't be a Hadley when you go on an assignment that involves any danger."

"... another layer on my background?"

"Perhaps several; the future remains shrouded in uncertainties."

"You're saying that me, myself, and I will all have different identities that I'll have to keep straight, depending on the circumstances."

"That's essentially it. Can you handle those complexities?"

"It will be like my being different people at different parties. So that's why you selected me."

"Your party performance with the old man's daughter gave us the idea."

Michael negatively shook his head. "I can improvise at a party, because I'm becoming someone who lives only in my imagination. The Hadleys are real people. You'll have to give me thorough coaching so that I'll know how to behave within the family. For instance, what's my occupation, and what's yours for that matter?"

Thomas retrieved a business card from his right-hand jacket pocket. "Allow me to introduce myself. I'm Thomas Hadley, Taxidermist, and I meet guild standards when I process wildlife. I have a small shop in a village near here, but I don't keep regular hours there."

"That's a convenient and slightly unique skill. What would you like me to be?"

Thomas removed a small stack of business cards from his left jacket pocket. "Here are your calling cards. There's a larger supply along with matching stationery in the office you will use for training purposes at the academy."

Michael read aloud, "Michael Farrell Hadley, Playwright and Journalist. I've never written a play."

Thomas said, "You wrote one for the old man's daughter, didn't you? It's best to keep your persona as close to reality as possible. You have the skills to play this role, and it's one that allows you to have an irregular schedule."

"I'll grant you that, but might it not suggest to someone I met on an assignment that I might not be what I seem?"

"You're forgetting that you'll be someone else when you do field work. Now, drink up, and we'll be on our way. I want you to meet your sister. You live with her."

CHAPTER 17 – ALICE

Thomas drove down rural roads traveling cross-country until he reached the village of Upper Benefield. Once there, he entered a long winding farm lane and stopped at a stone cottage on a land parcel behind and slightly to the left of one of the farmhouses. The lights in the cottage indicated that someone was at home. As they walked toward the door, Michael said, "Thomas, if you expect me to stay here, you'll have to get me a car. This is nowhere."

"I'll have one here for you tomorrow along with documents supporting your new identity. You won't need a car tonight. In case of emergency, Alice has a motorbike out back that she'll let you borrow."

As they reached the front door, Thomas extended his fist to knock, but the door opened inward before his knuckles could contact that wooden slab. A slender young woman with light brown hair greeted them.

"Good evening, Thomas. It's good to see you again. Come on inside."

They entered, and Thomas closed the door. "Hello, Alice. How's my favorite cousin? I've brought your brother, Michael, who has been in Scotland for the last year. He'll be living with you for several months while he receives training for his new assignment. I'm sure you two will have lots of family history to review. As I told Michael, someone will come by tomorrow to deliver a car for him to use while he is here."

She approached Michael and gave him a light kiss on the cheek. "As my brother, you rate a kiss, but Thomas, being a cousin, gets only a handshake."

Thomas reached for her outstretched hand and pulled on it, turning the expected handshake into a hug. "Alice is properly peeved at me for requesting changes to her normal routines. I'm sure you two will have a lot to discuss, Michael. Your wardrobe and other essentials will arrive with the car tomorrow, as will your training schedule and instructions."

Alice asked, "Can you stay for a while, Thomas?"

"I'd love to, but I have to go. I'll see you soon, Michael."

They walked out to the car with Thomas and then returned to the house as he drove away.

Michael put his jacket over a coat hook on the wall. "I hope this isn't a major imposition on you Alice. I do have one question. Are you my older or younger sister?"

"I'm your very slightly older sister, but thank you for suggesting I might be younger than you. I can see that we'll have to stay up late tonight so that I can give you at least a rough sketch of the family. There's fresh tea in the pot on the kitchen table. Grab some, and meet me by the fireplace. You'll sleep in the back bedroom, so feel free to look at it and leave your things there."

Michael walked to the rear of the cottage and entered the small corner bedroom. It contained a twin bed covered with a handmade eiderdown. An extra eiderdown and pillow sat on a card table. Two collapsed folding chairs leaning against the wall and a swing arm floor lamp completed the furniture. The room had no cupboard, but had empty shelves mounted on one wall that would serve for storage of clothing and other items. It was Spartan, but it would suit him adequately for the few months he would live here. Before returning to the front room and the planned fireplace session, Michael thought about the prospect of sharing the cottage with Alice Hadley. She was quite attractive in a small town way, if you looked past her severe hairstyle, overalls, and wellies. He was sure that their conversations about the Hadley family would prove stimulating and insightful. *If only they had appointed her to be his distant cousin instead of his sister ...*"

CHAPTER 18 – CLAN HADLEY

When Michael returned to the front room, he found Alice perched almost sideways on one end of the sofa. A tray bearing biscuits, cups, pots of tea and hot water, plus Nescafe instant coffee rested on a low table in front of the florally upholstered piece.

"I noticed that you didn't take the tea I left for you in the kitchen, so I added coffee to our menu. Which do you prefer?"

"I admit to being a bit non-traditional in my preference for coffee. If the Hadleys are devotees of tea, I'll switch. He mixed his instant coffee."

She waved him toward the other end of the sofa, where he settled mirror-imaged to her with his cup of coffee on his lap.

"Michael, blending you into the family will only work if you are relaxed about it. We Hadleys feel blessed to approach life informally. There are no ground rules for tea, coffee, or anything else. We reflect a wide range of views, and vary in how we value wealth. I am quite satisfied with this rural cottage, while Uncle Harold, our father's brother, needs the challenge of owning and operating a woolen mill."

"I appreciate that informality. Hopefully, it suggests a forgiving nature. I'm sure I will make social blunders and mistakes."

"Unfortunately, you won't have much latitude in the future. I'm supposed to weave you into the family fabric, but I'm also giving you experience for the time when you will have to assume a different identity in a much less forgiving context. Mistakes in a future social situation could prove fatal for you. We'll be rigorous in a relaxed way. Can you handle that?"

"I expect that I'll match the required standards, but you, sister dear, will have to refrain from bullying your younger brother as you did when we were children. I insist that we be equals at family events."

"That's very good, Michael. If we had been siblings as children, I undoubtedly would have looked down on you and the way you never clean up after yourself. In that, you're like Father, who left Mum for another woman and moved to Australia because he couldn't stand her insistence on organization and neatness."

"I'm glad I hit the right tone on our relationship, but I'm a bit puzzled. How do you square the informality characteristic of the family with the neatness and organization preoccupations of Mother?"

"The answer is that I can't square those two sides of the family coin, and neither can Mother. She has moved to Ireland, where she grew up. You're not likely to see her while you're here with me."

"So, Mother and Father, otherwise known as Annie and Gerald are probably out of the picture. That's good, because they would certainly know that Michael Farrell Hadley had been stillborn. How would we handle things if one of them were to visit you while I was still here?"

"That might be a problem. It's not likely, because you will be in training most of the time, but if it were to happen, we'd have to alter your name and our relationship during their presence. You would become Wilbur Maxwell, and I would be your fiancée."

"That's an interesting prospect."

"Don't get any ideas. That plan is for emergency use only."

"Right; I wouldn't much fancy the idea of being a Wilbur."

"Not even if I came with that name?"

"Don't get any ideas. That plan is for emergency use only."

"Touché; you've achieved the relaxed attitude."

"I have another question, Alice. Who owns this farm? Do we have to be alert for eavesdroppers?"

"That question shows that you're learning to watch your back, a necessary habit for your future success. The answer is that I own it, but rent the fields and other buildings out to a company that does the farming. Their people watch the area for any unwanted intruders or eavesdroppers. You'll be safe here, now and on any future visits."

For another two hours, Alice and Michael discussed various Hadley family members and the nature of their relationships with each other. Finally, Alice declared their first family tutoring session at an end and suggested that they continue in the morning.

As Michael lay in bed, trying to calm his thoughts in order to sleep, he decided that it had been a worthwhile day. He started it as a boring but familiar person and ended it as someone more interesting who had been inserted into an unexpected but stimulating context. His mission would start to take shape tomorrow.

CHAPTER 19 – TRAINING 101

At nine o'clock the next morning, someone rapped on the cottage door. Alice opened the door to find a green Austin Seven saloon and a small black van parked outside. She recognized the man who had knocked.

"Hello, Fred. What is all this?"

Michael walked up to the front room at the sound of Alice's voice and arrived in time to hear Fred's response.

"The car is for Michael's use, and the van contains items he might want while he's here. They're from his flat. He won't be going back there anymore. The rest of his belongings are in local storage."

Michael looked over Alice's shoulder. "Good morning. I don't know how you managed to do all that moving and secure that Austin Seven so early. Our project must have some priority."

"That it does, sir. Will you be ready to go soon? If you don't mind, I'll drive over to the academy, and you can start operating the car after today's training sessions. At that point, you'll have time to test out all of the car's features."

"That sounds fine. I'm ready to go now."

Alice introduced Michael to Fred Penwoody. Fred described himself as a jack-of-all-trades who handled those daily needs of the academy that were unusual or complicated. He told Michael he expected that they would find themselves working closely on several matters, but that details of their joint efforts would come from others. After a brief exchange between Fred and the van driver, Fred and Michael departed in the Austin, while Alice instructed the van driver as to where he should deposit his load from Michael's flat.

The academy turned out to be located in the town of Corby, within a building that had been a school in Victorian times and more recently an old people's home. The front of the building bore the faded blue sign, Windy Ridge Care House. The structure appeared abandoned, but upon entering a guarded fenced-in area at the rear, one discovered a car park containing more than ten vehicles of various types and an active entrance controlled by a second private guard at an inside desk.

Fred led Michael into the building, where they both signed the admissions logbook. Then, they went down a flight of stairs to a level with all windows blackened to prevent internal lights from being visible from the street. They entered an office where Fred introduced Michael to the training coordinator, Lawrence Bishop, a stout professorial gray-haired individual. Bishop dismissed Fred to his other duties and asked Michael to take a seat.

"First, I have to ask you, what is your name?"

"I'm Michael Farrell Hadley."

"What is your sister's name?"

"Her name is Alice Hadley."

"What's her middle name?"

"I don't remember."

"That's very good, Michael. A questioner might doubt your identity if you said that you didn't know it. Not being able to remember it is a forgivable sin."

"What are the middle names of your brothers and sisters, Mr. Bishop?"

"Call me Lawrence, and although I have three sisters, I can only remember the middle name of one of them. It's Doris. Even if you've lived with your brothers and sisters all of your life, forgetting is forgivable, because we rarely use middle names. Nevertheless, your first lesson is to be prepared to answer detailed questions, whether your situation requires research, as in assuming an identity that blends with an existing family, or creation and memorization, as would be the case if you were becoming someone unique. You must be consistent in both cases. When in doubt, change the subject or say that you don't remember."

"Lawrence, what will I be studying here, and how much time will I have to learn it?"

"I like the way you get right down to business, Michael. That's appropriate to training and business matters, but not to social situations. In those contexts you should beat around the bush and be more subtle and relaxed in your conversation and manner."

"Your use of the word *relaxed* suggests to me that you have spoken with Alice Hadley today. It reflects a conversation that I had with her last evening."

"Alice is informally a member of our staff, so I do get feedback from her as to your progress, but not the specific content of your discussions."

Michael stood and glared downward at the seated instructor. "If you want people to accept me as Alice's brother, you'll stop all monitoring of our conversations immediately. I will not have a *relaxed* relationship if you treat me as a guinea pig in an experiment. I have other things I can do with my life." Michael turned and took a step toward the office door.

Lawrence looked worried. "I agree to loosen our controls. Sit down, and I'll answer your earlier question about the training we have in store for you. My background is academics, and I'll have to remember that the appropriate amount of discipline for each student varies with the situation.

"Your training will include military tactics and weapons, even though you will not be operating within a formal military unit. You will learn how to attack a specific limited target as an individual or as part of a small offensive group. That portion of the curriculum may save your life someday. We will teach you intelligence techniques and clandestine communications. You will also study journalism and creative writing. You will receive frequent briefings on the political and military situations in Germany, and you will acquire sufficient German language skills to comprehend conversations and analyze written documents. In the field, you will conceal the fact that you have such language skills."

"In other words, I'm to be the proverbial fly on the wall in a German social setting."

"Michael, I can't tell you for sure how or where you'll serve our country. Our charge is to prepare you for any likely eventuality. Your curriculum may change as we learn more about your assignments, and there will be more than one of them."

"One final question, and then I'll quietly let you complete your orientation. How many others are you training to handle this type of work?"

"We're not at war yet, Michael, although we expect hostilities to start at any time. The people who are now in power within our government do not share our beliefs about the inevitability of war. Consequently, you are the only unofficial trainee in our system at present. I say unofficial, because you have no authorizing documents. Whether you turn out to be a success or a failure, you do not exist. You'll need to absorb everything you can from our training, because if you get into trouble, you will be on your own. At least until our government declares war on Germany, and probably for an extended period thereafter, we will not claim or protect you."

CHAPTER 20 – TRANSITION

The exhausting routine of the training sessions remained bearable for Michael only because those academic and physical tasks ended each day in time for him to return to the stone cottage for supper and family-related coaching by Alice. She delayed her evening meals to match his tedious schedule, and they both found themselves looking forward to their post-sunset hours together. After several weeks of Michael's formal plus informal education sessions, Alice made an announcement following supper.

"Michael Farrell Hadley, I have taught you absolutely everything I can about our family and its idiosyncrasies. I hereby declare you a graduate. Now, we'll have to spend our evenings talking about other matters."

"You've done a spectacular job, Alice. I don't think I could remember much about my pre-Hadley life, even under duress. You've been a great teacher and an equally great companion."

"Do you feel you're my brother now?" She arched her right eyebrow as she awaited his reaction.

He looked upward for a few moments, as though praying. "I both passed and failed that portion of the course. In a public setting, or when required for tactical purposes, I'm sure that I'll be a believable brother. I haven't quite decided on the amount of friction that we should display between us as siblings. No one would believe a perfect relationship between us. In a private setting like this, I find it much more difficult to regard you as my sister. Does that make me a failure?"

Alice walked to the table and prepared two cups of instant coffee. She carried one over to him and turned back toward the table.

Michael said, "Alice, what are you doing? You drink tea, not coffee."

She raised the second cup to her lips and took a sip with only a slight change in her expression. "That wasn't as bad as I expected.... Michael, your sister, Alice, drinks tea. Your friend, Alice, drinks coffee."

He walked toward her. "You must be the friend version. Are we close friends?"

She placed her cup on the table and approached him. "I think we're getting closer."

Michael surprised her by taking a step backward. "I need to know whether you're testing my ability to withstand temptation in the field, or if this is how you really feel."

She reached forward and clasped his left hand with her right. "I've wondered for weeks how long I could remain your sister. I held back because your training is more important than my feelings. Once you admitted you had feelings for me too, it changed everything."

He held her close and kissed her. "I did my best to keep my distance and act like your brother, but it has been difficult. Even now, I'm wondering how we can yield to our passions when we know they'll send me away soon."

"We won't be unique for long. The war with Germany is coming, and with it will come many scenes of last-minute passion as men and women go off to fight for Britain. Right now, I know you better than anyone else does. This is our moment." She took Michael's hand and led him toward her bedroom.

In the morning, it took him a few seconds to realize where he was. Alice had slipped out of bed and resumed her normal schedule of preparing to send him off to the academy for training. He woke up alone in the same stone cottage, but in a different bed and room. As his mind focused, he climbed out of bed and looked for Alice. He found her in the kitchen and laughed when he saw that she was drinking coffee with her sausages.

"Good morning, Michael. I took coffee to symbolize our new feelings for each other, and I'm actually beginning to like it. If and when you do leave, I may keep the coffee as a pledge and emblem of our love."

"I didn't realize how much of a romantic you are, Alice. I wish I could skip training and spend the whole day with you."

"Well, you can't, so get going, or you'll be late. Remember that we are brother and sister to the rest of the world. I'll feel horrible if they kick you out of training because you can't focus on your mission."

Michael kissed her and accelerated his preparations to make up for his slow start. Then he returned to bid a platonic adieu to his sister. Alice closed the door behind him and watched through the window until the green Austin drove out of sight.

CHAPTER 21 – FIRST STEP

Three honeymoon weeks later, Michael arrived for his morning Weapons and Tactics class and found Lawrence Bishop waiting for him in the empty room.

"No classes today, Michael; it's time to move to the next step along your journey."

"Have we gone to war?"

"Not yet, but disturbing events are happening on the continent. Germany has reoccupied the Rhineland. With that action plus their accelerating arms buildup, the fiction of the Versailles Treaty is at an end."

"What's my assignment?"

"We're moving you into a new position where you can have some leverage on future developments. Tomorrow, you'll sail for the United States, where you'll apply for a position as an editorial writer for the *New York Times*."

"But, I have no qualifications for that post. Who would hire me?"

"Your training here has included journalism and propaganda. You've written essays on the rise of Hitler and the dangers posed by German rearmament. You'll carry a resume that shows editorial experience at the *Manchester Guardian*. That newspaper, on a special arrangement basis, published several of your essays, with minor editing, in limited volume early editions. You will have copies of those newspapers including your editorials. You will also carry a letter of recommendation from John Russell Scott, Manager of the *Guardian*. We're confident that the *New York Times* will hire you."

"Lawrence, is some of that confidence based on your having connected with someone on that paper's staff who will lobby on my behalf?"

"I'm not at liberty to discuss people who may or may not sympathize with our efforts. You've performed well at every training task we've set for you, Michael. You're ready for action on your own, and believe me when I say that it will be important for Britain. Most Americans are isolationists. They view their country as protected by two large oceans, and they think Germany's aggressions in Europe will not affect them. You are going to help change their minds."

"I hope that I'll be sufficiently persuasive. Why would Americans listen to someone who is not one of their countrymen?"

"You raise a good point, but we've taken steps to counter it. American citizens are a mixture of people from all over the world. Newcomers are absorbed and given the same credence as those who have lived there for decades or centuries. You will become an American citizen. We have friends in their government who are already preparing to speed that process for you."

"It's not the assignment I anticipated, but I'll do my best." He shook hands with Lawrence and walked toward the door.

As Michael opened the door, Lawrence said, "The war is coming, Michael. You'll have additional assignments. Go forth for King and country."

CHAPTER 22 – DEPARTURE

Alice sensed the difference in Michael's manner as he approached the cottage door. He took an unusual amount of time gathering his papers and climbing out of the Austin. He interrupted his approach to the front door by pausing three times to look at the farm and its buildings. She understood and threw open the door before he could reach for the knob.

"Get in here, soldier, and give me a hug."

He obliged her with a long and tender embrace. "I have to leave you, Alice. They're shipping me out tomorrow."

"We've both known this would happen. It was just a question of the timing. We'll have a special evening tonight and firm up our memories."

"We still have so much more to learn about each other. I've avoided explaining my pre-Hadley past."

She grasped his hand and led him to the sofa. "Michael, I don't need to know anything more about you, but I would like to ask you one question related to your past history."

"Ask it."

"Why were you willing to enlist in this open-ended enterprise that quite possibly will not end well?"

"I'm not entirely sure, but a person who has never surpassed expectations at anything and who many times has run afoul of the rules, craves attention. No one ever thought that I would amount to anything special, but here I am in a position to help my country. I've found self-esteem and, in you, I have found love. The old saying is that opportunity knocks but once. I answered the door and invited him in. With regard to things not ending well, we're all going to be tested during the war that is coming, but considering that I never would have met you if I hadn't taken this path, it will all be worthwhile, however it ends."

"Goodness! That was quite a speech. You're becoming adept at expressing your thoughts, Michael."

"I hope so, because it turns out that projecting my thoughts in a convincing manner is the crux of my new assignment." He told Alice about his pending editorial career move, and was surprised when she laughed.

"What's funny about my writing for a newspaper?"

"I'm proud of you for qualifying to do that. I laughed because your recruitment stemmed from your having pretended to be an Oxford graduate at a party. Hundreds of Oxford graduates would give everything they have to write editorials for the *New York Times*. You've outreached them all."

He hugged her and said, "I'm an actor in a key role. I wouldn't have that role if it weren't for the people supporting me."

"I'll be supporting you with my love and thoughts from afar. I'll subscribe to that paper so that I'll be able to read your words and feel that I'm with you. Do me one favor."

"Anything ..."

"Whenever you can logically do so, insert our magic word into your essays so that I'll feel close to you."

"What magic word?"

"Coffee." Alice pulled his head closer and kissed him.

The next morning, Alice surprised Michael with a going-away present. She asked him to close his eyes and hold out his hands. Upon doing so, he felt something made of fabric placed across his palms. When she gave him permission to look, he saw that he was holding a pair of knit woolen socks. They had a red background, and each had a white coffee mug on the side filled with brown liquid. He folded and held them in his left hand while he hugged Alice with his right arm.

"I didn't know you were a knitter. They're handsome, and I'll always think of you when I wear them."

"That's one Hadley trait I didn't reveal to you. All of our women tend to have knitting or needlework as a hobby. I worked on these while you were away for training so that I could surprise you. If we both survive the coming war, we'll have a lot more to learn about each other."

Michael took a step away from her. "Enough of tingeing our outlooks with dread! We'll make it through whatever faces us."

They kissed and held each other tightly. Then Michael said, "I have a surprise for you too. I made a request, since approved by the authorities. Alice, you are hereby instructed to drive me to the academy this morning. I'll depart from there for my ship. Then you will return here with the Austin. It is now yours. Fred will deliver the official ownership papers in a few days. You'll have a memento of me also."

"You don't really think I need a physical reminder, do you?"

"Of course not, but I examined your motorbike out back. It hasn't much life left in it. I want you to have something reliable while I'm gone."

Alice hugged him again. Then she put on her coat. "I accept the car; I'm ready to drive you; but most of all I'll treasure your words *while I'm gone* as a pledge to come back to me when this is over."

CHAPTER 23 – NEW YORK

A major revelation occurred for Michael after boarding Cunard's R.M.S. Samaria in Liverpool, bound for New York via Boston. He sat at the bar, drinking a glass of Bass ale while he attempted to form an image of his pending interview at the *New York Times*. Michael's thoughts were interrupted by someone tapping him on the shoulder and asking whether he had a match. He started to say that he was without matches because he didn't smoke, when he discovered that the questioner was Thomas Hadley, standing behind him and grinning.

"I didn't know that you were going with me, Thomas. This is a welcome turn of events."

"Strictly speaking, I'm not accompanying you, but let's find a bit of privacy before we take this conversation further."

Thomas ordered a gin and tonic. Then they took their drinks to a corner table in the rear of the room.

Michael raised his glass in a salute to his supposed cousin. "I find it hard to believe that you're sailing with me, but you're not accompanying me. That's too coincidental."

"I said 'strictly speaking' when I made that comment. I'm supporting your mission, but I'll be leaving the ship in Boston. Hence, I am not accompanying you to New York."

"What will you do in Boston?"

"You'd better brace yourself for this one. I'll be arranging for you to meet your future wife."

"Excuse me, but I have no plans to get married, especially on a rush basis."

"We've learned that your expected supervisor at the *New York Times* insists that all of his key employees be married. He feels that the responsibilities involved in marriage will guarantee more balanced, responsible viewpoints in editorial writing."

"I don't think that's completely logical, Thomas. Do you?"

"It doesn't matter what we think. Our job is to get you writing for that newspaper in order to advance our arguments for the United States to support Britain in the coming conflict. You will be married, as required."

"Have you selected my wife?"

"You will be marrying Stephanie Wright. She's American-born, of British parents, and she's fluent in German, a skill that will help you while doing research for your editorials. She also, of course, works for us."

"You're saying that I should marry this woman because she has useful skills and is part of the organization. You make it sound as though I would be hiring her, not marrying her. Will this be a real wedding or a mock ceremony for business purposes? Will Miss Wright be right for me?"

"Michael, your humor is appreciated, but this marriage will definitely be genuine. Marrying an American will also help us expedite your becoming a naturalized American citizen, and that will be important to your future assignments."

"This is all quite manipulative, Thomas."

"Of course, it is, but we're counting on you to sell it as being natural and sincere."

"Will I at least get to meet Stephanie Wright before we gather for the church ceremony?"

"When you arrive in New York, our Ronald Windham will meet you and take you to your apartment near a station on the New York, New Haven, and Hartford Railroad. That location will let you travel by rail to

Bridgeport, Connecticut, where Stephanie lives, and to New York City for your work. We'll give you a day to become acclimated to the New York City area, and then you'll travel to Bridgeport, where Stephanie will meet you at the train station. You'll telephone her at nine o'clock in the morning to set up the schedule for that meeting. She will have the railroad timetable for coordinating your travel arrangements."

"How else will Stephanie work with me besides translating German documents and conversations?"

"That's for you two to decide. The primary requirement is that you convince people that you are married and not just working together. Will you have any problems with that?"

"No, Thomas; you and the academy staff have done a good job. I can separate my personal life from my assigned identity, even when it comes to romantic entanglements."

CHAPTER 24 – STEPHANIE

Over the telephone, Stephanie told Michael that she would be wearing a red hat to make it easier for him to identify her. He countered that he would wear a red tie. They agreed that he would take the train that arrived in Bridgeport at 2:35 p.m.

When the train arrived, he descended the steps along with three other men, two of whom wore red ties. He scanned the people on the platform, but couldn't see anyone with a red hat. Then he checked his watch and discovered that the train had arrived eight minutes early. He walked into the building and saw a woman with a red hat talking with one of the other red-tie men from his train. That individual shook his head negatively and walked away toward the building's street exit. Michael approached the woman.

"Pardon me, but are you Stephanie?"

"Michael? I'm so glad we found each other. I just embarrassed myself by approaching a different man with a red tie. I'm sure he thought I was trying to pick him up. How was the train trip?"

"The train was fine. I did worry that we'd have confusion when I saw two other men with red ties get off the train with me." He tried to be subtle as he absorbed the characteristics of the tall dark-haired beauty facing him. He guessed her age to be twenty-four, just about the same as Alice. He reminded himself that this was business and mentally apologized to Alice. "I don't quite know how to begin, Stephanie. Have you managed to make something natural out of our prospect of an arranged marriage?"

61

"We'll work that out. The first way to ease things would be for you to call me Steph. I consider Stephanie too formal for casual conversation. Do you prefer Michael or Mike?"

"I haven't been Mike since I was a lad, but I can see that things are less formal on this side of the pond, so if you prefer Steph, I'll be Mike to you, but Michael to most others. Does that work for you?"

"It does, Mike, but if you later feel you prefer the longer names, we can both change back."

"This might work out after all, Steph. We're already trying to accommodate each other."

"One other request, Mike ... now that we've identified each other, would you mind if I removed my hat? I know that current fashion rules demand that a lady wear a hat in public places, but I really don't feel comfortable in one."

"That's fine with me. I think you have it precisely. The most important characteristic of our relationship should be for us to feel comfortable with each other at all times. Let's aim for that."

She took his hand and led him toward the street. "My black Plymouth is parked at the right end of the parking lot, car park to you. I'll drive until you get used to our traffic being on the right side of the road. Would you like to go anywhere special?"

"Could we drive somewhere outside the city, and sit in a field or on a bench and talk about unimportant things?"

"I know a good place. We'll drive up the coast and sit near Charles Island where Captain Kidd was supposed to have buried treasure in 1699. I don't know how they got that precise date unless someone watched him bury it. You don't mind if I ramble a bit when I talk about things, do you?"

"The only way I'll get to know what goes on inside your head is if you tell me, so ramble away all you want."

They drove to the shore near Charles Island and parked. Michael removed his jacket and tie. Then they sat on a large rock, looking toward the ocean and the island.

After sitting in silence for a few minutes, Stephanie said, "This place is an enigma. The waves are always moving, so nothing really stays the same; yet a distant picture of the island and the ocean makes the scene constant. Add to that the suggestion of buried pirate treasure, and you have something special indeed."

"I think I have something special indeed sitting right next to me."

"Why, thank you, Mike. That's the nicest thing someone has said to me for a long time. Would you do me a favor?"

"Anything ..."

"Let me be impolite and stare at you for a while so that I might burn your image and personality into my subconscious."

"That sounds as though you've studied Freud."

"I have, but this is just for me. They're pushing us together to suit an agenda and circumstances, but I want to fool them by proving that we can run toward each other faster than they can push."

He leaned toward her, and she met him half way across their separation. They kissed warmly and embraced each other. Then he said, "Stare at me all you want, while I stare back at you. Tell me what you see."

"I see a man who's determined to make his life meaningful, but who has doubts about how he will measure up to his tasks and goals. I see someone who is kind, yet strong; complex, yet straightforward; adaptable, yet conservative. I see someone who is an unexpected gift to me. Now, what do you see?"

"I see a woman who is not to be taken at face value. She is much more than that. I see someone who is willing to go beyond the expected. She will cope under duress;

she will enjoy life when circumstances permit. I see a warrior, and I say that I also see a gift to me."

"Don't look now, Mike, but despite the tiny amount of time we've known each other, I think we've just written our wedding vows."

"More than that, Steph, I think we've performed our wedding ceremony in the sight of God and Captain Kidd's ghost."

CHAPTER 25 – INTERVIEW

Michael scheduled his initial visit to the *New York Times* for 9:30 a.m. the next Tuesday morning, based on his theory that the management would have been too busy with their weekly agenda-setting conference on Monday morning to hold a significant meeting with a new employee. It was, but it wasn't, to be an interview in the normal personnel department sense. Michael carried a Letter of Intent to Hire, issued by the General Manager of the paper, Julius Ochs Adler, based on his correspondence and telephone discussions with John Russell Scott, the Manager of the *Manchester Guardian* newspaper. Adler and Scott were colleagues who had great respect for each other. Michael also carried a Letter of Recommendation from that same John Russell Scott. The position would be his, unless he made a terrible first impression.

When he arrived at the *Times* and introduced himself to the receptionist, she said that he was expected, and that her instructions were to escort him to the editorial department conference room. Once there, she invited him to take coffee from a carafe on the side table, and then she left to notify the people who were on her list for meeting with Michael.

The first person to arrive was a woman, and Michael rose to meet her. She shook his hand. "Good morning. I have your name as Michael Farrell Hadley, is that correct? We have quite a few people around here who use all three of their names. I'm one of them. I'm Anne O'Hare McCormick, and I've recently joined the editorial board here, breaking up that old boys club for the first time. The

Times is a good place to work, although you may end up covering a lot of ground. I've done mostly field correspondence writing for almost fifteen years. I was born in England too, so we may have quite a few things in common."

While she spoke, two men entered the room, the second of whom closed the door, indicating that the gathering was complete. Anne turned to them. "Gentlemen, we have with us Michael Farrell Hadley, who aspires to join our group. Michael, this handsome individual with the military bearing is our General Manager, Julius Ochs Adler." They shook hands. "Our other associate to your left is Meyer Berger." Meyer waved in lieu of shaking hands. "Meyer is what we call a color writer. He specializes in human-interest events, local crime matters, and other stories that generate emotions in his readers. He's an expert on everything that goes on in New York City, so he'll be a great resource for someone looking to settle here. Let's sit down, and learn a bit about you, Michael. Julius, we defer to your opening comments."

"This place hasn't been the same since Anne reminded us that only half of the world's population is male. We received some major recommendations for your joining us from John Scott at the *Manchester Guardian*. You and your writing impressed him very much."

Michael did his best not to alter his expression due to the fact that he had never met John Scott, and had only had a few of his essays published in Scott's newspaper. The organization hiding behind Michael had prepared him well for this meeting.

Julius continued. "One of my main concerns is the development of an editorial group where all of the individuals work well together. To that end, I have to ask you several personal questions. Anne will work with you on our paper's viewpoints and style techniques."

Michael said, "Please proceed with your questions, sir."

"You just answered one of them. We do encourage politeness and deference to authority. Remember that this newspaper has a well-established reputation to uphold, and you represent our image when you conduct an interview or write an editorial. My second question centers on your family. Are you married or do you have plans for making that transition soon?"

"I have only recently arrived from England, but I have been here long enough to bring a relationship based on correspondence to fruition. Three days ago I proposed to Miss Stephanie Wright of Bridgeport, and we are planning to be married within the next fortnight, or if you prefer, two weeks."

"Congratulations, Michael; that statement shows your ability to make decisions and also your adaptability to our version of the English language." The others contributed their congratulations as well. Julius continued, "My final question is more of a comment. Your name, Michael Farrell Hadley, may be somewhat ponderous for a byline. What would you think of signing your pieces as M. Farrell Hadley?"

Michael said, "I'll follow your suggestion, but it may be ambiguous in France and French Canada. I'm sure you have many readers of the *Times* in those places."

"What do you mean by ambiguous?"

"M. is the abbreviation for Monsieur."

Julius laughed. "You're quick-witted. That's good. You'll be working under Anne's guidance, so I'll let her make the decision on your byline. I'll have to excuse myself now. I have another meeting. I'll look forward to reading your pieces and talking with you in the future."

After Julius Ochs Adler left, Meyer Berger said, "Why was he worried about bylines? He never said anything about my simple sign-off as Meyer Berger. Anyway,

Michael, I'm pleased to meet you, and welcome to New York. You'll find this town is rough and tough on the outside, but once people look on you as a character in the melodrama of life, they'll cherish you. We're all colorful here."

Anne asked, "Do you have questions for us, Michael?"

"I'm sure I'll have many as we go forward, but if you will be my supervisor as Mr. Adler suggested, where will I get my assignments, and to what extent will I have the flexibility to nominate topics on my own?"

"It will be a mixture, depending on whether it's a high intensity day with key events that demand the newspaper's attention, or a slow news day. On slower days, you will be free to select your own topic, but your piece will require approval prior to publication. As you accumulate seniority, you will earn more independence on topic selection. I suggest a simple topic for your first essay. Do you have anything you'd like to discuss for your first piece?"

Meyer said, "I have a topic. He comes from England where tea is supreme, and he's settling in America where coffee rules. Let Michael start with a piece relating tea and coffee to the countries they represent. What do you think, Michael?"

Michael leaned back, heard Alice's request in his mind, and smiled.

CHAPTER 26 – WEDDING

Calvary St. George's Episcopal Church was empty except for the six people who gathered around the altar table the next Saturday afternoon. Stephanie's parents, Joyce and Andrew Wright were her attendants while Thomas Hadley lent moral support to Michael. The Rev. Edward Newbody officiated. Stephanie's mother wanted to invite friends and relatives, but Steph objected because guests would question the reasons behind the arranged coupling of her with Mike. Her parents could be trusted to offset gossip by suggesting that their daughter had met her future husband years before during a visit to relatives in England.

Father Newbody frequently performed ceremonies for couples with few guests, so he stressed Christ's teaching that *where two or three are gathered in my name, I am in your midst*. Without the procession of a bridal party or hymns, the prayer book service was quite brief, but Father Newbody emphatically stressed the fact that the size of a wedding party does not predict the degree of dedication of the bride and groom to each other. This latter point was obvious to Joyce Wright who many times later told her close friends that Stephanie looked angelic as she smiled her love at Michael, who beamed his feelings back at her.

Following the service, the wedding party adjourned to an Irish pub owned by a close friend of Andrew Wright. They gathered there in a private room, decorated in white and silver for the occasion. Even Thomas Hadley agreed that Stephanie and Michael had truly become husband and wife, despite the tactical circumstances underlying their marriage. After dinner, Thomas and Michael walked outside with their ales. Thomas noticed that Michael looked worried.

"You can't have that shadow of gloom on your face today, Michael. You two make a perfect couple."

"That's my problem, Thomas. I didn't think it could happen, but I'm in love with two women at the same time. This marriage was supposed to be an arranged fiction to support our mission. It has turned out to be the real thing. I love Steph, and she loves me, even though for the long term, I'm committed to Alice."

"That won't do, Michael. Alice is supposed to be your sister."

"The operative words in that statement are *supposed to be*. Alice and I couldn't help falling for each other. Someday the coming war will be over. Then I will have to make a choice between my two loves. In the meantime, please don't tell Alice how much I'm enjoying this tactical marriage. You're the only one who knows how I feel about both of these women, and the old man designated you to be my mentor. Tell me, mentor, how should I handle my two loves?"

"All I can say is that you will have to keep putting one foot in front of the other. We all know a great conflict is coming. No one knows what its outcome will be, for countries or for individuals. You have the blessing of two loves. Love them both until you reach that decision point at the end of the war. I hate to have to be so realistic, but the war may make your choice for you. In the meantime, I won't tell Alice about the emotional dimension of your marriage to Stephanie."

"Thank you, Thomas."

"Just remember to treat each of them as well as possible. I'm jealous, you know. I'm older than you are, and I have yet to find even a single love."

CHAPTER 27 – PENNY'S RESEARCH

Debbie answered the telephone on the fourth ring after having fumbled wildly for her keys in order to open the door before the call went to voice mail. Jeremy followed her in, heading for the kitchen with two heavy bags of groceries.

From the other end of the phone line Debbie heard, "Slow down, Debbie; you're out of breath."

"Hi, Penny; I bet you called to give me a lecture on physical fitness and breath control."

"I hadn't planned on it, but those are good topics. How would you like to come over here later today? I've learned more about Jeremy's great-grandfather. You might say that I have a significant amount of material."

"We can be there in an hour. Would that be too soon?"

"Make it an hour and a half, and I'll have fresh chocolate chip cookies for you."

Debbie agreed to the schedule, and joined Jeremy in the kitchen.

"We have an invitation to visit Penny and Joe in ninety minutes to eat fresh cookies and learn more about your great-grandfather. Penny sounded as though she discovered something interesting."

As they sorted out the groceries, Debbie handed Jeremy four packages to put on the top shelf of the cabinet. "It's funny. Until I started my genealogy project, no one in your family discussed or even thought about your great-grandfather. Now, we all focus on him and his story. It's almost a form of time travel, learning more about your personal history. I'll be ready to go, and I'll take my notebook with me."

71

"Did she tell you anything about the information she found?"

"Penny likes to spring surprises on people. The fact that she's baking cookies for our visit tells me that she thinks her discovery will excite us. It has to be something significant – something that the aroma of fresh-baked cookies will enhance."

When they arrived at the Gonzalez's house, Joe answered the door and escorted them into the family room, surprising Jeremy.

"We usually have documentation and evidence sessions around your dining room table. Something must be different or unusual."

Joe leaned down to the low coffee table and opened the cover of his laptop computer. "Spoken like a seasoned detective, Jeremy. There is a reason for the change of venue. We're going to want to enlarge our computer graphics onto the large screen TV monitor. Sit down and relax. Penny will be here with her cookies and presentation in a minute or two. In the meantime, may I bring you something to drink?"

Debbie requested some water, while Jeremy said that he didn't want anything, perhaps because he suspected that drinks would delay the arrival of Penny's new information. Debbie rested her hand on Jeremy's knee as they sat on the couch, signaling that he needed to relax and wait patiently.

A few minutes later, Penny and Joe returned with the initial drinks, cookies, and a pitcher of lemonade in case someone wanted a drink later. Joe turned on the computer and the large monitor. The initial screen image displayed the words: Michael Farrell Hadley.

Penny announced, "It turned out that if you knew where and when to look, Jeremy, your great-grandfather wasn't hard to find at all." She pressed her mouse button to advance to the next slide on the large display. The image was an old copy of the *New York Times* newspaper. "He worked as an editorial writer for the *New York Times*. The difficult parts came in discovering when he left England for the United States and what he planned to do after he arrived here. He traveled here in July of 1936. By August, he was writing articles for the Times. We had no reason to expect him to be so successful with his job-hunting. His first article was a humorous comparison between England and the United States based on their cultural fondness for tea and coffee, respectively. In that article, he concluded that both countries are innovative and resourceful, due to the English being capable of deriving satisfaction from crumbled leaves in hot water, while the Americans base their morale on ground beans, similarly soaked. We had a slight difficulty spotting that article, because he signed it M. Farrell Hadley."

Debbie asked, "Did we have earlier knowledge that he was a writer?"

"We didn't have any evidence of his holding down any job. Up to the time when he went to work for the *Times*, he may have lived off of his family wealth, or he may have had a training scholarship. Perhaps he studied to be a journalist somewhere along the way."

Jeremy brightened at her words. "I like your suggestion that there was money in the family, Penny."

"Don't count on having any of it to spend. In any event, he became a journalist and went to work for the *New York Times*." She advanced to the next slide, an image of the *Times* dated August 14, 1936. "As reported in this issue, about one month after Michael went to work for the *Times*, President Roosevelt made his *I Hate War* speech:"

"We shun political commitments which might entangle us in foreign wars. We avoid connection with the political activities of the League of Nations ... I hate war. I have

Richard Davidson

passed unnumbered hours, I shall pass unnumbered hours, thinking and planning how war may be kept from this Nation."

"Roosevelt took this stand for domestic political expediency, even though many people thought that he was a closet internationalist. The interesting point that I want to make is that Michael was the *Times* writer who responded to Roosevelt's words one week later."

She advanced the slide to the front page of the *Times* issue of August 21, 1936, and then to an excerpt from an editorial article in that issue.

I thoroughly agree with President Roosevelt's recent remarks. Every rational person must hate war with all of its atrocities against both national armies and the human race as a whole. At present, America has the luxury of apparent protection from the troubles of Europe because of the ocean that lies between us, but the situation in Europe worsens by the day, and the protection of that water barrier will soon diminish. Already, the Germans have remilitarized the Rhineland and have greatly expanded their military forces, enough so that France has felt obligated to increase its forces too. German planes are dropping bombs in Spain in support of the Civil War there. Hitler has imprisoned tens of thousands of his own civilians and he speaks like God announcing which of them shall live and which shall die. Shall we forsake our British cousins? They stare across a thin stream of water at the continental madness. The situation is fluid and we must remember that future requirements and contingencies require advance planning if we are to have what we need when we need it. Let us all draw strength from that traditional motto: God helps those who help themselves. M.F.H.

Jeremy read the editorial several times before speaking. "Old Michael did have a way with words. I wonder why they let him write that response to President

74

Roosevelt's speech. I would have thought the *Times* would have assigned someone more senior to do it."

Joe laughed. "There's another old saying: Fools rush in where angels fear to tread. I'm sure they gave that assignment to their junior editorial writer because they could sacrifice him if Washington decided to apply pressure to their newspaper. The fact that he survived standing up to the president, undoubtedly gained him strength for future battles."

Penny contributed, "I agree, Joe. As I said earlier, Roosevelt may have been a closet internationalist. That's one reason why the *New York Times* didn't get a negative response to Michael's editorial. Roosevelt may have enjoyed it. He was in a position where he could say politically desirable things to suit the isolationists, and then count on a writer at the *Times* to issue the *support Europe* admonitions he really preferred."

Debbie said, "If you read between the lines of that article, Michael did the actual writing, but he was carrying out his assignment for someone named Churchill, who knew the British would need help from their American cousins."

They all looked at Debbie and nodded their heads in affirmation.

CHAPTER 28 – 1938

Events in Europe worsened in 1938. Hitler began the year by taking direct command of the German military forces. He did this by eliminating the War Ministry and replacing it with the *Oberkommando der Wehrmacht* (High Command of the Armed Forces). There was now no administrative buffer between Hitler and the military, no senior people to argue against his military desires and orders.

On February 12, he summoned the Chancellor of Austria and demanded more Nazi representation in his government. This step was the prelude to the March 12 *Anschluss*, the manipulated forced annexation of Austria into the Nazi German state. His next target was the Sudetenland, the German-speaking regions of Czechoslovakia, leading to a lengthy battle of threats and movements of armies.

During all of these developments, Michael continued to write articles arguing that the United States must protect itself by preparing for the possibility of conflict and must support its British kinsmen as they faced more immediate threats. A few of his readers remarked on the unusual number of times Michael mentioned coffee in the course of his serious editorials.

A decidedly unwarlike, but significant event in Michael's life occurred in January of 1938, when Stephanie issued her own headline. As they returned from a long early-evening walk, she suggested that they sit and talk for a while.

"Mike, it's time for us to discuss our future. I know that our relationship developed as an arranged marriage to support your assignment, but we both know it has turned out to be a sharing of our love."

"I'll confirm the love aspect, Steph. I couldn't be happier. Is there a problem?"

"I'd hardly call it a problem, but we have a new development that requires some serious discussion. We're going to have a child; I'm pregnant."

"That's wonderful, Steph. I have a good job, and the apartment is big enough to have a child's bedroom. There's no immediate difficulty."

"I caught that *immediate*, father-to-be. You spend your days writing about the coming war, and we both know your assignment here will end at some point. You'll receive instructions to go far away and take on a new identity. We both entered this marriage with our eyes open, but we've become a family, and it will soon have a third member. What's our future likely to be?"

He moved over to sit next to her, and he cradled her hand in his. "Steph, you're right; the war is coming. What happens to us will be no different than what will happen in any home where the husband has to go away to fight for his country. The only difference is that I now fight for two countries, both England and America. With God's guidance, we'll get through the nightmare, and then we'll be back together again. For now, we should enjoy the miracle of your pregnancy and the child it will produce."

"You're a hard person to doubt. I know there are pieces of your life that will remain secrets, and I'll cherish what we have, but I can only hope our relationship will survive the war. For now, we have a priority question to answer. What shall we call our child?"

"That's an easy one. The child should be Stephen if a boy, and Michelle if a girl. We're intertwined in many ways, and our children's names should be part of that pattern."

Stephanie put her arms around her husband's neck and pulled him toward her. "You are a unique person, Mike. I so want to believe that we'll come through the coming war in good shape."

"So do I, Steph; so do I."

CHAPTER 29 – TAKEOVER

Michael diligently interspersed articles about supporting England and preparing for the coming war among his other editorial assignments. During the early months of this pattern, several of the other editorial writers kidded him about being a Don Quixote who is on an impossible quest. The kidding tapered off as bad news continued to come out of Europe, and it ended completely on June 15, 1938, when Julius Ochs Adler called a meeting of the staff and editorial board to announce that the *New York Times* had a duty to alert the country to the coming danger.

"We have to go beyond Michael's admonitions that we cannot ignore what is going on in Europe. It's time for us to encourage the United States to free itself from the Neutrality Act and to prepare for what will inevitably come. We will prepare continuous editorials on the subject. Here is an excerpt from today's message:

The US would and should be prepared to defend a way of life which is our way of life and the only way of life worth living.

We will take this as a serious mission of this paper, and we will become activists."

Michael knew that members of the editorial board would write these new incarnations of his *prepare and support* messages. The marching orders presented by Julius Ochs Adler, the general manager, had originated with the publisher, Arthur Hays Sulzberger. It was good news and bad news at the same time. He rejoiced that the *Times* higher-ups had joined his crusade, but he knew that his next unknown assignment would come relatively soon. He sensed the pending acceleration of events that would lead to war and to the next stage of his life.

CHAPTER 30 – STORM AND AFTERMATH

Hitler gained the Sudetenland through the September Munich Agreement with British Prime Minister Neville Chamberlain and representatives of Italy and France. The appeaser, Chamberlain, returned to England and announced that the Munich Agreement meant *Peace for our time.*

On September 21, 1938, representatives of Britain and France announced to Czechoslovak President Edvard Beneš that they would not fight if Germany attempted to take the Sudetenland by force. Czechoslovakia yielded due to their refusal of support, and Germany moved its troops into the disputed territory. Another force moved into different new territory on that same date. An intense hurricane swept across Long Island and southern New England, leaving more than 600 people dead in its wake.

Shortly after the hurricane passed over their apartment in Fairfield, Connecticut, Stephanie and Michael heard a new small voice. Stephanie gave birth to Stephen Albert Hadley at Bridgeport Hospital after three hours of excruciating labor. When she saw her beautiful baby boy, Stephanie felt her pain had been worth the result. She knew Michael would also judge the baby amazing and special when he viewed his son through the nursery window set up for fathers and visitors. Stephanie's dread of her pending separation from Michael began to ease, because in Stephen she would have a piece of Michael forever.

Five days later, the hospital released Stephanie and the baby. Michael drove his wife and son home to their apartment, where he had completed his transformation of the second bedroom into a very blue nursery. It had been a rush job, undertaken after Stephen arrived and answered the gender question. Michael would soon return the alternate supply of pink paint to the hardware store.

Upon viewing the room, Stephanie proclaimed it perfect and promised to work on the final decoration touches as soon as her post-childbirth pains eased. She had seen a new periodical, *Action Comics*, and she thought she would paint its featured character, Superman, on the wall above Stephen's bed. The superhero even had an *S* on his chest, which in her mind would also signify *Stephen*.

Everything would have been idyllic in the aftermath of Stephen's birth, except for the lengthening shadow of Hitler's war machine in Europe. Both Stephanie and Michael knew that the confrontation with Britain would come soon, and with it would come Michael's next assignment. The countdown to their separation had started.

CHAPTER 31 – THOMAS

January of 1939 brought with it a *wait and see* attitude on both sides of the Atlantic, but at least for the British that status ended on 23 January when the German military intelligence agency, Abwehr, leaked misinformation that the Germans would invade the Netherlands in February in order to seize Dutch airfields for a major bombing offensive against Britain. This news disrupted Prime Minister Neville Chamberlain's policy of avoiding war through negotiations. At last, the unofficial elements that had organized covertly to prepare for war saw their opportunity to gain support for overt planning.

On the morning of February 4, the first Saturday of the month, Michael responded to a knock on the apartment door that interrupted his painting of the bookshelves he had built for their hallway. He answered the door after wiping his hands on a paint-spotted cloth, to find Thomas Hadley facing him.

"Hello, cousin, what brings you to our part of the world?"

Thomas entered the apartment and closed the door behind him for privacy. "Is Stephanie home?"

"She and the baby stayed overnight at her parents' house so that my paint fumes wouldn't bother them. Did you want to speak with her?"

"If she were here, I would speak with both of you. You'll have to relay my message to her. I'm here because events appear to be overtaking our schedule of preparations. We're going to need you back in England. Your efforts at the *Times* have succeeded, and now Michael Hadley will have to move on to his next incarnation. I know that your son is only five months old, but this transition has been in the cards all along."

"We knew that it would come, but we hoped that we would have more time. When will I have to leave?"

"We sail on Friday. That will give you a few days to disengage yourself from your employer and your family. I know that you'll find it difficult, but manage the change as smoothly as practical."

"Where and when will I meet you?"

"We'll rendezvous Friday morning at the British Consulate in New York City. You'll be traveling under a diplomatic passport, so that people won't ask questions."

"What name will be on that passport? Michael Hadley is a US citizen, thanks to your streamlining of the process."

"Michael Hadley actually has dual nationality and both US and British passports, but on this voyage you'll be Ralph Charters, an assistant to our commercial attaché. You won't have to worry about absorbing his background information, because you'll acquire a different persona once we arrive in England."

"I suspected you'd say something like that. You do realize that I've acquired more than a few Americanisms over here, and that I'm no longer a purebred Brit. Will that cause difficulty in my next assignment?"

"Don't concern yourself, Michael. Your assignment story will always match your experiences. It's time for me to make some preparations of my own. Pack for a one-week business trip. You'll receive any additional kit that you may need after we arrive. Be sure to leave behind anything that's monogrammed."

They shook hands, and Thomas departed.

When Stephanie returned with Stephen, she was enthusiastic about Michael's shelves. The additional storage there would allow them to move their books and knickknacks out of the living room and increase their open space. Stephanie wrapped Michael's neck with her arms and enthusiastically kissed him. Then she backed away from him.

"What's wrong? Something has changed."

"Thomas visited while you were away. I'm going to have to leave for a new assignment. Events in Europe are accelerating."

She kissed him harder than before. "I've dreaded this moment ever since our wedding. I love you, Mike, and I don't want to lose you. Will you come back to me someday?"

He returned her kisses and drew her close to him. "Steph, you're asking a question that has no answer. We'll be at war soon, and no one knows who will survive it. This will be especially difficult for us because they won't allow us to correspond or otherwise keep in touch with each other. Mike Hadley's thoughts and love will remain with you, but I'm likely to become somebody else for the duration of the war. Cherish our memories. You'll always have those and a big *perhaps*. In the meantime, prepare yourself for the uncertain future. If I'm not able to return, you'll have to move on to new things and new people."

Steph wiped her eyes with her forefinger knuckles. "When do you leave?"

"I have until Friday morning to make all of my arrangements and disconnect from my job."

"Correction – you have until Friday morning to handle those chores while making love with me during every spare moment."

CHAPTER 32 – ENGLAND

Lawrence Bishop, the training coordinator at the academy, looked across his desk at his visitor. "This is one of those awkward moments for an intelligence agent, and even though we didn't explicitly state it, that is your vocation. You have completed your New York mission with flying colors. I enjoyed reading some of your editorials, as did our higher-ups. Now, it's time for you to become someone else. State your current name and position."

"I'm Ralph Charters, and I'm the commercial attaché's assistant at Britain's New York City consulate."

"Pleased to meet you, Ralph, but that identification has expired. You are now George Millerson, an American of British ancestry who has run afoul of the law. You took a joyride in your employer's Jaguar, and even though he withdrew his complaint after you returned the vehicle, the local magistrate decided that you should spend two weeks in jail. Your employer at the import/export firm took the additional step of firing you."

"That sounds as though I'm an irresponsible bad actor, Lawrence. As an American, I probably wanted to experiment with driving a powerful car on the left side of the road."

"Exactly. You'll share a cell in the local jail with one Otto Krieger, a German language teacher accused of stealing fifty pounds from one of his private clients. At about the same time as the completion of your sentence, Krieger's complaining client will discover that he had simply misplaced the fifty pounds, and he will drop the charge against your cellmate."

"In other words, I have two weeks to build a friendship with Herr Krieger, following which the two of us may decide to undertake some new adventure together."

Lawrence shook George's hand. "Congratulations, Millerson, you're getting more adept at changing identities with each transition. You haven't asked yet, but I will caution you against renewing any acquaintanceships established during your previous assignment here. I say this, putting special emphasis on your connection with Alice Hadley. She has been warned to avoid recognizing you should you ever encounter each other. Such recognition could be detrimental to your mission, and it could be dangerous for Miss Hadley. Are we clear on that?"

"Your words are perfectly clear, Lawrence, but I won't commit to avoiding that person forever. You will have to assign a time limit to your sanction, or give Miss Hadley a new identity that would be compatible with my meeting her during the course of my mission."

"That may not be acceptable to our superiors. What happens if we cannot make such arrangements?"

"As you stated, I'm becoming adept at assuming new identities. There is always the possibility that Miss Hadley and I would both become different people and simply disappear."

"Apparently you have learned that all conversations are negotiations. I will request that the authorities comply with your conditions. Your suggestion of an identity change for the woman in question may be the solution to our impasse. In the meantime, following your period in jail, you will reside here at the academy, so that you won't be tempted to visit Miss Hadley."

George relaxed his stance. He hadn't noticed the tension in his muscles during their discussion, but felt vindicated by having stood firm on his refusal to turn his back on Alice. He reminded himself that Lawrence Bishop would always concern himself more with strategy and tactics than with accommodating the feelings of his agents.

"When does George Millerson report to jail?"

Lawrence handed him a file folder. "You have two hours to review and absorb your personal history and data from the enclosed documents. Upon completion of this study period, a uniformed officer will escort you to the jail."

CHAPTER 33 – DISAPPEARING ACT

Jeremy looked at the image on the large screen monitor. "So, you traced my great-grandfather, Michael Hadley to the editorial staff of the *New York Times*. How long did he work there, and where did he go after that?"

Joe Gonzalez shrugged his shoulders. "Jeremy, I'm afraid we have only partial information for you. Michael Hadley's personnel file at the *Times* indicates that he left his position there in February of 1939, supposedly because he needed to care for his sick mother in Ireland."

Debbie looked up from taking notes and asked, "Joe, why did you say 'supposedly?'"

"You're good at catching the subtleties. Michael said that he was leaving to care for his mother, but we have no record that he ever left the country in 1939."

"Perhaps his mother came to America."

Penny said, "We checked that possibility also, Debbie. Annie Hadley remained in Ireland until her death in 1947. She died in a car accident and had never been seriously ill."

Jeremy stood and started to pace. "If Michael didn't go to Ireland, then the story about his caring for his sick mother was an excuse to quit on short notice. When was the next time you found something on his activities?"

Penny looked at her papers. "At this point, we have nothing further on Michael Farrell Hadley until after the war. He disappeared from early 1939 until 1945. We may find new records in the future, but that's all we have for now."

"He couldn't have vanished."

Debbie patted Jeremy on his shoulder. "Relax; they found him again after the war. During the war, he must have done something that required what we today call stealth technology. He survived World War II, but he was undetectable."

CHAPTER 34 – CELLMATES

Otto Krieger stared at the new arrival without showing any emotion. Local jails had only one or two cells, so sharing was normal. The newcomer, somewhat younger and taller than Otto, put his coat on one of the two benches that also served as beds and nodded at Krieger.

"Greetings to you. Have you been here long?"

Krieger had an intense scowl on his face. "… long enough to have taken that bench as my bed. Put your coat on the other one."

The newcomer complied without commenting and then sat on his designated bench, waiting for the next comment from his cellmate.

"My name's Krieger. What do you call yourself?"

"I'm George Millerson. Sorry to intrude on your space, but they didn't have a separate cell for me. Do you have a first name?"

"It's Otto, but you call me Krieger."

"Fair enough, Krieger; you can call me George or Millerson, as you see fit."

"What is your accent? You don't sound like the other Brits around here."

"I could say the same for you. I'm American, but my folks came from England. Actually, I was born here but made the move across the pond as a child. I probably sound like some of each nationality. What's your accent?"

"I'm German, without anything else mixed in. I tutor British children in the German language. They may need it in the coming war."

Millerson said nothing for about a minute. "We Americans are determined to be neutral in any coming war, but I'd hate to have my British relatives and friends suffer."

"It will all depend on how much the Englanders resist when Hitler's forces come."

"That's a pleasant thought, Krieger. Will you be joining up with those forces?"

"As they say, that remains to be seen. You know, you may have German ancestry too. Many of the Millers were originally Muellers."

"I have heard that, but it may also come from a family's original occupation, milling grains."

"Ya, this is possible, but you probably don't know whether your family had that occupation or not."

"You have me there, Krieger. I never paid much attention to family trees or anything like that. Why are you here? What's your big crime?"

"I've done nothing wrong. The father of one of my students claims I took money from his house, but I didn't. I'm innocent."

"Well, I'm not innocent. I took my boss's Jaguar for a ride, and the cops picked me up when I returned the car. I didn't smash it up or anything. I just let that big cat race up and down a few roads between Corby and Birmingham, and then back to Corby by a different string of roads."

"Big cat ...?"

"They call the car a Jaguar, which is a big cat."

"Ah, I understand now. That was what you Americans call a play on words."

"You've got it, Krieger. I had a fine ride, and now I have to sit in this cell for two weeks to make them think I'll be a good boy again. I already apologized to my boss, but he was so mad that he rejected my apology and fired me. When I get out of here, I'll be looking for a new job."

"You said you'll be here for two weeks, Millerson. I don't know how long it will be before they take me to court, and what will happen after that. I may have a job for you if I'm still stuck in here when you get out. We'll talk about it at that time."

"You know, I can't teach people to speak German. I have trouble enough with the brand of English they use over here."

"You Americans have trouble with patience. We're stuck here, so relax. We'll learn more about each other while you're here, and then we'll determine what should happen later."

George rolled his coat into a neat bundle at one end of his bench. "I'll show you that I can relax. It's time for me to get a little sleep on this bench-bed. Try not to make too much noise while I'm sleeping."

"One question before you sleep, do you like German beer?"

George sat up. "Of course I do. Don't tell me you smuggled some into the jail."

Krieger smiled. "That proves your family was once Mueller. We will drink together after we leave this place."

CHAPTER 35 – FIRST OUT

Three days remained on George Millerson's two-week sentence. It hadn't been an unpleasant period, although the bench-beds were far from comfortable. Otto Krieger entertained him with stories of his camping and hiking adventures in Germany as a youth. Krieger also bragged about his carving skills, illustrating his story by carving their bar of soap into a wolf's head using a nail he had pried out of his shoe.

They were in the midst of discussing German card games when Constable Jeffries came to the cell door. "Good news this morning; you're going to get out."

George approached the door. "Wow, my sentence is reduced for good behavior."

"Not you, Millerson ... Krieger is the one who departs today. Otto, the party who complained about you stealing money now says that he found the amount in question behind a desk. He apologizes and has withdrawn his complaint."

"I told you I was innocent, Jeffries. You British are too quick to think all Germans are your enemies."

"We judge based on deeds, not ethnic background. You're free to go, but I'd love to have your Herr Hitler in my cell. I'd throw away the key so that he'd never get out."

Krieger picked up his coat and shook hands with Millerson. "George, when you are freed from this place in three days, please join me at the White Stag Pub at five in the afternoon. I owe you a pint or two for the good conversations we've had."

"They must have made an impact on you, Otto. You've never called me by my first name before. I'll see you there, and I challenge you to a game of darts."

Jeffries said, "That's enough chit-chat, you two. I have other duties on my schedule. Krieger, stop in the front office on your way out to sign some papers and retrieve the belongings you had when you arrived. Millerson, you'll partake of the same ritual in three more days."

"Wait, Jeffries, I have a going-away present for you." Krieger picked up the wolf head soap carving from the sink and handed it to Constable Jeffries. "Here's a sample of my German craftsmanship."

"It's good, but how did you carve that? I searched you for knives and other contraband when you arrived."

"Just call it magic. I am an elf from the Black Forest, you know."

CHAPTER 36 – THE WHITE STAG PUB

Three days later, George Millerson entered the White Stag Pub and saw Otto Krieger standing at a back table, waving his glass for attention. George stopped at the bar to order a pint of Guinness and then joined Krieger.

"Greetings, Otto, I'm here as scheduled."

"Your American pronunciation will take some getting used to. You'll recall that I said I would buy your drinks."

"That will be fine for any refills. I didn't want to wait for my first one. Two weeks in a cell makes one thirsty."

"Agreed, George ... I asked you here to see whether we might work together in the future. I'm looking for an assistant, and you said that your employer fired you after you took his Jaguar for a ride."

"I'll listen to what you have to say, and I'll enjoy my Guinness."

"I'm looking to do other things besides tutoring the German language to the children of rich people. I thought that given the likelihood of war between Britain and Germany, I might tutor German to military individuals and units."

"That sounds as though it might have potential. British soldiers would want to be able to communicate with prisoners and German civilians. How would I fit into your project?"

"I'd like you, as a neutral American, to visit military bases and ask whether they would be interested in language lessons."

"You could do that yourself, Otto. You don't need me."

"I need you for customer contact because they wouldn't trust me as a German citizen."

George drained the last of his Guinness. Otto rose to get him a new glass of the dark liquid and to get himself a refill of Harp. "Think about it while I get the refills. I'm trying to get used to Harp. German beers are already scarce over here."

When Krieger returned, George continued the conversation as though there hadn't been an interruption. "You want me to talk with potential customers because by doing so, I would be vouching for your honesty and loyalty to Britain. Are you honest and loyal to this country?"

Otto took a big swallow of his drink. "You know, this stuff tastes much better as you have more of it. My answer to your question is that you have identified the problem correctly. I knew you had brains. We already shared a cell, so you know I'm flexible about honesty, and as to loyalty, I'll need to be convinced that there's merit in supporting this kingdom. My easy path is to stay loyal to my German roots. These people here don't realize how much military strength Hitler has."

"How do you know about Hitler's military might?"

Otto scanned the tables around them and concluded that no one was close enough to overhear their conversation. Then he spoke in a low voice. "They told me and showed me during my last visit home."

"Who did?"

"The Abwehr ... the German intelligence service. They approached me because I have lived here for years. They want me to spy on the British and send coded messages back to them."

George raised an eyebrow, but answered in an equally low voice. "How did you respond to their request?"

"I told them I would have to think about it for a while. I also made immediate arrangements for my mother and father, my only relatives, to vacation in Scotland. They won't use their return tickets. I have friends in Edinburgh who have found them living quarters there. Whichever way

I answer the Abwehr people, they won't be able to use my parents for leverage on me."

"You're in an interesting position, Otto. I hope that Abwehr connection had nothing to do with your asking me to contact British military units on your behalf."

Krieger leaned back in his chair and stared at Millerson's eyes, looking for signs of nervousness. Not finding any, he said, "I figured that if I agreed to work with Abwehr, they would think well of me for having an American friend who had access to British military personnel. If I refused to work with Abwehr, it might protect me from reprisals to say I had a friend with military connections in England."

"Have you made that decision?"

"You're helping me to make it. I feel stronger with you as a friend. If we work together on a project, whether the one I described or a different one, I'll feel strong enough to refuse them."

George leaned forward and clinked his glass against Otto's in a toast gesture. Then he said, "Perhaps you shouldn't refuse them."

CHAPTER 37 – THE TWENTY COMMITTEE

Otto Krieger didn't know how to react to George Millerson's comment. "Are you saying that you think I should work for Abwehr as a spy for Germany in Britain?"

George drained his Guinness and set his glass on the table. Then he stood. "Sit here, while I call someone I know. He may be able to assist you."

George left for the telephone booth in the alcove off the main room of the pub and returned a few minutes later. Once back at their table, he suggested to Otto that they take a drive to meet the man he had contacted. Otto's reaction was less than enthusiastic.

"George, I want to trust you and work with you, but how can I be sure this meeting is not some kind of a trap for me. Are you some kind of government official?"

"There's nothing for you to worry about. I want to work with you too, but perhaps in a slightly different way. I'm not tied in with the government. For now, trust that I wouldn't ask you to do anything that might bring you harm. Come along with me to this meeting; I think it will be worth your time."

They went out to the car park, where George led the way to a black Vauxhall 10 saloon and opened the passenger door for Otto. Once he settled into the driver's seat, George removed a sheet of paper from his inside jacket pocket and studied the information on it. Then he started the engine and drove toward the north. Five turns and twenty minutes later, they arrived at a rural Anglican church where George saw Thomas Hadley waiting for them by the front steps. He parked and walked to meet

Richard Davidson

Thomas. Otto followed, lagging slightly behind his new friend.

They shook hands as George introduced them to each other. "Otto, this gentleman is Thomas Hadley, a friend of mine for some time. Thomas, Otto tutors the German language to private individuals, and we have discussed ways of increasing his business."

After shaking Thomas' extended hand, Otto asked, "Why are we meeting at this church? Is there something special about it?"

Thomas said, "A church is a welcoming place for people to have an informal meeting. It is usually open to anyone who desires a quiet sanctuary. In this instance, I've arranged for us to have a private office for our discussions. I hope that will be satisfactory. George, you look troubled. Is there a problem?"

"The idea of meeting at a church is fine with me. I'd feel more comfortable if you hadn't selected St. George's Church. I'm not the saintly type, having recently spent some time in a jail cell."

Thomas laughed and led them into the building, where they found the door to an office propped open for them. Thomas removed the doorstop that held the door open and invited Otto and George to enter the room. A bottle of mineral water and three glasses adorned the table. Once seated, George poured water for each of them.

Thomas acted as host. "I'm here at George's suggestion, and I hope to be of some assistance to you, Otto. We're all very aware of the threat that the aggressive German military poses to Britain and all of Europe. Several countries have already lost some or all of their territory to Hitler's forces. Otto, as a German national living in this country, you find yourself in an awkward position. How do you allocate your loyalty between your ancestral and adopted countries? On a confidential basis, George has informed me that you have already received

100

pressure from the Abwehr to support their efforts, and that you will have to respond to them soon."

"George, you disappoint me. I did not authorize you to discuss my situation with Thomas or anyone else. I thought I could trust you."

"You can, Otto. This meeting will help you resolve your dilemma. Listen to what Thomas has to say."

"Otto, I represent a group called the Twenty Committee. Our assignment is to identify German agents sent here to spy on British facilities and activities, with the goal of neutralizing them or otherwise rendering them ineffective. You are not such an agent, but you have received an invitation to become one. If you are willing to work with us, we would like you to accept the Abwehr proposition but to actually work for us."

"By us, you mean the British government?"

"Yes, I do."

"If I choose to work with you and put myself at risk of German retaliation, I will require several agreements from you."

Thomas looked slightly concerned, but he tried to hide it. "We anticipated that there would be some matters requiring negotiation. What agreements do you want from us?"

"First, and most important, I will not agree to be a traitor. In order to eliminate that outcome, you will have to obtain for me immediate British citizenship. That step would make me a patriot rather than a traitor if I worked with you."

"I see your point of view, and I'm sure we would be able to meet that requirement. What else do you need?"

"To eliminate the possibility of threats to my family from Abwehr, I moved my parents to Scotland. I would want them resettled there or in England with new untraceable identities."

"We'll agree to that. Is there anything else?"

"I have one final request. I have lived in England for several years as a businessman and language tutor. I will need to have a guarantee of a reasonable level of business income as compensation for any activities I perform for you. Whether I am in business alone, or with my new friend George Millerson, I will need obvious sources of legitimate income so that others will not perceive me to be a useless foreigner or a crook."

George said, "... or a possible German spy."

"Good point, George; can you meet my terms, Thomas?"

"I don't hear you asking for anything unreasonable, Otto. Assuming that Abwehr accepts you as a trustworthy agent, I'm sure we will be able to meet your requirements."

"In return I am to feed them false information you supply?"

"Yes, we will give you data to report that will contain just enough truth to be believable, but which may mislead your German handlers in a strategic direction. We would also hope that your becoming an Abwehr agent prior to a declaration of war, will lead to their entrusting later-assigned agents to your care and guidance."

"I see. I would then pass the identities of such new spies to your group."

"That's our hope. Do you agree?"

"I do, and I will enjoy being a British citizen doing my patriotic duty."

"Do you have any other questions, Otto?"

"Just one; what is the meaning of the name of your group, the Twenty Committee?"

Thomas laughed. "I don't think George knows the answer, and you'll both have to keep it highly confidential. Twenty is the equivalent of the Roman Numeral XX. That numeral refers to our double-crossing German intelligence officials by turning their agents against them."

George asked, "What will happen when you encounter agents who cannot be reliably turned back against their masters?"

"During wartime, captured spies are executed."

CHAPTER 38 – GEORGE AND OTTO

After Thomas left, George and Otto remained in front of the church to discuss the effects of the new developments. George could sense that Otto was not comfortable about what had transpired.

"Now that we're alone, Otto, would you mind telling me what you feel about this meeting?"

"It's not the meeting that was disturbs me; it's you, George."

"In what way? Did I do something to upset you?"

"I thought that you and I had enough commonality in background and outlook to work together in business. Now I have the feeling that you manipulated me into this Twenty Committee thing and that our long term relationship will disappear in the near future."

George knew he needed to word his response carefully. "Our relationship will remain intact and perhaps even strengthen, so long as you were sincere in your agreement to work with these people. Look at what you gained in this meeting. You're an outstanding negotiator. You protected your family from Abwehr reprisals. You obtained a shortcut to British citizenship. You even obtained a guarantee of a certain level of business income, even though I have no idea how that will work, since we haven't decided upon the nature of our business venture."

"Then you are going to work on a project with me. Thank you, George. Up to this point, I've felt like an outsider in this country. If we work together, I will feel that I belong. I did mean what I said about becoming a citizen and a patriot for Britain. One thing I've learned about this country is that people and institutions here are intentional about what they do, and by being deliberate, they make the future seem almost predictable. That is different from what the Hitler regime is doing in Germany. Everything there stems from the whims of a single erratic person. Even those who support him live in a state of fear, because Hitler could choose to turn on them at any time, for the least of reasons."

"You do realize that British stability will be sorely threatened by Hitler. He hates anything he can't control."

Otto extended his arm toward George for a handshake. "I told you that your family may once have been Muellers. You're beginning to think like a German. We love control and logical steps toward the future."

"If that's the case, then Herr Hitler should avoid a war with the Americans at all costs. Americans take an *anything goes* approach to the future and write their rulebook as they move forward. I'm hanging my hat on that philosophy."

"Fair enough, George, the firm of Krieger and Millerson will combine control with innovation in every project they undertake."

CHAPTER 39 – PARTY

The following day, as George sat eating breakfast in the residential section of the academy, his meal was interrupted by a page announcement that he had a telephone call. When the switchboard operator connected him, he heard the voice of Thomas Hadley.

"Good morning, George; I wanted to contact you before you ventured out on some undertaking. I need your analysis of how we did with Otto Krieger. I saw him talking with you as I drove away. How did he react to our meeting?"

"He was afraid that I had set him up for your pitch, and that I would soon abandon him to the clutches of the British spymasters. I assured him that we would, indeed, engage in one or more business projects together."

"Oh, yes, the man negotiated me into agreeing to support such an endeavor. He was considerably more demanding than I expected. Typically German approach to negotiations. What have you two decided to do?"

"At present, I have no idea, but I'm sure we'll come up with something that's marketable. He's being the stable, logical German, while I'm the American with the *I'll try anything* attitude. He finds my American accent fascinating, by the way."

"I'm sure that many times during the coming war we'll find his linguistic skills useful. My second motive in calling you this morning, by way of a reward for assignments well executed, is to invite you to a minor dinner party at my home this evening. Krieger has met me, so even if he follows you to that affair, he won't see anything alarming in it."

"Will a certain cousin of yours be there?"

"She will, and we will arrange for the two of you to disappear into a secure wing of the building while the rest of us carry on with idle chit-chat. It won't be the longest rendezvous, but it's the best I can offer right now."

"I humbly accept your kind invitation and offer. Thanks so much, Thomas. I've wanted to contact her ever since I returned, but lacked a suitable cover story."

"Just remember, she's officially visiting me and being introduced to George Millerson as a trivial side aspect to the gathering."

"Understood, Thomas; I'll be quite casual about it. Will anyone else there require my attention?"

"You'll meet Ruth Sisson who is a toymaker of French ancestry, but now a British citizen. She will tell you that she is looking to expand her business, a piece of information that you will pass to Otto Krieger. If things work well between them, you may have your business project with Otto."

"And you may have a honey trap for Otto, if he turns out to be less of a British patriot than he says he wants to be."

"That's one possible outcome, but I'm also looking ahead to the time when we will want Krieger to relinquish his partnership with you. You are too talented for us to pigeon-hole you into that relationship forever."

"Thanks for the compliment, but don't remind me about balancing complicated relationships. That's a topic we'll have to discuss before too many moons have come and gone."

"Agreed; just show up to renew your lapsed relationship with my cousin tonight."

When George arrived at Thomas Hadley's house he smiled at the sight of the green Austin Seven parked in the driveway. Alice had arrived before him. Now he would have to concentrate on being believable as a stranger to her.

He rang the doorbell and waited. A butler in formal attire admitted him and led him toward the gathering of guests. George noted the cheerful fragments of conversation emanating from the room ahead of him as well as a bulge under the butler's black morning coat. Thomas had instituted security procedures amidst the disturbing prewar news.

After an enthusiastic greeting, Thomas Hadley introduced George Millerson to his sister, Harriet, (familiar to George from his tutorial sessions during his earlier incarnation as Alice's brother) and to the various guests, including Ruth Sisson and Lawrence Bishop. The latter individual's presence was a surprise to George, who recalled Bishop's earlier admonition for him to avoid contact with Alice Hadley. At last, Thomas guided George toward his cousin.

"Alice Hadley, may I present a business associate, George Millerson. George is an American investor who is interested in establishing a British partnership of some kind. He hasn't shared his plans with me. George, Alice is my cousin. Our fathers are brothers."

"I'm very pleased to meet you, Alice. Are you involved in a business?"

"I suppose you would call me a devotee of the arts. I own a farm from which I derive rental income, but my interest is in culture and history. Thomas has a fine collection of antique books that I'd be happy to show you after dinner."

"I'm interested in such things also. I'll look forward to that tour."

They parted, and George engaged in conversation and an exchange of business cards with Ruth Sisson, following which a servant announced dinner. George noted that the two waiters possessed pocket bulges matching that of the butler. He took his assigned seat between Harriet Hadley and Ruth Sisson, being careful to turn his attention to those ladies rather than to Thomas' cousin. George estimated Harriet's age at about thirty-seven years, and observed that she had the disconcerting habit of thinking about something else while one talked with her. Ruth was somewhat younger; he guessed thirty-three, and she displayed an impressive mind that reached the logical conclusion of a discussion long before one presented it to her. Although this interfered with the planned flow of a conversation, it was preferable to Harriet's lack of attention.

During dinner, Ruth contributed a series of anecdotes regarding the British toy industry, while Harriet discussed family matters and tales of relatives in America. By the time they finished their individual custard tarts for dessert, the sound level of conversations had substantially increased as social awkwardness within the disparate group evaporated.

Following dinner, Alice approached George and reminded him of her offer to give him a tour of Thomas' library of antique books. He renewed his expression of interest and walked away with Alice. Harriet started to follow them, but Thomas intercepted her with a suggestion that she discuss her needlework and knitting skills with the wife of the local banker.

Alice led George down a hallway to a small room, which appeared to have a locked cupboard. She removed a key from her pocket and unlocked the cupboard door to reveal a second hallway. Locking the door behind them, they continued, past a small kitchen, into a secure windowless meeting room and the library beyond it. Once in the library, she locked the door and turned to George.

"It has been so lonely without you, George, or Michael or whoever you are now." They kissed, and clung to each other in a prolonged embrace.

"I've missed you too, Alice. We'll have to stick with my current name, George, to avoid slip-ups, but I'll always be Michael to you. This will probably be our only opportunity to be together for a while, but we'll share the future someday, even if you have to join into this name-changing business so that we'll be able to run away together."

"You know I love you and always will, no matter what. Even so, I need you to tell me about a rumored American marriage and how it might affect us."

George tried to avoid a pause before responding, but he wasn't successful. "... My mission over there required that I be married, so Thomas arranged for me to meet a woman named Stephanie Wright and marry her."

Alice separated herself from him and stared into his eyes. "I hadn't heard about my cousin's part in this. Did she turn out to be the *Wright* one for you?"

"My marriage to Stephanie was necessary to support my mission. It accomplished its purpose. Alice, you're the only *right* one for me."

"What about the rumor of a child with Stephanie?"

"Stephen was a few months old when I received orders to return here."

"You named him after her? Then you do love her!"

"Here we are, having our one chance to be alone together, and we're discussing our complications. That marriage was a device to support my mission as an editorial writer because the *Times* requires their key employees to be married. I played a part like an actor. My feelings toward you haven't changed. You are the person with whom I want to share my life, assuming we survive the coming war. Please marry me when it's over."

Alice relented and hugged George again. "Of course I'll marry you, but you'll have to worry about a bigamy charge. You'll also have to take responsibility for that other family that we will no longer discuss."

They adjourned to the sofa for brief, but passionate lovemaking, cut short because they would have to return to the party before their absence became a topic of general conversation. Then they straightened their clothes and inspected each other's appearance. After making a few necessary adjustments, they returned to the sofa and held hands.

Alice said, "I know we have a strange relationship and that your assignment required that other marriage. Despite that complication, I believe in you and your love. We'll make it through this mess."

Then, they wended their way out of the labyrinth of secure rooms and returned to the party as two diverging individuals. A few minutes later, as George talked with Thomas, Alice approached them and slipped a key into her cousin's pocket. Then she continued on her meandering path to join a conversation between Harriet Hadley and the banker's wife.

George guided Thomas toward a vacant space where they would not be overheard. "I've been reminded that a certain family in America will require support. What arrangements have you made?"

"I'd rather leave that topic for another time when we're by ourselves. It may have emotional overtones."

"Thomas, I need to know right now that Stephanie and Stephen will not be abandoned. A bad situation there will affect my performance here as well as my future with Alice."

"Then you two are long-term serious. Congratulations. In that case, please feel free to congratulate me also."

"What is your happy event?"

"Remain calm and expressionless, old boy, as I tell you my story. Others are watching us. This may push the limits of your ability to be calm in a stressful circumstance. I have to tell you that I sailed back to the United States a few weeks ago. Stephanie and Stephen are now living in a different apartment, and a few legal papers have been modified or replaced. Their apartment doorbell identification is now Mr. and Mrs. Thomas Hadley, but in case it becomes important, I also have a set of documents identifying me as Michael Farrell Hadley. At least for the moment, that identity is not in use."

"You can't take over a marriage out of a sense of duty, Thomas."

"Why not? You did when you married Stephanie to fulfill a mission requirement. Besides, my action wasn't truly the duty thing. I never told you, but Stephanie and I enjoyed each other's company before you entered the picture. Didn't you ever wonder how I managed to find you a suitable wife so quickly?"

George put his hands into his jacket pockets to keep them from shaking. "You knew Stephanie before I met her. Did you know her in the social or the biblical sense?"

"Both ..."

CHAPTER 40 – DEBBIE AND JEREMY

Jeremy entered the apartment, threw his keys onto the bookcase next to the front door, and called out to Debbie. "Deb, I'm home. You won't believe how much they charged me for my car repairs. I went in because I had a low air pressure symbol on my dashboard display, and ended up paying eleven hundred dollars to service that plus the suspension, and they talked me into buying two new tires. Sometimes I think they program the status displays to show trouble symbols at regular intervals, forcing you to return to the dealer for expensive services." He found Debbie working at her computer in her back room office. "What's happening? Do we have a new case to investigate?"

"Nope, I'm still trying to decipher the complex genealogy of your family. You'll remember that my original project encountered disaster when your great-grandfather, per a sheet of paper your mother found, turned out to be Michael Farrell Hadley, a person who died on the day of his birth."

"Right ..."

"Well, your mother discovered another document in her attic. This one says that your grandfather Stephen's father was Thomas Easley Hadley. That name does exist on your family tree as the cousin of the stillborn infant, Michael Farrell Hadley. It appears that your grandfather had two fathers."

"He had two fathers with the same family name?"

"Each of them was named Hadley, but the one we first found, Michael, was an impostor who took over the dead infant's name."

"That will complicate things, but at least Dad will be back to feeling he's a legitimate Hadley."

She stared at him. "It's not funny. Your family tree is a mess. I have no idea how to decide which of Stephen's fathers is the one responsible for his birth and which one is his stepfather."

"Perhaps you've discovered at least one of the reasons why my grandfather refused to discuss his parents."

"You should question your dad as to whether Stephen ever hinted that his family was unusual. I think the key clue has to lie in the fact that both fathers shared the same family name. Perhaps one died, and his cousin married the widow. I've read in the Bible that Moses and others said a man should marry his deceased brother's widow if she had not produced children for her dead husband."

"I don't know whether that rule would gain any traction in today's age of independent women."

"I was simply speculating. How else would you explain Stephen having two fathers with the same family name but two different first names?"

Jeremy looked smug. "You're making too much of this, Debbie. It's possible that there was only one father, but that someone entered an incorrect first name for him on that new document."

She had done her homework in anticipation of this question. "I didn't mention that I informed Penny Gonzalez of this new, second father, result. She researched the naturalization records and found that Michael Farrell Hadley became a US citizen in 1938, while Thomas Easley Hadley became a US citizen in 1946."

"I'll admit that my single person theory was questionable. At least we now know which of the two fathers came first."

Impostor

"That logic is also questionable. Thomas could have been in your great-grandmother's life long before he became a naturalized citizen."

CHAPTER 41 – TOYS

Ruth Sisson's toy studio was an enterprise barely touched by the industrial revolution. Located in a barn behind her farmhouse home, her four young workshop assistants performed almost all of their manufacturing operations with hand-powered tools and general-purpose electrical devices. Ruth knew that her business needed more professional management than she could or even wanted to give it. She firmly believed that her tops, puzzles, and building blocks were superior to similar products sold by larger companies, but marketing and distribution were not her strong suits. She needed help, and she hoped that the seeds she had scattered at Thomas Hadley's party would take root and blossom. The banker there sounded sympathetic to her plight, and that American investor, George Millerson, told her that he and a partner were looking to undertake a new business venture. Thomas Hadley even hinted that he had some funds he wanted to match with a worthwhile investment opportunity.

Her next step in cultivating these leads would come in an hour. George Millerson had called to arrange a visit for himself and the partner he had mentioned. In anticipation of this visit, Ruth instructed her lead assistant, 18-year-old Heather Watkins, to lay out samples of everything they made. Heather said that she would do that, but that she would also set up displays of each item at different stages of fabrication. Ruth appreciated Heather's initiative in going beyond her assignment. She hoped her cash flow would permit her to keep the girl on board as a permanent staff member.

As she completed tea time, Ruth heard an automobile arriving outside the barn. Glancing out of the office window, she saw Millerson and another man stepping out of a black Vauxhall. Ruth checked the arrangement of her hair in a mirror and met them in the reception area as they came in the door. From the second man's posture and slight bow as they entered, she assessed him as not being British.

"Good morning, gentlemen; Mr. Millerson, it's so good to see you again."

"Good morning to you Miss Sisson, allow me to present my business associate, Otto Krieger."

Millerson shook Ruth's hand. Krieger accompanied his holding of Ruth's hand with another slight bow.

Ruth said, "To clarify matters on the assumption that we will be talking and meeting beyond today's visit, I'm actually Mrs. Sisson. I'm a widow, my husband Paul having died in a car accident five years ago. We started this toy business together."

Both men murmured their sympathies to her.

"I mentioned Paul as background to any business discussions. He and I jointly developed our designs and techniques. I hope you won't find me impertinent, but Mr. Krieger, are you a German citizen? There will almost certainly be war between Britain and Hitler's Germany, so I would not look forward to working with someone whose loyalties were to the other side."

Otto shrugged his shoulders. "My national background is a curse I will have to bear throughout the coming war, but I am pleased to advise you that I have been a naturalized citizen of the United Kingdom of Britain and Northern Ireland since the past two weeks. My loyalties are with my new adopted country."

"Bravo, Mr. Krieger, I welcome your becoming one of us."

"Add my congratulations, Otto. I hadn't realized that your British citizenship had become official. If you will pardon my American brashness, I suggest that we all converse using first names. I find formality difficult and disconcerting."

"Very well, George and Otto, you may call me Ruth. Now, as to the purpose of your visit today, I understand that you two are looking to work together on a new business project. Have you worked together in the past?"

Otto motioned that he would respond. "George and I have only known each other for a short time, but we have found each other sufficiently compatible that we want to be in business together. Earlier, I assumed that we would start a business of our own, but George's report on your desire to expand your existing business, has us intrigued. We would welcome a discussion of how we might assist you and your toy company."

"Paul and I named our company Seasoned Toys. It's a play on our name, Sisson, but it also indicates our interest in making durable toys that are classics. We weren't interested in creating novelties or technical curiosities. Right now, we are making and selling tops for spinning, sets of wooden blocks, and jigsaw puzzles. These are all items we can manufacture right here, supported by local machine shops, with a low level of overhead cost. Our toys have become popular. Now, I have to learn how to distribute them better and to market them through a larger number of outlets. In short, my problem is that I am a toymaker rather than a business executive."

George said, "If your traditional toys are of high quality and reasonable cost, I suspect that you will find stable markets for your products, even during the coming war. The men will be off in the military services, but the women and children will find themselves confined within homes and shelters. They will need products to distract the children from war worries and help them pass time during long periods of isolation. Your toys may serve a great need, especially the jigsaw puzzles and the blocks. I suggest that we may be able to reach a meeting of the minds with regard to working together. What do you think, Otto?"

"I agree, and I may have suggestions for expanding your products through contacts I have in neutral Switzerland."

George raised a questioning eyebrow over Otto's comment but didn't respond to it. Instead he said, "Ruth, we would appreciate your giving us a tour of your facility and an opportunity to examine your products."

Having expected this request, Ruth agreed and led George and Otto from the office into the open section of the barn. There they found Heather Watkins prepared for their inspection visit. Following Ruth's introductions, Heather first demonstrated the spinning tops, including one model with a heavy flywheel that could balance on a taut string or a flat surface. It would continue spinning even though the board upon which it spun was moved in various directions. Then she demonstrated the ease with which the wooden blocks would snap together to form tall and strong structures, using a special tab-in-slot joint design. Heather's final demonstration was to show that a Seasoned jigsaw puzzle, once assembled, had such strong connections that she could lift the entire puzzle from its horizontal position on a table and rotate it for mounting on a wall without any pieces falling out of the assembled picture.

Following her demonstrations, Heather asked whether the guests had any questions.

George asked, "Are your puzzles made of wood like the blocks?"

Heather looked to Ruth for permission to answer, and after receiving a nod said, "We use a cardboard base material compressed from paper pulp and shreds with enough sawdust content to make it nearly as durable as wood. A local firm produces the base material for us using a process developed by Paul Sisson. We avoid the need for a huge stamping press for the cutting operation by stamping out only one row of pieces at a time. After mounting the artwork to the machine table, we trim it to a rectangle. Then we cut one row of individual pieces, index the stock, and repeatedly cut additional rows one at a time. The process is time-consuming, but it makes quality puzzles. The slight variations in the angles of the cuts due to our index-and-cut repetitions cause the assembled puzzle pieces to interlock with greater strength than would be the case if all cuts were made at once and were precisely parallel."

George pulled a magnifying glass from his pocket and examined a puzzle piece. "I'm impressed. You studied each step in the process and developed cost-controlled procedures for doing everything on a minimum capital basis. I like the way you think and your capabilities for making specialized tools and fixtures. Ruth, you have developed quite a business here."

"Thank you, George. Other small firms in the area support our efforts. At this point in our discussions, would you and Otto like to confer without us present, to decide whether you want to work with us?"

Otto said, "I don't think that will be necessary. George has already voiced his approval of your operation, and I agree with his statements. Let's say that we agree in principle to work with you. The next step will be for the three of us to sit down together to determine our division of responsibilities and the amount of additional investment that you will need. Do you agree, George?"

"I do, Otto, but we'll have to give Ruth time to decide whether she feels we would be acceptable associates. This is her business, and she should remain in control."

"Thank you, George and Otto, I won't need additional time. You two will be considerably easier to work with than would some of the bankers that I've consulted. It's rewarding to find people who appreciate one's products and work philosophy. Let's meet here again tomorrow to assign responsibilities and define our relationship."

George and Otto left and walked toward the Vauxhall. As they were getting into the car, George asked, "What are you thinking about your Swiss contact? You have something unexpected up your sleeve."

Otto smiled. "Thanks for being so observant, George. I do have something special in mind, but I'll save it for another time."

CHAPTER 42 – ABWEHR

The following day's meeting at the toy factory went well. George agreed to review current manufacturing and distribution procedures with the goal of suggesting improvements. Otto accepted the longer-term assignment of determining whether to recommend expansion of the firm in the face of the likely wartime economy. George noted that Otto was unusually pensive during the discussions, but didn't question him about it. Ruth appeared to be quite satisfied with her two new associates, especially since George kept insisting that she remain the leader while he and Otto worked in supporting capacities.

Following the meeting, Otto asked George to contact Thomas Hadley to schedule a new meeting of the three of them. They stopped at the White Stag Pub, where George telephoned to Thomas. Otto stood next to the slightly open booth door and strained to hear George's end of the conversation over the background noise in the pub.

"Hello, Thomas; it's George here. I have some new developments to discuss with you. Would you set up a private meeting? It will be you, Otto, and me. That same location would be fine, unless you want to meet someplace else."

George waited for the response from Thomas. Then he said, "Fine, we'll be there."

As he rejoined his friend, George could sense Krieger's tension from his posture and the expression on his face. "We're all set, Otto. We'll meet at 4:30 this afternoon at the same place."

"That's good. I need to give him some new information as soon as possible."

George could see that Otto felt his input would be important, but he decided to wait for the meeting rather than to press him for an advance summary of his news.

Promptly at 4:30, George parked the Vauxhall outside St. George's Church. He and Otto entered the church and went to the room they had used on their previous visit. There, they found Thomas in the midst of a telephone conversation. Thomas' last few comments before he replaced the handset on its cradle suggested that he had been on the defensive in a debate with someone in a superior position. After a slight pause, he greeted them.

"Welcome, you two; please pardon my being on the telephone when you arrived, but the Germans are accelerating their aggressive actions on the continent. They're demanding that the League of Nations return the Free City of Danzig to Germany, and they've given Lithuania an ultimatum to cede to them its Klaipeda Region. Each incremental step they take brings us closer to a full-scale war. It can only be a matter of months now." He shook hands with each of them.

"Otto, George requested this meeting on your behalf. I assume you have new developments to report. Please present them to us."

"Thank you, Thomas. Pardon me if I am a little excited, but I agree with your comment about events moving rapidly. First, I must announce that I have informed my contact at the Abwehr that I will work with them. In return, I received information about how well everything is proceeding on the continent. The German military leaders feel that they can simply ask for one country after another to yield some of its territory, and those countries will agree in order to avoid war. My other news is that following an agreement with Ruth Sisson for George and me to work with her company in the toy business, I contacted a toy-making associate in

Switzerland. I intended to see whether his products might be of interest here. During our conversation, he mentioned a publisher there named Rudolf Roessler, who appears to know about everything that happens in Germany as soon as it occurs. This publisher told him that an operation codenamed *Fall Weiss* is in progress. This operation indicates that Hitler will no longer settle for grabbing isolated regions from smaller countries. They are preparing to invade Poland."

George whistled a short tone. "If they invade Poland, full-scale hostilities will begin. Britain and France have guaranteed Polish independence. What do you think, Thomas?"

"You're correct. This is how the big wars start. An attack on one country pulls in its allies. I'll pass your information to those in the British government who will have to act on it. This is very high quality input, Otto. Thank you for your diligence."

George completed writing something in a pocket notebook. "Thomas, I suggest that someone in the government should try to cultivate a relationship with this man Rudolf Roessler. He appears to have inside information from the German military establishment."

"I'm sure our agents will have heard of him, but perhaps they haven't realized his potential value. I'll make a few phone calls to people in a position to act upon Otto's information. I'm sure that Switzerland will again remain neutral, at least nominally, during the coming war. It will be the perfect listening post location for as long as their transportation and communication links remain open. If I were Herr Hitler, I would assign high priority to isolating Switzerland from the rest of the world."

George said, "Otto, what did you have in mind when you contacted your toy manufacturer associate?"

"My friend, Dirk Grossen, manufactures jigsaw puzzles, just as Ruth does. I still have some reliable contacts in Germany. I thought that such individuals might photograph German military installations and then smuggle those pictures to Grossen in Switzerland. If Seasoned Toys had a marketing agreement to sell his Swiss puzzles here in Britain, he could include one puzzle of the military picture, marked with a code, as part of the normal shipment. Because puzzles ship unassembled, it would be difficult for customs agents to realize that one puzzle was different from the others. When the shipment arrived here, we would assemble the marked puzzle to reconstruct the intelligence photograph."

Thomas leaned over the table to shake Otto's hand. "Congratulations; that is a creative way to pass secret information. It would work until the German Army moved to block Swiss commercial export shipments. The Swiss are landlocked and vulnerable to a blockade. What do you think, George?"

"First, I think that Otto is showing us that he is no longer an outsider, but thinks and acts like the British citizen he has become. Bravo, Otto! Second, I suggest a backup plan for use after the Germans blockade commercial shipments from Switzerland. Newspapers have started to transmit photographs by scanning them and producing a radio signal corresponding to the variations in brightness of each dot in the original picture. Matching equipment at the receiving location prints a new copy of the picture matching the received sequential dot signals. The equipment is currently bulky, but I'm sure that engineers will soon improve the design, especially if it can help the war effort."

This time, Thomas Hadley congratulated George Millerson. "You've just hit on the difference between past wars and the one that's coming. The winner of this war will be the side with the greatest technical innovations. Right now, the Germans have the advantage because of their years of preparation, but as we and other countries enter the conflict, civilian and military technologists will have a major role to play. You've hit on one area they should address, improvements in sending all kinds of information by radio signals, not just voice messages."

"Thanks for the pat on the back, Thomas, but I think we've overlooked a topic of major importance."

"What's that?"

"Otto told us that he agreed to work for the German Abwehr and that they were pleased with his decision. I would like to know what they asked him to do for them."

Thomas asked, "How about that, Otto? Do you have any specific Abwehr instructions?"

"They instructed me to wait until Britain declares war on Germany, and then I'm expected to find a way to sabotage the electrical mains system."

"You're not an engineer, so they can't expect you to do anything large-scale or particularly technical. When the time comes, we might be able to arrange for a brief power outage in a nonessential area. Then we could have a few reporters write stories exaggerating the event's importance. That should satisfy them that you're following their instructions."

"Thank you Thomas. I didn't realize that you were in a position to arrange such things, or that you would be willing to do so."

"Our mission, Otto, is to convince the Abwehr that they are successfully developing a spy network in this country, while minimizing the impact of their efforts and turning their agents to serve our objectives. Assisting you with a minor power outage reported as major exactly fits our mission statement. That action will enhance your standing with them."

George said, "The flaw in that tactic is that they'll be so pleased with Otto's success that they'll ask him to repeat that sabotage in additional places. You can't continue to assist in causing multiple outages."

"We'll offset that possibility by including Otto among a large number of suspects who are questioned about the sabotage. If the Abwehr know that the police are interested in Otto and will be watching him, they'll tell him to restrict himself to normal business activities. That instruction will give him time to set up his jigsaw puzzle spy network and get it working."

Otto reacted to Thomas' comment by standing and hitting his left palm with his right fist, as a physical sign of his enthusiasm. "Then you are approving of my puzzle concept and are telling me to proceed with it."

"We endorse creativity and initiative. If your contacts can supply the Swiss puzzle maker with photographs of key German military installations and troop movements so that he can send them to us as disassembled puzzles, we'll have a new weapon in our arsenal of spy techniques. Implement your importation of the Swiss puzzles. You'll have to convince Ruth Sisson that the second puzzle line will improve her business, without hinting that there is a hidden extra dimension to that new affiliation. You'll also have to realize that Swiss commercial exporting will eventually dry up as enemy forces move to sever Switzerland's normal transportation channels."

Otto smiled. "I'm sure we'll obtain valuable new information for the government through the special puzzles. Later, as necessary, we'll modify the technique, perhaps through George's suggestion of scanning the picture into a radio signal and reconstructing it on this end. I'm going to enjoy playing an active part in this covert war."

George said, "Just remember that you also committed to playing an active part in growing Ruth's toy business."

"Don't worry; I won't abandon Ruth."

CHAPTER 43 – FEEDBACK

Startled by the knock on the apartment's front door, Jeremy rose from his chair to answer it. Out of the corner of his eye, he saw Debbie standing in the kitchen doorway. The person at the door would have had to pass through the downstairs lobby door along with a resident, defeating the security system. Jeremy prepared himself mentally for the possibility of seeing someone hostile when he opened the front door.

The unannounced visitor turned out to be Joe Gonzalez, unaccompanied by Penny. Jeremy relaxed from his alert stance. "Hi, Joe; why the stealthy visit?"

Joe entered, closing the apartment door behind him. He waved to Debbie, standing at the entrance to the kitchen. "When Debbie asked Penny for naturalization details regarding Thomas Easley Hadley, I did a double-take but tried not to let Penny see it. The Easley middle name triggered my reaction. Since then, I did a bit of research to refresh my memory so that I would understand his significance to our puzzle. I called Penny and asked her to meet me here. I'll brief everyone on my findings once she arrives. In the meantime, would you have a cup of coffee for a stealthy stranger if he joins you in the kitchen?

Debbie said, "You didn't go unnoticed by Penny. She told me that you have been acting strangely lately, and that she might have to hire me to shadow you in case you were hiding a girlfriend." She set a mug of black coffee on the table for him.

"You women all stick together. I'll save you the trouble. Penny is the only *girlfriend* I can handle. I did think that I managed my research without alerting her to anything being unusual. I'll have to take a refresher course on masking my thoughts and movements." He sipped his coffee and tilted the kitchen chair backward in a relaxed pose. "...coffee tastes great."

The doorbell rang, and Jeremy went to answer it, returning a few minutes later with Penny.

"Hi, Debbie; thanks for finding my wandering boy. Should I worry about his secretive activities?"

"He promised to confess to everything after your arrival. Would you like anything to eat or drink?"

"I'll take one of those apples in the bowl. As he talks, I'll decide whether it should be a snack or a weapon."

"Just don't hit me in the head with it. I might lose the memory I worked so hard to reconstruct."

"Was this memory blond, brunette, or redhead?"

"By the time I met him, his hair was gray. Jeremy, come over to my side of the table. I need some male support. I'm getting nothing but aggression from the women. Anyway, the person I've researched while I've been out of your sight is Thomas Easley Hadley. When I first ran into him, I didn't know you or your family, Jeremy, so I never considered that he might be connected to you."

Penny looked surprised. "You actually met Thomas?"

"He gave a classified lecture I attended during my first round of intelligence training. I've determined that his subject matter is now declassified, so I'll be able to discuss it with you."

Jeremy asked, "Was he considered someone important?"

"He was a member of the Twenty Committee, and they did something never done before or since."

Debbie took notes and then looked toward Joe. "What's the Twenty Committee?"

"They were a secret intelligence group in the UK during World War II that managed to identify all the spies that Germany sent into Britain."

Penny asked, "All of them?"

"As far as we know ... they even managed to turn most of them around so that they worked for Britain, identifying other spies and supplying misinformation to Germany. Those few spies that wouldn't cooperate faced prison or execution."

Jeremy asked, "If they couldn't feed damaging information to the Germans, why did they have to execute some of them? They could have just locked them up."

"In wartime, the rules are different. Spies for all countries are subject to execution if they are caught, Jeremy."

"That's barbaric, but so is war itself. Was the Twenty Committee a group of twenty counterespionage agents?"

Joe said, "I'm surprised that it took so long for someone to ask about that name. That group was named for the number twenty and not the number of people in it. Twenty in Roman numerals is XX. The significance of XX is that the group was charged with double-crossing the Germans by turning their agents around to spy on them and supply their former masters with misinformation. The committee members were very good at it. Had you heard of them, Penny?"

"No, I'll admit that this is new information for me. What do you remember about Thomas Easley Hadley, Joe?"

"As I said before, he had gray hair when I encountered him. I recall a lively sense of humor and a dynamic speaking voice. He wasn't one of those speakers who lull you to sleep with a monotone delivery. We were all concentrating on his words, anyway, because we had the opportunity to learn from someone who had personally made a significant contribution to the war's outcome."

Jeremy said, "The fact that he was in some way a part of my family makes me feel proud, even though the details of his fit within my family tree are still obscure."

Debbie touched his shoulder. "We'll figure out those details before we're through. I started to add *with this case*, but I'm not sure what to call our joint effort."

Penny said, "If it's not a case, it's at least a case study. I think we're all learning some key history from it. I'll authorize continuing low-level effort on it from our agency."

CHAPTER 44 – POLAND

The good news was that transatlantic airline passenger service was initiated in July of 1939 by Pan American Airways, followed on 5 August by the start of similar weekly service by Imperial Airways. The bad news started to arrive on 25 August with the bomb set off by the Irish Republican Army in Coventry, killing twenty-five people. One week later, on 1 September, Germany invaded Poland. Britain and France had guaranteed Polish independence, so on 3 September 1939, Britain declared war on Germany. The war news arrived via Prime Minister Neville Chamberlain's 11:00 speech on BBC, followed soon afterward by his establishment of a War Cabinet that included Winston Churchill as First Lord of the Admiralty.

Thomas Hadley left for London to consult with Churchill.

George Millerson, sensing that his toy business associates, Ruth Sisson and Otto Krieger were becoming romantically involved, felt that he would not attract curiosity if he dropped out of sight for a short while.

That evening, he knocked on the door of a farm cottage. The door quickly opened to admit him.

Several intense hugs later, they sat together on the sofa. "Alice, I couldn't stay away now that it has started. I don't know what's in store for either one of us. Whatever happens, we have to survive so that we will finally be together permanently."

"If you hadn't come for a visit right away, you might have missed me. I have my orders. By the end of the week I report to an estate north of London called Bletchley Park for a highly classified mission involving code work. I'll finally be applying my university work in mathematics. I've felt a bit *stored on the shelf* out here. I'll live on the premises there, but I might get an occasional night out, especially if you have the right kind of intelligence assignment. You may want to angle for something suitable."

"Of course I will if I can. If they don't ship me to the continent, I'll do my best to arrange something compatible with your work. Up to now, I've been moved around at the whims of your cousin. Now that the war has started, I may seek to free myself from his direction."

"Hold up, George; do I detect a conflict between you and Thomas?"

"If there is, it's a strangely comforting type of conflict. You see, without any prior discussion, Thomas took over my mission marriage in America. According to all official paperwork, he's now Stephanie's husband, and I'm free of any obligations over there. I'm yours and only yours."

She studied his face and stared into his eyes. "Don't you have any misgivings about that? What about your son, Stephen?"

"I do wonder how well I would have done as a father to him. He won't remember me. I came back here when he was only a few months old. I should probably keep track of him as he grows up, but I probably won't spend appreciable time with him again."

"Is that you or your sense of obligation talking?"

"I'll have to say that I don't know. I've turned my back on the family that raised me, so it wouldn't be too much different. I didn't ever feel I was part of that group. I probably feel a stronger connection to my son than to my original family, but I'm still a bit of a lone wolf. All I know for sure is that I could never turn my back on you."

"My mother told me that I should never say 'never'. You do understand that if we marry, Thomas, Stephanie, and Stephen would be part of our extended family."

"Of course I do, Alice, but we'll face the implications of that much later."

"I'm sure we'll cope, so long as we have each other. I hope we'll always stay in love." They kissed and sat silently.

"George ..."

"Yes."

"If we make it through the war and stay together, I will call you Michael or I will call you a new name, but at least to me, you're not a George."

CHAPTER 45 – OTTO

Ruth studied the kneeling man as he packaged the jigsaw puzzle pieces that had dropped into the receptacle beneath the complex cutting blade. His sandy hair was thinning. His nose was crooked. After years of avoiding manual labor, he had started to display calluses on his hands.

"Otto, I don't understand how we've reached this point."

He concentrated on his work as he off-handedly answered. "What point is that?"

"When I was young and living in France during the last war, I promised myself that I would avoid activities with anyone who was German because the Kaiser's troops attacked my country. I also told myself that I would not hire anyone older than twenty-five to work in my toy business, because young employees are the only ones who will agree to follow my procedures exactly. Further, I find myself no longer framing each day's activities in terms of similar jobs done alongside my husband, Paul."

Otto stopped working. He concentrated on Ruth's face and cool blue eyes. He could see his silhouette reflected in those eyes as Ruth faced the bright lights behind him. "I thought I would always be treated as a foreigner by British people. I thought I was too much of a professional to do manual labor. I doubted that I would ever find a woman with whom I could be comfortable at all times."

She held out her hand for him to grasp and helped him to his feet. They continued to hold hands after he stood. "We haven't worked together for a great amount of time, Otto, but I already know this partnership is right for both of us."

"You don't know everything about me, Ruth. I might have unpleasant secrets."

"And what's to say that I don't, Otto? We'll learn about each other as we continue to work side-by-side."

"Are you saying that you want our relationship to be restricted to the working variety?"

"No, I'm opening the door to something much more special, if you feel the same way."

"I do, but I'll have to consider whether this changes our business relationship with George."

"That's something totally separate from the way we feel about each other." She led him into her office and locked the door so that they would have privacy. Then she put her arms around his neck and kissed him."

Otto returned the kiss with fervor. "I grew up thinking that English women were completely reserved and non-demonstrative about their passions."

"And I swore that I'd never allow myself to have romantic feelings toward anyone who was German." Ruth started to unbutton her blouse. Amidst a great deal of fumbling and caressing, they negotiated their new relationship.

Two hours later, George arrived at the toy factory and asked Otto to step outside for a few minutes. When they were by themselves he said, "Now that the war has begun, I'm going to have to beg off from our working agreement. You can stay here, assisting Ruth without interfering with your wartime assignment of dealing with Abwehr and future German agents. I need to determine how I can best contribute to the war effort. I hope you'll understand."

Otto shook George's hand. "I agree with your thinking. You're released from our agreement about working together."

"What about Ruth? Do you think she'll resent my leaving?"

"Ask her yourself." They went back into the barn to join Ruth.

George approached Ruth, not knowing what to expect. "Ruth, I'm afraid I'll have to drop out of our working agreement in favor of taking on a war-related assignment. I hope you won't mind."

"George, you're not obligated to stay here at all. We all have our parts to play. Let's have a final drink together." She removed three glasses from her desk drawer and momentarily debated whether to select the port or the scotch. She chose the scotch and poured it generously. "Here's to accomplishments we've made together and to future victories wherever fate may find us."

They clinked their glasses together and downed the strong liquid.

Ruth shook hands with George and then said, "Who knows? Otto and I might soon be manufacturing war supplies."

George saw the way Ruth and Otto exchanged glances and walked out of the building smiling.

CHAPTER 46 – ASSIGNMENT

Thomas Hadley had disappeared into the inner circles of London's intelligence establishment. George Millerson knew that with the British declaration of war against Nazi Germany on 3 September 1939, it was essential that he obtain a new assignment while he still possessed significant contacts and some measure of control. Given the absence of Thomas, he decided to approach Lawrence Bishop, the training coordinator at the academy.

As he entered the academy, George observed a new sense of urgency in the hustled movements and strict discipline of the military personnel around him. The preparation stage was behind them. The students graduated there would leave to apply their learned skills.

He waited for two other individuals to complete their discussions with Bishop before he received permission to enter the office. Once inside, he and Lawrence shook hands; then Lawrence took his seat behind the large desk, awaiting the anticipated petition from George.

"Lawrence, I've completed my assignment of bringing Otto Krieger on board with the Twenty Committee as an agent, while obtaining a viable cover enterprise for him. Otto is content and dedicated to his business and his partner in it. With the recent declaration of war, I need a new assignment."

"I take it that you are here this morning because Thomas Hadley is not available for your consultation; hence the value of a flexible chain of command. As it happens, your proper assignment is obvious. You will report to the Ministry of Information, where you will find that you have some standing, at least under your former name. They will determine how to best use your skills at this time. You've come a long way since our first meeting, George. I hope that your future efforts produce results equally as good as those from your activities up to this point. This will be the last time we meet, at least for a long while. I'm returning to military service, where I will be in a position to have a more direct effect on events."

"I appreciate everything I've learned under your guidance, Lawrence. Good fortune to you in your new position."

"Thanks, George. Between you and me, I'll need some good fortune. As a nation, we spent too much time refusing to believe that the war would come. Hitler's forces are infinitely better equipped than we are, but we will catch up with them. Right now, we don't even have enough weapons to arm every soldier. Hopefully, the major battles will not occur before we build up a satisfactory supply of arms and equipment."

The next day, George parked the Vauxhall across the street from the new Ministry of Information headquarters at the Senate House of the University of London. Once inside, he presented the documents prepared by Lawrence Bishop's staff to the guard at the front desk. That individual directed him to the office of Welby Marsh, the assistant director. As George followed the guard's directions to Marsh's office, he observed a high level of activity due to a steady stream of new people and equipment arriving and circulating through the corridors.

He knocked on Mr. Marsh's door. That individual, a thin man with rimless glasses and a pencil mustache, hastily donned his jacket and opened the door to the visitor. "Pardon our appearance, but we're just moving into this building. We've only been formally organized for two days, and the Minister, Lord Macmillan, received his official appointment today. Are you one of my new staff people, or are you from another department?"

"I didn't appreciate that the Ministry of Information was only now getting assembled." He handed Marsh the paperwork. "I'm George Millerson, and I'm here because Lawrence Bishop said I should come here for an assignment."

Welby Marsh opened the envelope and studied the papers. "You didn't read your documents, did you?"

"No, I didn't think that would be proper. They were intended for your eyes."

"Having seen them, I want to extend my welcome to you, Michael. You see, the paperwork details your activities in America for the *New York Times* under your former name of Michael Farrell Hadley. The Ministry of Information existed during the last war and was then closed down, having been revived officially only two days ago. When you were writing editorials in New York, you were serving effectively as the entire Ministry of Information. I read a few of your pieces, by the way. They were quite good."

"So, you want me to revert to being Michael Farrell Hadley?"

"That will be essential for the work we will desire from you."

"What will be my position, and what will be my assignment?"

Welby Marsh laughed. "You probably won't believe this, but your position is to be invisible. Michael Farrell Hadley is an American citizen. We will want you, as an unbiased American, to write materials that will encourage your fellow Americans to like and support the British. You will have to convince the neutrality-loving Americans that it is right and proper for them to support and supply their British cousins. This will not be an easy job, especially while we are warning British writers and lecturers to avoid anything that conveys the same message."

"In other words, British writers may not openly encourage American support of British war efforts for fear that Americans will resist lectures from foreigners, but American writers may do exactly that, preferably in subtle ways."

"That's it exactly. In order to support your authenticity and lack of bias, you will not be housed here. We will want to be able to substantiate an arm's length relationship with you, should someone enquire. You will be an American academic, doing research on the American War of Independence from the British viewpoint."

"That's fine, but from our viewpoint we call it the Revolutionary War."

"Spoken like a true American. You'll do well. We'll have continuing informal contacts through your secretary, but we'll only occasionally have in-person meetings, usually in the context of accidental encounters. We will, after all, be operating on the same university campus, so chance contacts would be expected. Do you have any questions or comments?"

"I hope you'll tell me that I have a little budget, and I hope I'll be free to travel throughout the country to research travel pieces for American consumption. I would also like to know whom I contact to get my stories published in various outlets of the American press."

"As I said earlier, you will have a secretary. She will have high-level credentials and will negotiate an arrangement with an agent based in the United States. That person will handle all of your freelance negotiations and contract details. Your job will be the writing part, but we'll welcome your proposals for new projects."

"Well, thank you Mr. Marsh of the British government, would you have someone show me to my new quarters?"

"I'll cater to American informality. Make it Welby, Michael. I'll take you there myself. You'll be using an office that the university has reserved in the past for visiting dignitaries. They assigned it to us without any limitations on how we may use it. The office is in King's College, sufficiently removed from the Senate House to eliminate any suggestion that you are connected with the Ministry of Information."

Once he parted from Welby Marsh, Michael tried out his new desk chair and made a telephone call. "Good morning, Alice. I have both good and bad news. The good news is that I'm Michael again. You will no longer have to deal with George. The bad news is that I'm back to being your brother, which may make social events awkward."

CHAPTER 47 – THE PHONEY WAR

The consequences of Britain and France having pledged to guarantee the independence of Poland greatly increased in significance as Germany unleashed its new *blitzkrieg* tactics on the Poles. On 1 September 1939 Large numbers of tanks, operating as an independent force penetrated Polish territory at lightning speed from the west while similarly large numbers of bombers, including the new dive bombers, attacked overhead. As Polish forces withdrew eastward, they encountered a new threat. Stalin's Soviet Army attacked Poland from the east, in accordance with an agreement between German and Soviet foreign ministers a week earlier to divide Polish territory between their two countries.

In response, the British Expeditionary Force (BEF) and thirteen RAF squadrons entered France on 9 and 10 September. The British forces arrived too late to save Poland, so instead they took up positions to protect France, principally along the fortified 280-mile-long Maginot line that stretched along the entire border between France and Germany. The British and French forces counted on support of their left flank by the small defending militaries of Holland and Luxembourg, with Belgium armed but remaining neutral.

For seven months, the Germans did not attack, and the front remained stationary, allowing the British forces to receive improved weapons and equipment. Neville Chamberlain's government began to express hopes that they would be able to negotiate a peace treaty to end the impasse.

Richard Davidson

Then the Germans completed their own buildup and struck. On 9 April 1940, the Wehrmacht armies and Luftwaffe aircraft invaded Denmark and Norway. With the fall of Norway, Parliament forced Chamberlain from office and replaced him as prime minister with Winston Churchill. That same day, Hitler's armies and aircraft attacked Holland, Belgium, and Luxembourg and then began an end run around the stationary fortified lines manned by the British and the French. Those fixed barriers had the available French and British tanks strung out along their entire length, positioned to counter an attack across the barriers. Instead, by early May, the Germans sent their massed tank divisions at high speed along the French side of the barrier lines and rolled up the spread-out defenders. The Phoney War ended as British and French forces fell back, searching fruitlessly for defendable positions.

CHAPTER 48 – WRITER'S DILEMMA

Now established in his University of London office, Michael sat at his desk and meditated on the best way to tackle his writing mission. The facts that the British troops had limited and poor-quality supplies plus their having been handily out-maneuvered by the Germans could hardly rate as good selling points for the Americans to come to their aid. He would need a message that went beyond the facts in addressing the American public.

As he contemplated his options, Michael remembered a comment made by Welby Marsh during a recent evening discussion at a local pub. They hadn't intended to discuss anything particularly consequential, but an interesting tidbit bubbled into the stream of their conversation. Welby recounted the observation of a British Embassy official in Washington concerning the way that Americans didn't absorb raw information. He said that Americans digest information only when it is fed to them as part of a story or drama. As Michael remembered that comment, he printed it in large letters on a blank sheet of paper and underlined it twice. He had his key. His thrust in writing successful articles would be: once upon a time ... or bust.

Michael added to that watchword his own experience from conversations with native-born Americans that they see the British as being too aloof and class conscious. His stories of British people would have to stem from the working class or from those to whom the concept of class was an obsolete idiosyncrasy. He rolled a fresh sheet of paper into his typewriter and began to hammer the keys to forge a first draft.

Richard Davidson

Early this morning, I decided to acquire a walking stick to accompany and support me while hiking on one of those famous walking tours across the English countryside. While not too practical in the vastness of America, such tours are both educational and healthy in an island nation where no inland point is more than seventy miles from the coast. My inquiries as to a suitable supplier of a hiking staff led me to Jason Burns and Sons on London's New Oxford Street. Founded in the West End in 1830, this maker of canes, walking sticks, and umbrellas has been owned and operated by members of the same family ever since. They are precision craftsmen and well known for their products, even in the United States. The manager told me that one American customer once requested that the company make him a walking stick in every English wood that was available. That customer received more than seventy walking sticks.

Impostor

Imagine my surprise this morning when I entered the front room of the Burns & Sons establishment, only to be told that my order would have to be placed on a waiting list, because they currently allocate only ten percent of their production to the civilian market. Once the British government entered the war against Nazi Germany, the owners decided that their patriotic duty was to support the war effort, using their more-than-century-old skills. Today, ninety percent of the production of Jason Burns and Sons takes the form of buttstocks and forestocks for Lee-Enfield military rifles. According to Dwight Harvey of the Burns firm, they were not exceptional in asking the government what they might do to support the war effort. Many small and medium-sized firms have made similar decisions to convert their manufacturing, partially or totally, to war-related products and services. Their actions remind me that the small firms that serve as the backbone of the

United States economy, developed from similar local

family efforts. Whatever our personal ancestral

heritages, as Americans, our work ethic and our

individual desires to go out on our own in a small

business, stem from the traditions and skills of our

British cousins.

By the way, I did order that walking stick, and

even though I won't receive it until next year, I know

that it will give me long and sturdy service.

Michael reread his draft twice and then called for his secretary, Joanna. "Please take this draft to Welby Marsh for his opinion and suggestions. If he and you like it, make any necessary improvements and send it off to Hank Murray in the States for his distribution to periodicals that might have an interest."

"That's very humble of you, Michael, but based on unofficial government connections, you know that at least a few magazines will accept it."

"You're right, of course, but I still enjoy thinking that I have to earn the right to appear in print."

Joanna scanned the draft. "I do have one suggestion for you."

"What's that?"

"Americans like informality. I suspect that at least for this kind of piece, you would receive a better response if you dropped the Farrell middle name. You may want to consider signing it as Michael Hadley or even Mike Hadley."

"That's a good suggestion. I'll take the middle road and sign the piece as Michael Hadley. I'm not sure I'm ready for public use of just plain Mike at this point ... maybe later, after I get used to hearing more people call me that."

CHAPTER 49 – ALICE AND MICHAEL

Three months later, Michael answered the telephone and received the pleasant surprise of hearing Alice's voice. "Hello, stranger; how would you feel about buying a girl some dinner?"

"Hi, Alice; it's great to hear from you. I thought they kept you cloistered at all times."

"They're allowing us a one week break four times each year. We can't do any shop talking, of course. Do you have any plans for this week?"

"I do now. Where shall we meet?"

"I'll come to you. I'd like to see your office and appreciate your new status as an American academic."

Michael looked around at the institutional furniture and blank pale green walls in his ten foot square quarters. "This place is pretty bare bones, but you're more than welcome to visit me. At least, I have a window that looks out on people walking back and forth between the buildings."

"Is your desk piled high with research documents?"

"I haven't been here long enough to achieve that seriously academic look, but I'll work on it if that's your preferred style."

"It sounds perfect the way it is. I'll be there in thirty minutes. Then let's go somewhere within walking distance to eat. I need to spend time in the outdoors, after all my on-duty confinement."

Precisely thirty minutes later, Alice knocked on the frame of Michael's open door. She bore a big smile and a stuffed toy bear wearing a blue and white apron.

"Greetings, Michael; it's so good to be face-to-face again." She entered his office and shut the door behind her to give them privacy.

After several warm kisses, he asked, "Who's your friend?"

She placed the bear on his desk facing his chair. "Allow me to introduce you to Alicette. She is your slightly smaller representation of me to keep you company when we're apart. Feel free to talk with her in my absence."

"Is she fitted with a listening device, so that you'll actually hear what I tell her? I might have to be very careful if that's the case."

"You're safe. She's just what she appears to be, as am I."

"You're much more than that, Alice. I'm not putting you on a pedestal, but you're the center of my universe."

"Spoken like a ridiculously enthusiastic American writer – let's get out of here before we get too mushy."

Michael introduced Alice to Joanna as his sister, causing her to arch a skeptical eyebrow. He told her that they would be at the London Arts Pub if someone needed to find him.

They were bringing each other up to date and enjoying their pub lunch forty-five minutes later, when Welby Marsh entered and headed straight for their table. "I'm sorry to have to intrude on the two of you, but there has been an emergency. I'll give you more details when we're outside and away from the crowd."

Michael left some money on the table and followed Welby out the door, shepherding Alice in front of him. Welby led them to a small spot of greenery under a tree on the edge of the campus.

"I regret that our first meeting had to come under these circumstances, Alice, but nowadays one must be prepared for anything. Joanna told me that you are

Michael's sister, which would bother me if I did not know that our mutual friend changes identities like the latest fashion styles. In any event, Michael, your pieces for American consumption have been sufficiently impressive that the Germans decided to do something about them. They sent an agent to assassinate you in your office."

"Is Joanna safe? Give me more details."

"Everything is under control now. When this man pulled out a pistol and pointed it at her, Joanna distracted him by calling out a warning to you over his shoulder. As he pivoted, she disarmed him and hit him on the head with his own gun. I did tell you that Joanna is highly qualified, didn't I? We consider you a major asset, Michael, so we made arrangements for your protection. Your German visitor is now in the custody of MI6 for questioning."

Michael withdrew his notebook and pen from his jacket pocket. "What is the agent's name, and was he known to the Twenty Committee?"

"The identification he carried was his British alias, John Jones. He was known to said committee and supposedly had received the blessing of a previously turned Abwehr man as having been converted to our side. MI6 will give him priority attention because his action against you may implicate someone else in the system."

"Then, I've failed."

Alice asked, "What do you mean?"

"As George Millerson, I recruited the apparently harmless German language teacher, Otto Krieger as a primary asset for the Twenty Committee. We had him in place with Abwehr German Intelligence before the war so that Abwehr would send subsequent agents to him for orientation, and Otto would bring them to the attention of the Twenty Committee. It appears that Otto is serving both sides in this war. He sent this agent after me because Otto knows me as George Millerson. Michael Hadley is a stranger to him."

Welby patted Michael's shoulder. "We're at war now, so there will be harsh consequences for both the agent that Joanna overcame and your man Krieger. Would Krieger's demise bother you?"

"It would if he were the man I thought I knew. His actions show that he remained a stranger to me, and a dangerous one. There will be many more betrayals before this war is over. I should check in with Joanna and thank her."

"Tomorrow will be soon enough for that. Joanna is a professional. You and Alice should take the rest of today for pleasant pursuits. We want you to be in a proper frame of mind for tomorrow. In the meantime, we'll move your office to a private and guarded section of King's College so that any future agents will be less likely to locate you. Joanna will guide you there from your current office in the morning."

Michael thanked Welby before walking away with Alice. They walked in silence without apparent purpose for about fifteen minutes before Alice brought Michael to a stop by pulling on his arm. "You're more upset by Otto Krieger's action against you than you admitted to Welby."

"I am upset, but less because of its effect on me than because of what it will do to Ruth Sisson. She's the toy manufacturer you met at Thomas' party. She's in love with Otto, and now, as was the case with her deceased husband, she'll again lose the central man in her life."

Alice squeezed his arm. "I'm determined to never lose my central man."

CHAPTER 50 – DUNKIRK

In April of 1940, the British Expeditionary Force (BEF) retreated after having suffered large losses as German forces attacked their static positions from flank and rear directions at the end of the seven-month-long Phoney War. By 21 May, the Germans encircled the BEF, the remainder of the Belgian forces, and three French armies in an area along the northern coast of France. Seeing that the only escape from their dilemma would be a withdrawal across the English Channel, BEF Commander General John Vereker planned for an evacuation from Dunkirk, because it was the closest location with acceptable port facilities and beaches.

In order to get the trapped forces to Dunkirk, a delaying battle against the Germans would be required. Given the relative strengths of the two sides, success by the BEF and its allies could hardly be guaranteed. Then, on 24 May, the unexpected happened. The German High Command, either with Adolf Hitler's approval, or at his instigation, issued an order for its forces to halt and cease further advances. Many of the German ground forces commanders argued against this tactic without success.

Because of the halt order, the Allies had time to move their forces toward Dunkirk. They took up positions behind a canal system, flooding it behind them to delay a future German advance. They also constructed defensive obstacles for the same purpose.

The Germans captured the port of Boulogne and encircled Calais, leaving Dunkirk as the only port in the area suitable for the evacuation. The German High Command halt order enabled the allies to reach Dunkirk despite the great odds against them. The apparent reason for the Germans' failure to advance was that Hermann Göring, Commander of the Luftwaffe, convinced Hitler to let his aircraft finish off the allies as they sat penned up against the English Channel. Hitler's resulting order was transmitted without coding, and the British intercepted it.

Upon receiving Hitler's halt order, the British sent sixteen squadrons of RAF aircraft against the Luftwaffe, which, combined with bad weather in the area, diminished the effectiveness of the German air forces. On the ground, German Army Group B, the only unit allowed by Hitler to continue advancing, was met by the remaining 40,000 men of the French First Army in a crucial delaying action.

The evacuation of British and allied troops from Dunkirk was christened Operation Dynamo. It utilized every available naval vessel plus many unofficial civilian ships and small craft of various types volunteered or requisitioned without permission for the purpose.

Michael's telephone rang seven times early on the morning of 27 May. When he finally dragged himself from his bed to the instrument, he heard Thomas Hadley's voice.

"Wake yourself up, Michael; we have an emergency."

Michael shook his head to clear his brain and slapped his cheek for emphasis. "I'm functional. What needs to be done?"

"They've minimized the publicity, but the remains of the British Expeditionary Force plus French and Belgian units are trapped on the northern French coast at Dunkirk. They have to be evacuated across the channel before the Germans annihilate them. I have requisitioned a large motor boat. Will you be able to crew for me, and have you any nautical experience?"

"Thanks to our mutual wife, I have some. Stephanie took me out in her father's boat off Bridgeport a number of times, and she taught me the basics."

"Connecticut women are always raised with some sea experience. Meet me at Folkestone in two hours. We'll leave from the wharf there. I have copies of the necessary charts for channel, sandbank, and minefield markings. We won't be able to plot a direct course. You'll want proper clothing and a supply kit. We'll make multiple trips over several days."

"You may want to arrange for a second crew, to keep the boat working even after we get too tired for a safe passage. Thanks for including me. I'll see you in two hours."

Neither the Hadleys nor any of the other civilian, commercial, and military crew members of the evacuation fleet would forget their Dunkirk experience. Avoiding all the other vessels in the motley fleet plus underwater obstacles required intense application of all of their skills. They quickly learned that they would be under fire whenever they went in to pick up soldiers and that luck would be a major factor in their survival. The soldiers waiting for evacuation were the targets of bombs and strafing, despite the protective efforts of many RAF fighters that continually battled the assaulting German aircraft. During the operation, which lasted from 27 May to 4 June, 1940, 226 of the 693 participating vessels were sunk by German ordnance, whether air or ground-based. The Royal Navy lost six destroyers, while the French Navy lost three. Due to these losses, the Royal Navy ordered eight destroyers diverted to their home ports to save them for future actions. The class of vessels with the highest losses was the *other small craft* category, which had 170 sunk out of a total of 311. Throughout the operation, there was friction between the British and French militaries due to informal and formal preferences for British over French evacuees. At the end of the operation, 35,000 French soldiers of the 2ⁿᵈ Light Mechanized Division and the 68ᵗʰ Infantry Division who had protected the troops during the evacuation, surrendered to the Germans. All the heavy equipment of the BEF had to be abandoned in France.

Despite all the logistical difficulties and tragic losses, by the end of Operation Dynamo 338,226 troops from the several national commands had been successfully evacuated to England. There was so much euphoria among British citizens that Prime Minister Churchill felt obliged to make a cautionary statement.

We must be very careful not to assign to this the attributes of a victory. Wars are not won by evacuations.

On the American side of the Atlantic, the *New York Times* disagreed. On June 1, 1940, its Dunkirk message was:

So long as the English Tongue survives, the word Dunkirk will be spoken with reverence. In that harbour, such a hell on earth as never blazed before, at the end of a lost battle, the rags and blemishes that had hidden the soul of democracy fell away. There, beaten but unconquered, in shining splendour, she faced the enemy, this shining thing in the souls of free men, which Hitler cannot command. It is in the great tradition of democracy. It is a future. It is a victory.

When Thomas and Michael completed their final trip carrying six wounded but determined French soldiers, they collapsed on the beach, leaving their passengers' care to the many assigned and volunteer caregivers lining the shore. Michael's left upper arm ached beneath a crude and soiled bandage due to a strafing bullet that had passed completely through it during one of their trips. He felt the sudden impact while they were positioning their boat close enough to the Dunkirk shore to pick up wading soldiers of various forces. Michael knew that he would have to visit one of the many doctors who were assisting the incoming wounded soldiers before he left the arrival facilities for home.

After a ten-minute rest break, Thomas left the area, returning five minutes later with a bucket of black paint and a brush. Without a word to Michael or to others standing nearby, he waded out behind the boat, where he used the paint to cross out the boat's original name, *Durgin's Folly* and replace it with a new title, *Dunkirk Queen*.

Years later the *Dunkirk Queen*, along with the other surviving civilian vessels would be granted the right to fly a new ensign, the Dunkirk Jack, bearing the St. George's Cross defaced with the arms of Dunkirk. No other boats or ships would be entitled to fly this flag.

CHAPTER 51 – SCRAPBOOK

Early December brought a festive Saturday morning for Debbie Danforth and Jeremy Hadley. During their recent visit to Jeremy's parents' house for the Thanksgiving holiday feast, Jeremy enhanced the occasion by proposing to Debbie and giving her a ring of his own design. It had a centered solitaire diamond surrounded by six smaller stones. He announced that the design signified his desire for them to have six children. Debbie was thrilled to accept his proposal, but insisted that he had misinterpreted the symbolism of the ring setting. She declared that the six small diamonds indicated that they would have two children, two dogs, and two cats.

Her exact response was, "I love you, Jeremy, and of course I'll marry you, but you're asking too much if you think I'll go through that pregnancy and birthing process six times."

Following Debbie's conditional acceptance, Shirley and Walter Hadley welcomed her into the family circle with six toasts to support the ring symbolism conversation.

Now, one weekend later, Debbie and Jeremy worked together to prepare their apartment for their first Christmas as an officially committed couple. Jeremy volunteered to assemble and trim their newly-purchased artificial Christmas tree, while Debbie would decorate every room and niche of their apartment to spread their Yule mood. She even recorded a special holiday message for their voice mail system.

Two and a half hours into their decking of the halls, the telephone rang. In keeping with her holiday preparation mood, Debbie answered it with, "North Pole decorating services, Debbie the Elf speaking."

Penny Gonzalez laughed at the other end of the line. "Now that's very appropriate, Debbie. I was calling to ask whether it would be convenient for us to visit. We have an early Christmas present for you."

"Wow! That really matches our theme for today. We're in the process of putting up all our Christmas decorations. In case you covert folks haven't yet detected the joy in our apartment, I'll tell you that this will be our first official Christmas celebration. Jeremy proposed on Thanksgiving. We're engaged, and I have the ring to prove it."

"Well, best wishes or congratulations, whichever is the appropriate phrase. I always mix them up."

"Thanks, Penny. I'd settle for 'Hip, Hip, Hooray', anything to signify that we're past the transition from day-by-day to long-term relationship."

"You're too hard on yourself, Debbie. I don't think Jeremy was ever close to abandoning you."

"I'll admit that I might be slightly irrational, but I frequently felt the shadow of his old flame, Michelle Caspar, leaning over us."

"That's behind you now. Jeremy has declared his choice to all who will listen. We'll be over in about an hour, bearing something that should contribute to your good mood."

"Thanks, Penny. We'll look forward to it."

When Penny and Joe Gonzalez arrived, Jeremy met them outside the open apartment entrance after having buzzed them through the lobby security door.

"Welcome to Hadley's Christmas Village. The tree has been trimmed, and we elves are doing all we can to assure that your visit will be a cheerful one. Even though we have a while to go before Christmas, we have some spiked eggnog to share with you."

Joe said, "That actually sounds good. I'll accept your offer of that liquid refreshment."

Once inside the apartment, Joe and Penny settled into chairs near the Christmas tree, while Jeremy went to get Debbie. When they returned, they carried a tray of glasses filled with eggnog and another with homemade chocolate chip cookies. Debbie passed the glasses while Jeremy followed with the cookies.

Joe stood to take his glass and held it high. "I propose a toast to the pending marriage of Debbie and Jeremy. May their ceremony be memorable; may their love for each other never cease; and may their children have Debbie's beauty and Jeremy's athletic skills." They clicked their glasses together and then sat.

Penny asked, "Have you discussed the matter of children? Will you be trying to have them right away?"

Debbie responded after making eye contact with Jeremy. "We discussed the number of children we'd like to have, but not their timing. Jeremy wants more children than I do, because he won't have the burdens of pregnancy and childbirth. We do want kids, but they aren't our main reason for getting married."

Penny laid her package on the coffee table in front of the couch where Debbie and Jeremy sat. "The events of your marriage before, during, and after childbirth deserve documentation. To put you into the right frame of mind for that, we have prepared a little present for you. Please unwrap it now, and we'll discuss it with you. Jeremy, would you do the honors?"

Jeremy carefully removed the brown wrapping paper to reveal a large black book bearing the hand-lettered white ink title: The writings of Michael Farrell Hadley.

"This looks very impressive. Does it contain all his editorials from the *New York Times*?"

Penny said, "It has some of those editorials, but it also has later pieces. We discovered that your great-grandfather had a gap in his writing work following his work for the *Times*, but that he again published pieces for a variety of newspapers and magazines after Britain declared war on Germany. Joe found most of the later articles."

Joe continued the conversation following Penny's cue. "I discovered several interesting aspects of the later work. First, he wrote almost all of his articles under the less formal names of Michael Hadley and Mike Hadley. It took more time for me to find them because I didn't have the uniqueness of the Farrell middle name to help me. There were many Michael Hadleys in the world, but he was the only one writing a special type of material. That was my second point of interest. He wrote editorials for the *Times* advocating America's support of Britain as war with Hitler's forces became inevitable. However, his later articles emerged after Britain had already declared war against Germany. They took the form of stories rather than editorials or essays. I found it interesting that they were written in England but published in America."

Debbie said, "I'll bet that they still carried the message that Americans should support the British."

"That they did, but in a more subtle way. The new articles reminded Americans that the British were just like them in many ways. They essentially argued that despite the Revolutionary War and the War of 1812, the Brits were so like Americans that we should think of them as extended family, and that in tough times, family members have to assist each other."

Jeremy asked, "How did Michael overcome the fact that the British were losing all their battles? That couldn't have impressed the American reading public."

"He tried to turn their weakness into strength in the eyes of American readers. Michael emphasized the dignity and resourcefulness of British individuals as they stood up against stronger forces. He tried to make as many

Americans as possible abandon their isolationist tendencies in favor of feeling kinship with the British as they faced invasion threats and bombings."

Debbie asked, "What did he hope to accomplish? A few stories about the British couldn't be expected to get Americans to petition their government to enter a war."

Penny shook her head negatively. "That wouldn't have been his goal. Historians have revealed that President Roosevelt wanted to support the British, but he couldn't do so because Congress and the general public preferred to think that we could stay out of any war. That attitude was based on the popular belief that the Atlantic and Pacific Oceans would keep the war away from our shores. Michael was trying to generate enough empathy for the British, as they stood up against the overwhelming German forces, to convince Franklin Roosevelt that he had sufficient political support to openly send supplies and equipment to England."

"So FDR was basically the audience-of-one for Michael's articles."

"That was the indirect result, Debbie, but of course he was playing to the American population as a whole. A good politician like Roosevelt would sense any shift in the public's attitude."

Joe added, "Don't forget that Roosevelt's friend, Winston Churchill was whispering the same message into his ear."

Jeremy opened the scrapbook and started to leaf through it. "I have to admit that I'm impressed that my great-grandfather conducted a campaign to convince Americans in general and President Roosevelt in particular that America should help England fight Hitler's aggression. Weren't many British writers doing the same thing, Penny?"

"A few may have been writing similar things in letters to friends and associates, but the British Ministry of

Information told many academic and press voices that Americans would resent being told what to do by the British. American voices would have to be the ones addressing the American population."

"So that's why it was important for my great-grandfather to get his American citizenship as soon as possible after he came here to write for the *Times*."

"Churchill and his associates definitely planned ahead in their dealings with Michael. They must have had a great deal of faith in him."

Debbie said, "One thing bothers me. He wrote his stories as an American in England after the onset of the war. When we lost track of him, he was still living in Connecticut, well before the beginning of World War II. How did he get to England, Joe?"

"My guess is that they gave him a different assignment between his two writing efforts. They probably gave him a different identity during the missing period, so we would have no way of knowing what he did. I should point out that it was important for him to be writing from England after the British entered the war. If he had written his stories from America, they would have represented his speculative thoughts, and he wouldn't have stood out from the many other American writers having articles published. As an American in England close to the war, he had on-site information that many back here wanted to know. He was in the position that made Edward R. Murrow so famous after the United States entered the war."

Jeremy said, "Wow, I'm even more impressed with my great-grandfather. He knew Churchill, wrote to influence Roosevelt, and could be described as an early version of Edward R. Murrow. This scrapbook will be my treasure forever. Thanks so much for all the work that went into assembling it."

CHAPTER 52 – KRIEGER

After having obtained as much information as practical from the German agent who called himself John Jones, Albert Samson of MI6 and two associates traveled to the Seasoned Toys factory, where Michael Hadley had suggested they would find the German agent supervising John Jones, Otto Krieger. Hadley sounded regretful when he passed along the information, but explained that he once thought Krieger to be trustworthy and a friend. Samson could appreciate Hadley's mixed feelings. He was still trying to recover from the shock of learning that his former Dutch girlfriend had actually been German and that she sabotaged a Dutch power station in advance of the recent bombing of Rotterdam. The devastation from that concentrated bombing, along with the use of paratroopers to take over widespread airfields, led to the surrender of the Netherlands within one week of the invasion's start.

Michael Hadley assured Samson that Ruth Sisson, the proprietor of Seasoned Toys was a loyal citizen who had erred only by falling in love with Otto Krieger. He added that he didn't expect Krieger to resist arrest by MI6.

Upon arrival at the barn that served as the Seasoned Toys factory, Samson directed the agent who was driving to park behind the building to interdict any possible escape attempt via the rear door. Samson and his other associate would enter through the reception area.

Once inside, Samson tapped the plunger on the counter call bell to ring it. A short time later a woman appeared and slid the window aside.

"Welcome to Seasoned Toys. May I help you?"

"Are you Ruth Sisson?"

"Yes, I am. And you are?"

"My name is Albert Samson, and I'm here to talk with Mr. Otto Krieger. Is he here?"

Ruth wasn't sure whether this man represented a threat. "Otto is working on a piece of machinery right now. May I assist you?"

Michael Hadley had told Samson that Ruth knew him as George Millerson and that she would be receptive to that name. "Mrs. Sisson, we have a mutual friend in George Millerson. Would you mind my coming in while I wait for Mr. Krieger to become available?"

"If George sent you then there is no problem. As a matter of fact, Otto should be finishing up right now." She opened the door to admit Mr. Samson, and was only slightly disturbed that his associate followed closely behind him. She asked them to have a seat in the alcove that served as the company conference room while she fetched Otto to meet with them.

Otto was washing his hands as Ruth approached.

"It's working now, Ruth. Do you have another machine that needs attention?"

"Not a machine, but a person; you have a Mr. Samson here to see you."

"I don't know that name. Did he tell you his reason for coming or who he represents?"

"I assumed you would know something about him. He came with another man who didn't introduce himself. Samson said that George Millerson suggested he come."

"I suppose that could signify a business opportunity. I'll see him now."

"I told him to wait in the conference alcove. Do you want me to join you?"

"No, you have a newly repaired machine to set up. I'll call you if it becomes important for you to join us."

They held hands briefly and parted. Otto walked to the conference alcove. He was surprised to see only one man sitting there, but then he turned and saw that a second man was behind him, following him while walking very softly. That man must have walked into the factory behind Ruth, without her noticing him. *Something unusual is happening, but I won't react to it.*

He approached the seated man. "Good morning, I'm Otto Krieger. May I help you?"

The man rose and shook hands with him. "Mr. Krieger, I'm Albert Samson. I've learned quite a bit about you from a man who calls himself John Jones." Samson observed only a flicker of reaction in Krieger's facial expression, but noted that it definitely was there.

"Mr. Samson, I was told that your visit had something to do with George Millerson, a friend of mine. Is this not the case?"

"Oh, he is indeed the reason for our visit. I'll further inform you that I represent British Intelligence, MI6, and that we are here to arrest you."

Otto's surface calm was beginning to melt into his inner pool of tensions. "I haven't done anything wrong. I'm a simple toymaker."

"You're a simple toymaker who also works for Abwehr and who directed a German national, temporarily using the name of John Jones, to assassinate one Michael Hadley."

"I don't work for the Germans. I'm a British citizen, and I don't know this Michael Hadley."

"You should acknowledge that you know a man named Thomas Hadley, who is now very disappointed in your lack of loyalty to your adopted country. He had high hopes for working with you as a loyal British subject. You've thrown that opportunity away."

Otto didn't notice Ruth standing slightly behind him and to his left. She heard the entire conversation. Otto said, "I don't know this John Jones, and why would you believe anything he says about me if he is a German spy?"

"I said that he was a German national, but I didn't use the word spy. He told us that you supplied him with the pistol he used in his attempt to kill Michael Hadley. After we stopped him before he could complete that mission, we checked that pistol and found that it had been registered to Paul Sisson, since deceased."

Ruth gasped behind Otto, making him aware of her presence. "How long have you been standing there?"

"I've heard everything, Otto. How could you take Paul's pistol for such a purpose? He purchased it when we first moved here, because our property was remote and far from any police protection. I didn't think you knew about that gun. I hid it in the back of my bureau drawer."

"Your comments are not helping me, Ruth. I'll speak for myself. I suggest that if this man John Jones had Paul's pistol, he must have broken into your house and stolen it. I never met John Jones, and I know nothing about his coming to our toy factory or the house. You mentioned George Millerson. George is my closest friend, and I'm certain he will vouch for my trustworthiness. I am not loyal to the Germans, and I only agreed to work with Abwehr at the suggestion of Thomas Hadley and the Twenty Committee. Is Thomas Hadley related to the Michael Hadley that this John Jones tried to shoot?"

Samson smiled. "Thomas Hadley is not related to Michael Hadley, but Michael Hadley is the name currently being used by the man you acknowledged to be your closest friend, George Millerson. You assigned John Jones to murder your closest friend."

Otto lowered himself into the nearest chair, no longer having the energy to protest anything. Ruth walked over to him and slapped his face as hard as she could. Then she began to cry.

CHAPTER 53 – WELBY MARSH

In September of 1940, The German Luftwaffe began nightly bombing raids on London and other cities. Everyone grew used to carrying on an approximation of normal life while keeping one ear cocked for the beginning of air raid sirens that would require hustling to the nearest air raid shelter. There, one would face hours of close contact confinement with strangers. Most of the students at King's College, where Michael's office was located, were in the process of evacuating to temporary facilities in Bristol and Glasgow.

As the first week of this new stage of warfare drew to a close, Welby Marsh began his workday by knocking on Michael Hadley's office door.

"Good morning, Michael. I have news for you, along with a high priority assignment."

"Good morning to you, Welby. How did you fare during last night's bombing raid?"

"It was the usual thing, tight quarters in the sub-basement of a hotel after an early-evening meeting. At least I live far enough out of the city that we haven't seen much damage near my home. You're place is local. Did your neighborhood get hit?"

"A stray bomb damaged a building on the next block with minor injuries from flying glass, but nothing too serious. Officials did some boarding up over there, and declared that the damage did not make the building uninhabitable. Mr. and Mrs. Keene will have to close off a room or two, but life there will go on with some inconveniences. What do you have for me today?"

"First, I'll give you some good news. The British Library of Information in New York has taken some discrete public opinion surveys, and their results indicate that a larger percentage of the American populace favors giving aid in the form of war supplies to Britain. Your writing efforts have won over some of the people there. President Roosevelt has been talking with Prime Minister Churchill about swapping a large number of their older ships for land leases. The US wants to establish military bases in British dependencies in the Americas. Churchill wanted the ships for free, but he has little choice but to accept Roosevelt's terms. FDR has to have compensation in order to avoid violating their neutrality law. Word has it that he's trying to develop an alternate arrangement but that it will take some precious time."

"You're right, Welby; Britain needs good news sooner, rather than later. What's the high priority job you mentioned?"

"We've decided to produce a documentary film for distribution through American movie theatres. It will be about the way our citizens are reacting to living in the midst of bombing attacks. I'd like you to be part of the script writing group. We have to get this completed within two weeks, so that it will reach American audiences while they're still shocked by the nightly German attacks on our cities."

Michael leaned back in his chair. "I think I see the approach we should take. It should be low key, and it should show how ordinary citizens are taking everything in stride rather than panicking. Who will do the narration?"

"We thought we would use someone with a reassuring voice from the BBC."

"Sorry, Welby, but as in the case of your having me flout my American citizenship while writing my magazine stories, you should have an American narrator report this story to his fellow citizens."

"Do you have any suggestions?"

"I met one possible candidate who's over here reporting on the war for *Collier's Weekly*, Quentin Reynolds."

"See, you're already contributing to our project. I'll have a talk with this Reynolds chap. I haven't met him, and I'll need to get a feeling for his voice and the degree to which people would regard him as a trusted source. In the meantime, come to my office at three o'clock this afternoon, and I'll introduce you to the rest of the writing crew."

Richard Davidson

CHAPTER 54 – *LONDON CAN TAKE IT!*

Before the end of September, 1940, the same month in which the bombings transitioned from occasional to nightly events, Warner Brothers released to American Theaters the ten minute film, *London Can Take It!* The film, narrated by American Quentin Reynolds, displayed only his name on the credits, hiding the fact that it had been produced by the Crown Film Unit of the British Ministry of Information. It was screened so many times in so many theaters that this propaganda film actually made a profit.

Using Michael's principle that Americans respond more readily to stories than to lists of facts, the film opens with scenes of ordinary British people performing their normal jobs until air raid sirens and explosions punctuate the serenity of the night. As the citizens of London move quickly to their nearest marked air raid shelters, Reynolds intones, "These are not Hollywood sound effects. This is the music they play every night in London, the symphony of war."

Later in the film, ordinary people retrieve possessions from damaged homes, sweep the debris from the streets and sidewalks, and rescue a live cat that was buried as a home collapsed. Volunteers serving in secondary war-related occupations attend to the injured and eliminate hazards. Buses again drive through damaged neighborhoods. Without any labeling of the event, the king and queen walk through a bombed area looking at the damage, and the queen pats a damaged wall as though consoling a cherished pet.

Reynolds summarizes for the viewers, "I am a neutral reporter. I have watched the people of London live and die ever since death in its most ghastly garb began to come here as a nightly visitor five weeks ago.... I can assure you there is no panic, no fear, no despair...among the people of Churchill's island.... London can take it."

The impact of the film was immense, having within the first two months been shown to sixty million people in twelve thousand theaters. Americans, who looked on the British as having lost every confrontation with the Germans and having little chance of defending their islands, began to see the courage and calm under duress of their cousins across the sea. Many became sympathetic and even outraged by the German blitz on London. US government leaders who wanted to provide aid to the British would find a more receptive citizenry than they had in the past. The tide was turning, but would assistance come too late for Britain? (To see the newsreel film, *London Can Take It*, on your computer, go to: https://www.youtube.com/watch?v=Shst3xVmJrQ)

CHAPTER 55 – BLETCHLEY PARK

At Bletchley, Alice Hadley regularly mingled with people possessing ultimate brain power, but she refrained from treating them with awe and deference. Each of the elite code-breakers had some variation of clay feet. Quirks among the staff of Bletchley Park were the rule and not the exception. Within this unique setting, Alice was one of the few who stood out for being unusually normal. Her normality made Alice readily approachable by all staff members and enhanced her effectiveness in meshing the minor decoding discoveries of many key individuals into a coherent mosaic. Her work required a sophisticated effort to discover patterns in the unrelated fragments of data deciphered by the many star-quality geniuses surrounding her.

The absolute secrecy requirements of Bletchley did not daunt Alice; she had always been self-confident and content to tackle problems without assistance. One of her key solo achievements as a child had been the assembly of a thousand piece jigsaw puzzle with all the pieces turned over to their uniformly gray side.

The Bletchley security level was Ultra Secret, exceeding the normal highest classification of Most Secret. Staff members were required to avoid casual conversations connected to their work whenever they were off duty, whether within the Bletchley facility or elsewhere.

Very few people within the government and military were allowed to know of Bletchley's existence. When Bletchley staff members did decode a message with tactical or strategic value, they fabricated a cover story to document their having obtained the information through normal channels, prior to delivering it to the applicable military command or government department. Alice was frequently assigned to cover story fabrication because of her ability to generate logical and reasonable fictions. On occasion, a critically-important message had to be withheld from the military even though lives would be lost in the absence of the new information, for fear that the resulting actions taken might alert the enemy to its codes having been broken.

Alice, like the other staff members, worked around the clock in one of three eight-hour shifts. Each of her assigned shifts lasted for three weeks before she would be rotated to a different shift. The transition day required sixteen hours of work. This brutal schedule enhanced her anticipation of the next quarterly one-week break with Michael. Bletchley being fifty miles northwest of London, Alice did not have to worry about the nightly German bombing assaults, but she had periodic nightmares about Michael not surviving them. As a coordinator of the various fragments of decoded information, Alice knew more about the status of the war than most of her fellow staffers, but her inability to discuss that information with anyone beyond those with a need to know it, added an extra mental burden.

The pace of the code-breaking efforts was frenzied. Bletchley's success in constructing machines that would break the German Enigma and Lorenz ciphers came about because of many lapses in judgment and understanding by German and allied Italian users of the original machines. Each failure to encode a message properly gave Bletchley a clue to the process. Eventually, the staff processed thousands of messages each day with sufficient success to reduce the expected duration of the war by two to four years.

CHAPTER 56 – BREAK TIME

One sunny morning, Michael had finished eating his porridge and was taking his first sip of coffee when he heard a knock on the door of the flat. He opened it to find Alice smiling up at him from her seated perch atop a suitcase.

"Hello there, Alice; are you my gift for today?"

"I certainly am. I have my quarterly week-long break, and we should make the most of it."

She stood, and they hugged their way into the flat while Michael carried her suitcase with his free hand. Then they spent several minutes kissing and clinging to each other.

Michael was the first to speak. "I like your comment that we should make the most of this week. Would you really like to do that?"

"Absolutely, Michael; what do you have in mind?"

"I think it's time for us to declare our commitment to the world. Let's get married."

"I'll require a more formal proposal than that before I respond." She took one step backward.

Michael held her right hand as he knelt before her. "Alice Hadley, I've loved you ever since I first met you at your farm cottage. I want to spend the rest of my life with you as the focus and support of my existence. Together, we're much more than two individuals. Let's build something special. Will you do me the honor of becoming my wife?"

She wiped away a slight tear. "Of course I'll marry you, Michael. I agree that we should do it as soon as possible. I'm not going to let some new assignment pull you away from me again." He stood, and she kissed him long and hard.

Michael walked over to his desk and opened a small drawer. "Rationing makes the purchase of new things a bit difficult. I can only offer you my mother's ring. It's the sole item I have of hers. That family is gone for me, but through your wearing this ring, it will continue." He slipped the ring onto her finger and was pleased to find that it fit.

"Michael, it's beautiful. I'll wear it with pride and feel a connection to your mother through it." As she examined the ring, Alice realized that Michael's original family must have had more wealth than she had imagined. She would let him keep his secrets.

Michael called his secretary, Joanna Shore, and told her that he would not be in the office until the late afternoon. Then he and Alice left for London City Hall to obtain their marriage license. Once there, they learned that a regular license would require a delay of fifteen days, but that under the circumstances of the war and the nightly bombings they could obtain a Special License and have a civil wedding in the office of the registrar if they had two witnesses. They chose that approach, both because of their limited time and the fact that Michael's local church had been hit by a bomb three nights earlier. Following the processing of the license paperwork, Michael called Joanna and gave her instructions to find Welby Marsh and then come to the London City Hall with him to serve as his wedding witnesses.

"You're getting married, Michael? I didn't see this in the offing. I was about to go after you myself. Who is the lucky lady?"

"I'm marrying Alice. You met her earlier."

"You can't marry your sister!"

"Sorry, Joanna; I forgot about that introduction. When you find Welby, he'll explain how and why it is acceptable for me to marry Alice. She's not really my sister. After the ceremony, we'll all go out for a celebration."

When Michael returned to Alice, he laughed as he told her about Joanna's belief that they were brother and sister. He was surprised when Alice didn't laugh with him.

"What's the problem Alice? Didn't you find her reaction humorous?"

"It would be a lot more comical if I were absolutely convinced that we won't have a problem because of Stephanie in America."

"Thomas has assured me that my marriage to her was nullified and that he is now her husband. He also stated that he is committed to her and that he will shortly take on a second diplomatic position so that he will be able to spend more time with her in the States."

"Michael, you do understand that our marriage will make you Stephanie's cousin. Your son, Stephen will also be your second cousin. Can you handle those relationships?"

"Alice, I love you and want to be yours forever. Do you have a problem with Thomas being married to Stephanie?"

"You're right; our marriage is the important one. In the words of that American film, *Gone with the Wind*, my answer to your question is 'Frankly, my dear, I don't give a damn!'"

A little more than an hour later, Joanna Shore and Welby Marsh arrived, walking arm-in-arm. They announced that they were thrilled to be involved in the wedding. The four of them exchanged hugs all around. Then Michael left the group and advised the registrar that they were ready to proceed with the ceremony.

When Michael returned, he told the others that the wedding room was available for them and that the registrar would meet them there. Michael whispered something into Alice's ear, and she responded by kissing him. Then the four of them went into the wedding room.

The ceremony was brief and efficient, the registrar doing his best to put everyone at ease so that they felt that the proper emotions of the event. Alice and Michael saw little more than each other as they proclaimed their vows. Welby offered Joanna his handkerchief to blot her tears, and when she returned it, he touched it to his own eyes. At the conclusion of the ceremony, Alice and Michael kissed and locked each other into a tight embrace. Then they followed the registrar to sign the official wedding register. A round of hugs and handshakes later, they left for a local pub to celebrate.

Once at the pub, Welby ordered the first round of drinks and, upon their arrival, toasted the happy couple for their creativity, their flexibility under harsh conditions, and the fairy-tale quality of their love. Then he turned to Michael. "If you don't mind, and if it's not too personal, would you mind telling us what you whispered to Alice before the ceremony?"

Michael looked at Alice, who nodded her agreement. "I promised her that once this war is behind us, we will reconfirm our vows in a proper church ceremony." This statement drew a new exchange of kisses between the newlyweds. A few minutes later, the waitress arrived with a fresh tray of drinks, delivered with the compliments of the management.

Their party continued for about an hour, at which point Welby announced that he would have to leave in order to prepare for a presentation he had to make the following morning. Before he left, he asked, "Will you two go anywhere by way of a honeymoon?"

Michael looked at Alice. "Things have moved quickly, so we haven't really discussed that, but if you're agreeable, Alice, I'll suggest a train trip to Scotland."

Alice answered that suggestion with a nod, a smile, and a kiss.

Welby and Joanna stood to go. Welby said, "I'll take Joanna home. Congratulations again, you two." Then he winked at Alice and smiled. "Tell me, Alice, are you going to take Michael's surname?"

"That won't be necessary, Welby. He already took mine."

Everyone laughed, Joanna the loudest, indicating that she finally understood the premarital relationship between Michael and Alice. Michael noted that, as Welby and Joanna walked out, again arm-in-arm, she leaned her head against his shoulder.

It had been a romantic day, of great significance to all involved; but those individuals, focused on romance, failed to listen to the news reports. In rare afternoon air battles RAF fighters, outnumbered five to one, did their best to counter huge flights of German bombers and escorts coming in from the North Sea, from the Calais area, and from another origin point north of Calais. The South London airport and RAF facility suffered major damage, along with several coastal RAF bases, but dreary weather accompanied by low visibility led several German formations to bomb incorrect low-value targets.

CHAPTER 57 – SCOTLAND

When they arrived in Glasgow, Alice and Michael consulted the stationmaster, and determined that they had an hour to wait before departure of the train for their final destination, Ballantrae, on the west coast facing the Irish Sea. They spent that interval walking the neighborhood and having tea and coffee, respectively, at a tea shop across from the station. They noticed reconstruction work on several buildings that had been hit in a German bombing raid during July, but there was nothing like the destruction that surrounded Alice and Michael when they were in London.

The train ride southwestward to Ballantrae was uneventful and liberating as they passed through rural terrain, moving farther away from evidence and gloomy thoughts of the war. They would have only two days of honeymoon, but at least they would enjoy them within a peaceful setting. Michael had made a reservation for them at the Kings Arms Inn, adjacent to the ferry embarkation point for Northern Ireland. It would be picturesque, but their time would be too limited to include the ferry trip.

They arrived at the Kings Arms in time to register and take a walk along the shore before dinner. As they walked hand-in-hand, Alice took inventory of her new husband. Michael was several inches the taller one, with a firm jaw line but a typically relaxed expression on his face. He was muscular, but not overly so, athletic in a casual way, and he had a soothingly deep voice. In short, he was ideal. For his part, Michael thought that, in having Alice as his wife, he had achieved every goal he had ever sought. The best part was that, at least for the brief now, they were alone together.

They sat down on an outcropping of rock. Michael skipped a few flat stones across the surface of the water.

"Alice, what percentage of perfect would you assign to this place?"

"As long as I'm here with you, it rates a hundred and ten percent. What more could we want, except to stretch out our time here?"

"Those were my thoughts exactly. Let's keep in the back of our minds the possibility of having a home here."

"That's your sky's-the-limit American style showing. You said 'a home' suggesting we might have more than one."

"If we're going to dream, we might as well dream big. Besides, I wasn't visualizing something grandiose like that Glenapp Castle we passed. A small cottage with you amidst these surroundings would suffice quite well. I expect you'll want to keep your stone cottage and farm as well, and then, we'd have to consider whether we'd want a place in America too."

"You are thinking ahead. I hope I won't completely deflate your bubble if I suggest that we each try to get through this war in one piece before we make grand plans."

"I know. We have to be practical, but having you with me enables me to tackle anything."

"I have something I have to ask you. Answer it once, and I won't return to the subject."

"Go ahead."

"Michael, if you were to fly across that Irish island we're facing, and keep going, you'd reach the New England coast where Stephanie and Stephen live. She was your wife; he is your son. Will thoughts of them affect our marriage?"

This time there was no hesitation before he spoke. "You are my one and all, my alpha and omega. I can't cut them out of my past, but you are my present and future. I love only you, now and forever."

Her newly relaxed body pivoted to embrace him and to assure him that all was well in their private world.

CHAPTER 58 – UNOFFICIAL PROGRESS

The various British attempts to win America to their cause, including Michael's magazine articles and film script writing, were gaining traction. Unofficial personal vows of support were becoming common.

A few voices from the American side demanded to be heard. One of these was the poet, Edna St. Vincent Millay. She had grown tired of both isolationist pontificators and those, like Anne Morrow Lindbergh who wrote that the irresistible wave of the future would be driven by Nazis, Fascists, and Communists. Millay responded in June of 1940 with her poem *There Are No Islands, Any More: Lines Written in Passion and in Deep Concern for England, France, and My Own Country* (excerpts):

Dear Isolationist, you are
So very, very insular!
Surely you do not take offense? -
The word's well used in such a sense.
'Tis you, not I, sir, who insist
You are an Isolationist.

And oh, how sweet a thing to be
Safe on an island, not at sea!
(Though some one said, some months ago-
I heard him, and he seemed to know;
Was it the German Chancellor?
"There *are* no islands anymore.")

Impostor

Dear Islander, I envy you:
I'm very fond of islands, too;
And few the pleasures I have known
Which equaled being left alone.
Yet matters from without intrude
At times upon my solitude:
A forest fire, a dog run mad,
A neighbor stripped of all he had
By swindlers, or the shrieking plea
For help, of stabbed Democracy.

Startled, I rise, run from the room,
Join the brigade of spade and broom;
Help to surround the sickened beast;
Hear the account of farmers fleeced
By dapper men, condole, and give
Something to help them hope and live;
Or, if democracy's at stake,
Give more, give more than I can make;
And notice, with a rueful grin,
What was without is now within.

(The tidal wave devours the shore:
There *are* no islands any more.)

With sobbing breath, with blistered hands,
Men fight the forest fire in bands;
With kitchen broom, with branch of pine,
Beat at the blackened, treacherous line;
Before the veering wind fall back,
With eyebrows burnt and faces black;
While breasts in blackened streams perspire.
Watch how the wind runs with the fire
Like a broad banner up the hill-
And can no more... yet more must still.

185

Richard Davidson

New life!-To hear across the field
Voices of neighbors, forms concealed
By smoke, but loud the nearing shout:
"Hold on! We're coming! Here it's out!"

(The tidal wave devours the shore:
There *are* no islands any more.)

...

On English soil, on French terrain,
Democracy's at grips again
With forces forged to stamp it out
This time no quarter!-since no doubt.

Not France, not England's what's involved,
Not we, --there's something to be solved
Of grave concern to free men all:
Can Freedom stand? -Must Freedom fall?

(Meantime, the tide devours the shore:
There *are* no islands any more.)

Oh, build, assemble, transport, give,
That England, France and we may live,
Before tonight, before too late,
To those who build our country's fate
In desperate fingers, reaching out
For weapons we confer about,
All that we can, and more, and now!
Oh, God, let not the lovely brow
Of Freedom in the trampled mud
Grow cold! Have we no brains, no blood,
No enterprise-no any thing
Of which we proudly talk and sing,

Which we like men can bring to bear
For Freedom, and against Despair?

Lest French and British fighters, deep
In battle, needing guns and sleep,
For lack of aid be overthrown
And we be left to fight alone.

One of the unexpected results of Michael's writing had been the development of a following for his articles and opinions. Each month he received more American fan mail than he had previously. While some of the letters commented on the quality of his writing, others reported small progress steps made toward supporting the British and their Commonwealth allies. He learned from many correspondents in American industry that company managers were developing plans for conversion of their factories to production of war-related equipment and supplies. Michael was surprised to receive a fan letter from a Florida resident describing RAF pilots and aircraft training in his area. Michael passed this report to Welby Marsh, who said that the Ministry of Information had no knowledge of American training facilities.

Canada, as a member of the British Commonwealth, entered the war in September of 1939, shortly after the British did. As the American populace began to favor support for Britain, Michael's fan base reported rumors of training facilities for US spies in Canada and flights of many American aircraft across the northern border.

Michael concluded that the prospect of war was now real for Americans, but that the new first steps in that direction were not officially recognized. The American government's new stance was *anything short of committing troops*. Nevertheless, he saw in these first small steps a

Richard Davidson

shift in direction of US policy, and movement that would gain momentum.

CHAPTER 59 – TURNING POINT

One day in December of 1940, Welby Marsh arrived unannounced at the open door of Michael Hadley's office.

"Good morning, Michael; I never get over the way you Americans work with your doors open. Doesn't the outside world intrude on your concentration and productivity?"

"Good morning to you, Welby; I suspect that you're really asking me to close my door so that I won't see you getting familiar with Joanna. I saw her leaning her head on your shoulder as you left our post-wedding celebration."

Welby colored a bit as he entered Michael's office and closed the door behind him. "Not so loud, please; Joanna will hear everything."

Michael reached out to shake hands with his friend. "You're going to have to decide where you stand, Welby. I've noticed your recent frequent visits, ostensibly to confer with me, but really to touch base with Joanna. If you care for her, be open about it. I won't interfere with the blooming of a love blossom."

"It's not exactly that, old boy. I am here with some important developments to discuss with you. A word with Joanna on the way past her desk simply improves my day."

"And how does she feel about you?"

"I think that I amuse her."

"Don't look now, my friend, but all women are amused by men who want to be with them but are fearful of discussing their emotions or a relationship. Americans do have the advantage of an informal outlook that minimizes dancing around romance issues."

"Michael, you do realize that you're somewhat of a Frankenstein monster. You're actually a Brit by birth and upbringing that we enabled to quickly gain American citizenship in order to assist our cause. Now you talk as though you've always been American."

"That's the nature of that special country. With very few exceptions, every citizen's family came from somewhere else, so once one becomes a citizen, he or she is the same as every other American, regardless of vintage."

"Where will you stand, should there be a conflict between American and British leaders after the US gets into this war and becomes our ally?"

Michael stared long and hard at Welby. "In answer to your question, I hope I'm objective enough to take my stance based on the merits of the arguments in the specific matter at hand. However, you implied when and not if. Are you here with information that there has been movement on the American front toward joining us?"

Welby sat and leaned forward across the desk. "This is very preliminary, so keep it under your hat, but President Roosevelt has reacted to Churchill's declaration that Britain can no longer pay for American supplied war materials, by developing a concept he calls Lend-Lease. Roosevelt wants to help us, but he has to work his way through the minefield of isolationist sentiments and neutrality acts. This time he may have taken the step that cannot be reversed."

"What does Lend-Lease mean?"

"You'll remember that in September Roosevelt agreed to send us fifty naval ships, destroyers, in exchange for ninety-nine year military base leases in Newfoundland and the Caribbean. That deal took America past the insistence by many officials that armaments must be sold on a cash basis. Roosevelt convinced the opposition that the military base leases would enhance US security and were at least as good as cash payments. Now that Churchill has refused future immediate payments of any kind, Roosevelt is developing a system of deferred compensation that has a more subjective nature."

"I write fiction, Welby. I'm sensing a hint of that here."

"Just don't say that too loudly. Roosevelt is willing to give us and other countries opposing German aggression war equipment in exchange for our services in defending America from German hostility, and for commitments toward liberal economic arrangements after the war is behind us. He's even extending similar terms to Asian countries like China who are fighting Japanese aggression."

"That still sounds as though he's willing to give something for nothing in return."

"None of this is actual law yet. He'll have a tough fight in Congress, but I think he'll get Lend-Lease passed within a few months if he keeps working on it."

"I agree, Welby, but I think all the fancy reasoning about what America gets in return will mean very little to Congress. Don't forget, I used to write for the *New York Times*. Lend-Lease will pass because Congress will see it as a delaying action. The legislators will gladly trade surplus military equipment for American lives saved by delaying their unavoidable entrance into the war. They won't admit that waging war is inevitable, but they're realistic enough to see what's coming. They'll also have the industrialists supporting them because old weapons given away will have to be replaced by newly manufactured ones. Americans who have been out of work because of the depression will get jobs making new weapons and supporting equipment. The American public will love Congress for approving this bill. The economy and patriotism will flourish, but they'll be more committed than ever to keeping their people out of the fight."

"So, Michael, you think we'll win the Lend-Lease battle, but we're far from winning our propaganda war to get the Americans to fight on our side."

"It will take something with major impact to gain that goal. In the meantime, why don't you turn your propaganda expertise toward winning the affections of Miss Joanna Shore?"

CHAPTER 60 – ALICE

Her Bletchley supervisor, Dr. Stanley Rokle, was not at all pleased.

"Alice Hadley, I've learned from several sources that you got married during your last break period. You know that our Ultra Secret standing requires that no one may make a family status change until the new member is cleared by MI6. Were you not aware of this policy? I heard that your husband is an American citizen. That probably makes him completely unacceptable from a security standpoint."

Alice smiled at him. "I don't expect there will be a problem. Michael works with MI6 and the Ministry of Information on several special projects that are so classified that they aren't documented anywhere. You will have no problem obtaining confirmation from MI6. I personally attest that we never discuss my duties here."

"Be that as it may, by getting married without authorization, you have jeopardized your position here. Your husband's assignment cannot be as important to the war effort as ours. Breaking the enemy's cyphers and simulating enemy encoding devices are of paramount importance to our country's survival. I'm putting you on probationary status, requiring you to file a weekly report documenting your detailed activities and to certify in each report that you have followed all proper procedures. I'll also request expedited investigation by MI6 of your husband's security worthiness."

Alice returned to her department wondering how administrative dotting of i's and crossing of t's could possibly be compatible with the out-of-bounds thinking required by staff members to unscramble cyphers.

Two hours later, Dr. Stanley Rokle visited Alice at her desk. His attitude change was obvious. "Alice, please disregard my earlier peevishness and those remarks about probation. Just carry on as usual, and let me know if you need any assistance."

She looked up at him with a puzzled expression. "What happened since I last met with you?"

"I spoke with the security clearance people at MI6 to request an investigation of your husband. They laughed at me and informed me that Michael Farrell Hadley is listed as being on a special assignment for the Prime Minister and is to be accorded all requested assistance. What does he do?"

"Sorry, Stanley, I can't discuss that. It's a matter of National Security."

CHAPTER 61 – RUTH SISSON

Ruth was halfway between her house and the barn that served as the Seasoned Toys factory, when a car pulled into the driveway. The driver tooted the horn and waved before getting out. Ruth ran toward him.

"George, I didn't know whether I would see you again, after that horrible business with Otto." She hugged him.

"Call me Michael now, Ruth. I'm Michael Hadley; George Millerson has served his purpose and moved on. I was in the area and felt compelled to check in with you."

"Perhaps I should call the constable, Michael. You're driving George's car."

"I'm afraid the change in name did not come with a new vehicle. We have to conserve, what with rationing and the war situation. I've been worried about you, Ruth. I know that you and Otto became close before he surprised us all with his mixed loyalties. How are things working out for you now that he's out of the picture?"

"You worded that well. 'Working out' is the proper terminology. I've thrown myself into increased toy production plus a small government contract to manufacture a pocket tin opener for military field rations. I bought a new metal shear and forming machine to make that one. I also work with a nearby shop that supplies my hardened blade piece."

"How did you do that? You were short on capital. I can help with the payments if you'll let me."

"You were a sweetheart when you were George, and you still are one. I should have made a play for you instead of Otto. Now I see you're wearing a wedding ring. Is she someone related to Thomas Hadley? We first met at that party at his house and I sensed your interest in someone there."

"I will always appreciate your clear thinking. Yes, I married Alice Hadley. She was indeed at that party. I'm afraid we were already pretty committed to each other at that time, so you and I getting together would not have been a possibility."

"It's interesting to me that you took her name. That's unconventional. Do you want to share that story?"

"I'm afraid that tale is both complicated and classified, so I'll have to sidestep it. I was serious before, though. I'm more than willing to help you finance things here."

Ruth surprised him with another hug and added a kiss. "I hope your wife won't mind my expression of love for you. She got someone special. With regard to financial support, the contract for the pocket tin opener is paying the bills, and my former associate George Millerson predicted correctly that families required to spend long hours in air raid shelters are buying puzzles and other toys to help their children pass the time usefully. Nevertheless, I'll keep you in mind in case I run into new money problems in the future."

Michael gave her his business card. "Keep this and call if you need me."

"Can you stay for tea?"

"Only if coffee is an option; I like beans much better than leaves."

CHAPTER 62 – PASSAGE

Welby Marsh knocked on the doorpost of Michael's open office. "What day is this, Michael?"

"I'm going to have to buy you a calendar so that you won't have to ask me every time. Today is 11 March 1941. Do I win anything by giving you the correct answer?"

"That's only one of the correct answers. Today is the day President Roosevelt signs the Lend-Lease Act, making it American law. Today, our forces know they will get improved equipment. Specifically, Roosevelt will sign a document that permits him to:

"... sell, transfer title to, exchange, lease, lend, or otherwise dispose of, to any such government [whose defense the President deems vital to the defense of the United States] any defense article."

"I hadn't read the exact wording before. That's a blank check. We'll have to celebrate at the pub."

"That sounds good to me. I'll meet you there in twenty minutes."

When Welby Marsh entered the London Arts Pub, he received a pleasant surprise. Smiling at him from a corner table were both Michael Hadley and Joanna Shore. He approached them, trying to look serious but having a hard time of it. "Greetings; I didn't realize there would be three of us here. Who's minding the writing shop?"

Michael replied, "That shop will take care of itself quite nicely, thank you. Joanna deserves to celebrate too. She expedited all of my articles to get them published. Of course, she has a say as to whether we should let you join us. Is he acceptable, Joanna?"

"I think he'll do quite nicely."

She patted the seat next to her. As Welby sat, she patted his thigh, leading to a slight amount of additional color in his face. Michael left to place their drink order with the barmaid.

Welby gripped Joanna's hand briefly. "We're in a public place. I have to be circumspect because of my position. Please be careful."

She teased him by pouting. "How can you be circumspect and celebrate at the same time? Do you have a secret wife you haven't told me about?"

"Of course not; I'm independent and unclaimed."

"And how do I go about establishing a claim?"

"You remain discrete in public, and you keep me from having too much to drink during this celebration."

Joanna puckered her lips. "Keeping you sober might be anti-productive for me."

Welby was trying to come up with a glib rejoinder when Michael returned to the table with his tray of drinks.

They toasted the new Lend-Lease Act. They toasted the King. They toasted the Prime Minister. They toasted each other. Then Michael decided to present them with an old American joke.

"Why did the chicken cross the road?"

Joanna said, "I don't know. Why?"

"Because the loo was on the other side. I'm going to visit the one in this establishment, and then I'll be leaving you to enjoy each other's company." He departed, weaving only slightly on the way to his first destination.

CHAPTER 63 - PEARL HARBOR

The Japanese attack on Pearl Harbor on Oahu Island in Hawaii at 7:55 a.m. on a December Sunday morning, was unexpected and devastating. The loss of more than 2300 military personnel plus at least 180 aircraft and many ships almost crippled the United States military in the Pacific. Fortunately, the Pacific Fleet's three aircraft carriers were out at sea, far from Pearl Harbor. Eight battleships were hit but only two, the Arizona and the Oklahoma would not be repaired eventually. All over the United States people ran up to each other on the streets exchanging news of the shocking attack and asking where Pearl Harbor was.

The following day, with only one congressional vote against it, the United States declared war on Japan in response to President Roosevelt's address:

"Yesterday, December seventh, nineteen forty-one -- a date which will live in infamy -- the United States of America was suddenly and deliberately attacked by naval and air forces of the Empire of Japan. The United States was at peace with that nation and, at the solicitation of Japan, was still in conversation with its government and its emperor, looking toward the maintenance of peace in the Pacific ...

"No matter how long it may take us to overcome this premeditated invasion, the American people in their righteous might will win through to absolute victory...

"We will not only defend ourselves to the uttermost but will make it very certain that this form of treachery shall never again endanger us ...

"I ask that the Congress declare that since the unprovoked and dastardly attack by Japan on Sunday, December seventh, nineteen forty-one, a state of war has existed between the United States and the Japanese Empire."

Three days later, on December 11, 1941, Germany and Italy declared war on the United States. Congress responded by declaring war on them.

Prime Minister Winston Churchill is said to have declared, "We have won the war!" Later, he would write that *only silly people, and there were many, underestimated American strength.* He added that following America's declaration of war against Germany and Italy, he *went to bed and slept the sleep of the saved and thankful.*

Churchill also mused about the amount of time and effort he and his countrymen had put into trying to bring the United States into the war on Britain's side, while the Japanese had caused that to happen in a single day.

For his part, Michael Hadley felt vindicated. He had told Welby Marsh that it would take a major event to drive the Americans into the war. After he learned that Congress had declared war on Germany and Italy, he had mixed feelings. The goal of allying the United States with Britain had been achieved, but what would be his future mission as those allies marched forward together?

Michael's contemplations were shattered by the ringing of the telephone. It rang several times before he became conscious of it. He picked it up and heard Welby Marsh singing *Rule, Britannia* in a raucous off-key voice. When the singing stopped, he said, "Bravo, Welby; how much have you had to drink?"

"I'm allowed to imbibe tonight. It's celebration time. Please come over to my flat. I have secured two bottles of champagne for a special party."

"We're not each supposed to drink a whole bottle of that bubbly stuff, are we?"

"That sounds like a fabulous idea, Michael, but I have a few people from the office coming as well. We've been working toward this day for what seems like eons. Please join us."

"Your invitation is tempting, Welby, but I have some things to do here. I'll check in with you at your office tomorrow."

"Be a friend, and make it later in the day, would you? I also suggest that you not be too upset if you're without a secretary in the morning."

"That sounds promising for you. Tell her I'll be fine on my own. Enjoy your party."

CHAPTER 64 – OPTIONS

The problem with achieving your goal is that you have to follow it up with a new goal or take on an entirely different project. Michael had devoted a vast amount of time and effort toward accelerating the entry of the United States into the war against the Germans and their allies. Now he faced the identification of his next project. If he did nothing and simply waited for a new assignment, he was sure his future work would be considerably less significant. He wanted to propose a new high priority effort for which he would be well-suited, but what would it be? He had been guilty of failing to plan ahead. He spent close to an hour wrestling with this dilemma without success. Then the telephone rang.

"Hello, Michael; this is Welby. I'm back in the office and ready to carry on with peak efficiency. Would you mind joining me down here?"

"Will this be the session where you fire me because we've achieved our objective and I'm now excess luggage?"

"You are feeling sorry for yourself this morning. First of all, I can't fire you because you work for the Prime Minister with Thomas Hadley as your intermediary and immediate supervisor. You're merely on loan to the Ministry of Information. The second point is that you're not excess luggage because we have a huge amount of work to do. Now, come to my office, and we'll get more specific."

Thirty minutes later, Michael sat facing Welby Marsh at MOI headquarters. He cradled a cup of coffee, brought with him as an alternative to Welby's ever-present tea.

Welby proceeded with his pep talk. "Michael, you seem to have the idea that your value to the British government disappeared with America's declaration of war and their becoming our partner against Hitler's forces. Nothing could be further from the truth. Now that we have the Americans on board, we have to learn to live with them and work as an effective team. You, sir, speak their language and are known to many of their leadership people. For the duration of this war, you will have the unenviable task of helping to coordinate logistics and assuage conflicts between American and British leaders, both civilian and military. At the same time, you will be expected to continue writing articles for American consumption that will convince their civilian population that the two military forces are working well together."

"It is nice to feel needed, but if I'm to do all that, I'll expect an increase in pay."

"An increase? I didn't realize that we'd been paying you for your efforts.... That is not likely to be a problem, because you will be given a title and pay that are appropriate for you to deal as an equal with leaders of both allies. Do you have any other questions?"

Michael thought for a moment. "Will I be the only one trying to convince the American populace that the American and British forces are working well together?"

"You'll have support from our MOI people, because preaching the effectiveness of British/American cooperation will be part of our ongoing effort to convince the enemy that things are going well for us and poorly for them. You'll also be aided by British actors, actresses, and producers in California who have been asked to remain there and to develop films that emphasize the affinity of Americans and Brits as they work together."

"It all sounds like significant work. Do I stay in my current office, and will I have a staff?"

"That's up to you. You're in charge of this effort. It comes with a significant budget. You'll enjoy the part that I saved for last."

"What's that?"

"I've been nominated to be First Assistant to the Director of Interalliance Coordination. I work for you now."

CHAPTER 65 – RETHINKING THE QUEST

Arthur and Irma Blake, after returning from their vacation in Florida, requested that their friends and associates join them for an evening at their home in Amboy, Illinois; attire to be rigorously informal. No specific reason for the event was mentioned, but everyone assumed that the Blakes wanted to discuss their recent vacation and catch up on events that had occurred during their absence. Positive responses to the invitation came from Penny and Joe Gonzalez plus Jeremy Hadley and Debbie Danforth, but Bobby and Renee Andrews would be in Cleveland at a conference of chiefs of police.

On the appointed evening, the four guests arrived together along with Rex, the Blakes' golden retriever whose excitement at going home was obvious. The carpooling foursome plus Rex drove up the hillside driveway to the century-old white Queen Anne house, and parked near the more modern separate garage. After walking across the pavement between the garage and the house, they found Irma waiting for them on the porch. She hugged Rex as he jumped up on her, and invited the four guests to open the front door and go inside. Upon entering the front door, they were greeted by a bench and a sign that read *bare feet only beyond this point.* Individual cartons for shoes, socks, jackets, and purses surrounded the bench. One glance at their surroundings revealed the reason for the sign.

The Blakes had transformed their ground floor rooms into a Florida beach scene. They had removed the furniture and had covered the floors first with blue plastic tarps and then with a thick layer of sand over them.

Plastic palm trees surrounded the central area of the entrance hall, where cushions were arranged under beach umbrellas for seating. Overhead, additional blue tarps suspended from the ceilings had been irregularly dabbed with blotches of white paint, simulating a tropical sky.

Seeing the scene that faced them, Penny said, "Oh, I feel warmer already. This is much nicer than a picture postcard or a slide show about your vacation. Joe loves to play in the sand."

Irma responded, "We have an area near the kitchen where you're allowed to wet the sand if you want to build a sand castle. We also have a collection of seashells including conch shells you can hold up to your ears to hear the ocean waves."

Arthur joined them and added, "We won't go into the physics of the sounds you hear with the shells. Just use your imagination."

Irma led Rex to his food and water bowls in the kitchen and latched the door behind him while the visitors removed their shoes and socks. Then the barefoot guests walked to the drink cart and table in the center of the sandy beach to select tall rum drinks and appetizers. Once supplied with refreshments, they lowered themselves onto cushions under umbrellas.

Irma said, "Welcome to our beach party. I'll start by apologizing to Joe for not asking him to pick us up at the airport, but we decided to come back on a flight that arrived quite late in the evening. We drove ourselves home in a rental car to avoid making you stay up into the early morning hours, Joe. Tonight's gathering is due to our having had a great time hanging around on the sand in Miami Beach. We recreated our beach to share that environment with you. While we were there, we stumbled onto a mystery for Arthur to solve. That helped him to enjoy our vacation too. No matter where he goes, he finds something to investigate. Tell them about it, Arthur."

"Irma was speaking literally when she said I stumbled upon a mystery. I tripped on a woman's leg sticking out of the sand. The leg turned out to be a prosthesis. Its owner had been approached by some unsavory characters who wanted to take her away with them. She uncoupled her artificial leg to make it difficult for them to force her to go. They reacted by carrying her away minus the detached leg. Others on the beach witnessed the scene, but did nothing about it because they were afraid of getting involved. When Arthur found the leg and heard about the kidnapping, he checked the prosthesis for clues. The leg had an identifying serial number and manufacturer website link, allowing us to computer search the kidnapped woman's identity on our smart phones and obtain additional information about her. Once we had that, we notified the police, and they caught the kidnappers in a roadblock near Fort Lauderdale. The bad guys turned out to be wanted in three states in connection with a series of ransom kidnappings of rich young women. If this victim hadn't left her leg on the beach, we wouldn't have known about the crime or caught her abductors. She was smart and a survivor."

Jeremy said, "It also helped that you happened to be on that beach. How many others would have reacted by quickly tracking the owner of the prosthesis and getting the police on the trail?"

"Anyway, it added a touch of excitement to our vacation. Despite that, our vacation was primarily quiet time for us. Did anything significant happen while we were gone?"

The four guests all started to talk at the same time.

Arthur said, "I'll take that as an affirmative answer. Who wants to tell us about it?"

Joe said, "Debbie deserves the honor. She's the initiator and primary investigator of our mystery. Go ahead, Debbie."

"It all started when I decided to trace Jeremy's roots and give him the gift of a family tree graphic layout. Then I discovered that his great-grandfather Hadley had taken the place of a stillborn infant...."

The recounting bounced back and forth among the four guests, culminating in the description of the scrapbook in which the Gonzalezes had collected many of Michael's articles and stories written to influence the American public.

After they finished their story, Arthur commented. "Michael Farrell Hadley appears to have been a talented and unique individual. He contributed toward speeding up the entry of the United States into World War II. Have you jumped to the other end of the war to see whether he had an official position or received government recognition for his efforts during the war?"

Irma said, "You may also want to check marriage and death registers. Assuming he remained in Britain during the war, something official may have been recorded. The British are quite diligent about vital records like births, deaths, and marriages. Their long history as a nation has taught them to preserve such data for future generations. Of course some records will have been lost due to bombing by the Germans."

Penny wrote a few items in her pocket notebook. "You raise some good points. We have been tracing Michael's activities with the passage of time on a fairly linear basis. If we follow your suggestion we'll be looking back from their future. For the first time, we'll be working from the other end of the time line. We have a few data points when Michael used his American and British passports after the war. There's no need for us to discover what he did during the entire conflict. We can skip to the end of the war and even beyond that time."

Jeremy called for attention by banging his glass with a seashell. "I think it's time for me to take the podium, so to speak. I realize that I'm not likely to find a podium on a beach. All of our combined efforts have been aimed at helping me to understand my family tree. I'm grateful for everyone's assistance. Arthur and Irma do not yet know that during our family's Thanksgiving gathering, I posed the question and Debbie consented to marry me. I think it's time for us to set an early wedding date and for the two of us to honeymoon in England, checking out old records while we celebrate our union. How does that sound to you, Debbie?"

"That sounds perfect. My passport is current. I'm ready to go when you are, Jeremy."

Irma said, "You surprise me Jeremy. I've never known you to be so quick to make a decision and take action."

"That's evidence of Debbie's spontaneous nature influencing me. I suspect that it will be easier for Penny and Joe to check American documents than official British records. Debbie and I will check those plus original hard-copy document files after we arrive in the United Kingdom. Arthur, we'd like you to perform the wedding ceremony. Will you be able to get a church, and how long will that take?"

"I'm currently on leave of absence, but I'm sure I'll be able to arrange something. It may not be the Parkville church, will that bother you? The new pastor there has some strong opinions including a dislike for me. I'm sure I could set something up in this area. The Amboy church is still in the process of reconstruction, but I occasionally preach at the church that is the temporary home for the Amboy congregation."

"That will be fine. Mom and Dad will be happy to come down here. I expect that we won't have that many guests beyond you folks, our families, plus Bobby and Renee Andrews. Debbie, how would you feel about going for our license this week?"

Debbie had been reclining under a different umbrella. She crawled over to Jeremy and kissed him. "The sooner we're married, the better. With all of the effort we've put into exploring the Hadley family tree, I want to be part of it as quickly as possible. I'd settle for Arthur performing the ceremony right here and now."

"Sorry, Debbie, that's a little too soon. You'll still need that license, and I suspect that your parents will want to attend."

CHAPTER 66 – HONEYMOON

The quickly-arranged wedding and subsequent celebration behind them, Jeremy and Debbie relaxed on their big Boeing jet. Debbie, in a window seat, stared intently at the ocean whenever it became visible through breaks in the clouds. Jeremy watched her concentration with amusement.

"Hey, wife-of-mine, why are you concentrating on the ocean? Are you thinking that the plane isn't safe?"

"Hardly that; I'm reminding myself that when your great-grandfather Michael first crossed from England to the United States and later journeyed back from our country, he would have traveled by ship. Flying across the ocean was experimental and hazardous before World War II. I'm also thinking that those apparently small ripples on the ocean's surface are probably major waves. How would you enjoy getting tossed around by large waves while crossing the ocean in a ship? I'm not sure I would cope with it well."

"Flying in a big jet is just one of the things we have easier than those who came before us. The wartime years were dangerous in many ways. Those fancy ocean liners you mentioned were converted to troop ships and filled with large numbers of young people, many of whom would never make it home again. They were also susceptible to attack by German submarines. Today, we have terrorism and civil wars, but nothing like the Second World War."

"If you're in the wrong place at the wrong time, the result can be just as bad. Let's change the subject. Honeymoons deserve better topics than that."

"Let's plan our initial time in London. I booked us into the Astors Hotel which claims to be a converted Victorian townhouse. We can stay there while we decide whether we want to move to a different area. It's centrally located on the map, so we should be able to use public transportation. If we decide after the first couple of nights that we would prefer moving away from town, we'll rent a car and cover more territory."

"How will you feel about driving on the left side of the road? That should be an interesting experience."

"If it turns out to be a problem, I've heard that the train system is reliable. The important thing is that we'll be on our first major vacation and adventure together. We will be having fun while trying to learn more about Michael and the rest of my family."

"Correction, that's our family now. I can hardly wait to be considered part of it by new people we discover. You do get brownie points for looking forward to sharing an adventure with me."

"Debbie, when you initially worked on the family tree, did you find a particular area the family came from?"

"Some of them were located near Corby and Upper Benefield in East Northamptonshire. That's north of London. It should be easy driving distance, or there may be a bus that goes there. We're going to have to learn to travel the way local people do."

"Do you have any current-generation names to try to locate?"

"Not in your direct family line; your immediate ancestors are all in America. Stephen's second father or stepfather, Thomas Easley Hadley, has some relatives in the Corby area. I still don't know how to refer to Thomas. Perhaps we'll find a relative who will be able to clarify family ties."

"Records for Michael could be on either side of the Atlantic Ocean."

"That's true, Jeremy, but we're flying to the United Kingdom, so we'll be concentrating on locating whatever records he has there. You do realize that the London Blitz and subsequent bombings destroyed public records as well as buildings. My notes say that files were lost at the Greater London Record Office and at the Public Record Office at Kew, in Richmond."

"We'll search whatever is still available and hope for the best. Even if we find nothing, our trip is worthwhile, because it's also our honeymoon. Let's not lose sight of that."

Debbie cuddled up against Jeremy. "Honeymoon is a magic word. I'm thoroughly enjoying having you as my husband."

After landing and clearing customs, they took a taxi to their hotel and pledged to remain in pure honeymoon mode for at least two days. They would spend that time taking bus and walking tours, pub crawling, visiting museums, and paying as much intimate attention to each other as possible.

CHAPTER 67 – ARCHIVES

Debbie had noted from the scrapbook of Michael's published articles that his credits included being a researcher at the University of London. Her computer indicated that the central library for the university was the Senate House Library, so she and Jeremy made that facility their first stop on the third day of their stay, following their two-day honeymoon preamble to their research project.

When they arrived at the library on Malet Street, they asked a reference librarian about old university telephone directories that would indicate the room numbers of researchers during past years. They learned that while old directory copies had been preserved, they had not been digitized and made searchable by computer. Debbie and Jeremy would have to physically browse through those documents in the library stacks located in the sub-basement.

Guided by the reference librarian's assistant, they descended two levels into the stacks and found a table where they could work between sets of steel shelves. The assistant showed them the shelves that held old University of London telephone directories and then departed for the main floor.

Debbie opened her notebook and started to delve into the directories. Jeremy spotted some documents on another shelf related to the London Blitz of 1940. He decided to browse through them while Debbie did her assigned task.

Jeremy had scanned about half of the clippings and other papers in his pile when Debbie called out, "I found him. Michael Farrell Hadley is listed as having had an office on the third floor of the Strand building of King's College. We'll be able to find that office and see exactly where he worked."

"I don't think so, Debbie. Record the information on his office location for our scrapbook, but the historical papers I've been reading say that the Strand building, along with the quadrangle and the chapel suffered bomb damage during the London Blitz. They didn't reconstruct the buildings until the 1950's. Michael probably exchanged the office you located for a temporary one after the bombing. The current buildings have undergone substantial changes from the original layouts."

"Sometimes we Americans forget how much damage and loss of life there was here during the bombings. I'll make a copy of the page where I found his listing, and then let's go to the Greater London Record Office and see whether we can find anything there."

One hour later, they repeated their *search the archives* scene at the Greater London Record Office. Both Debbie and Jeremy examined old record books, but neither knew exactly what they were likely to find. The two of them were working their way through a huge amount of longhand and typed data that they had to examine manually. They had just heard the announcement that the office would be closing in twenty minutes, when Jeremy exclaimed, "I found something!"

"What do you have?"

"Michael Farrell Hadley married Alice Manning Hadley on Thursday, 15 August 1940 in a civil ceremony at London City Hall."

Debbie slammed her notebook shut. "Damn the Hadley family!"

"What's wrong?"

"That's the second time we learned about one Hadley marrying another Hadley. Thomas Hadley married Stephanie Hadley too."

CHAPTER 68 – COUNTRYSIDE

Having searched the University of London library and the Greater London Record Office, Debbie and Jeremy decided it was time for some field work. They had previously noted that earlier generation Hadley family members frequently came from the Upper Benefield and Corby areas. When they found Michael's wedding record, they discovered that his address at that time was in London near King's College, but that Alice Manning Hadley's address was listed as being in Upper Benefield. It was possible that some family members still lived in that ancestrally popular area.

After consulting the Astors Hotel staff and Debbie's computer about train service to Corby, Jeremy checked them out of the hotel and called for a taxi to take them to the London St. Pancras railway station. As their vehicle approached their destination, Debbie and Jeremy were both surprised to see that the official name of the station was St. Pancras International, but the taxi driver explained that the term *International* indicated that at that station one could board a Eurostar train to France through the Chunnel, in addition to domestic trains northbound from London.

The station had many facilities and shops and a modern arched glass roof. Jeremy and Debbie visited several shops while waiting for their train. Once on board, they relaxed and took in the scenery as their surroundings transitioned from urban sprawl to rural countryside. The train trip took slightly more than ninety minutes. In Corby, Jeremy rented a blue Mini Cooper D 3-door Hatch.

The rental agent gave him a map marked with the route to take to get to the old address for Alice Manning Hadley.

At last, they were off on their exploration adventure. Jeremy first drove a test pattern of several blocks in Corby to be sure that he could handle driving on the left of the road within a high-traffic area. Then he returned to the rental office as his starting point for following the agent's directions. They left the city surroundings of Corby and took a two lane road headed toward Upper Benefield.

Jeremy summarized their directions. "The agent said that we go toward Upper Benefield, but we don't get all the way to it. We should see a bed and breakfast sign on a building on the left. It will have a stone wall covered with ivy in front of it. Immediately beyond that building, we'll see an unpaved track that goes away from the road at a shallow angle. We're supposed to take that track to the fifth set of farm buildings. Your address is a farm that will be on the left."

"At least you found someone who knows the area. There can't be many people who go to our destination."

"Debbie, you do realize that a lot of water has flowed under the bridge since Michael married Alice. They may never have lived at her address here, and even if they did, it's unlikely that anyone in that building will remember them."

"Those are very practical arguments, but the romantic side of me tells me that it will be a good starting point. We'll at least see where and how Alice lived at one time, and we'll be able to take some pictures for our friends and family back home. By coming to the country, we may also be able to get some referrals to other Hadleys in the area."

"Fair enough; we're coming up to some buildings. Look for a bed and breakfast sign."

"Slow down and pull over; I think I see it. Park in front of the house. The car rental agent said that the wall would be covered with ivy. It's not. Instead, there are trimmed bushes growing inside the wall and rising above it. The bushes are trimmed to also cap an archway where a walking person enters through a wrought iron gate. There's a brass plate on a rock next to the archway. It says *Historic Whimsey Cottage Bed and Breakfast.*"

"Either it has very unusual and whimsical architecture, or Lord Peter Whimsey lived there."

"You do know that he was a fictional character, don't you?"

"So was Sherlock Holmes, Debbie, but tourists attempt to visit him at 221B Baker Street."

"That's different. There was no such address, but a building society at that location added a plaque in homage to Mr. Holmes. They've since dedicated a museum to him, but it's located farther down the renumbered street. The management earns a substantial amount by playing along with the devoted Sherlockians."

"Anyway, just beyond this building should be our unpaved byway. If we strike out on making contacts with current members of the Hadley clan, we can come back and spend a night at Whimsey Cottage."

They turned off the road onto the unpaved track, little more than two ruts with grass growing between them. Jeremy intently watched for rocks and deep holes which might damage their little rented car.

They drove about one half mile and had passed several small farms when Debbie nudged Jeremy. "You'll have to find a place to pull off. I think I see a car headed toward us, and there's no room for us to pass each other."

"I was enjoying the single lane because I didn't have to remember to keep to the left. I'll move off the road and squeeze under that tree up ahead. They should be able to drive past us."

They pulled off the road as far as possible and waited for the oncoming vehicle. Debbie gasped slightly when she saw that it was a large Land Rover that had seen many years of service. It might be too wide to pass between their car and the trees on the other side of the road. The Rover approached, but stopped short of them. A tall gray-haired woman wearing a red pullover sweater and blue jeans climbed out and walked toward them.

"Either you folks have lost your way, or you're headed for my farm. There's not much else ahead of you. I'm Micki Banyon."

Jeremy said, "This may sound crazy, but we're looking for the farm where Alice Hadley once lived. I wonder whether you might have known her."

"Possibly, but who are you and why are you looking for that place?"

Debbie said, "I'm sorry; we're being quite impolite. We're Jeremy and Debbie Hadley. We've come here from the United States on our honeymoon, and we thought it would be fun to search out some of Jeremy's ancestors and relatives."

"I'm pleased to meet you two. Congratulations on your marriage. How are you related to Alice Hadley?"

Jeremy said, "She married my great-grandfather, Michael Farrell Hadley. You hinted that you might know of her. Do you?"

"I'll have to answer that in the affirmative, since Alice was my mother. By the way, my nickname, Micki, is short for Michelle. I was named after your great-grandfather who was also my father. Get back into your car while I pull into a field to turn this Rover around. Then follow me to my place so that we can sit and have a chat."

Micki reversed the big Rover and then turned it in a continuous arc through the adjacent rocky field, causing Jeremy to think she was showing off her vehicle's capabilities and her driving skill. Then he pulled away from the tree and followed her.

As they drove, Debbie said, "They won't believe this when we get home. We're actually going to learn about

Michael and his wife Alice from their daughter. How much did you learn about them from talking with your grandfather?"

"If you mean Stephen, I didn't learn anything at all. Dad said that his father wouldn't talk about family matters. Anyway, I don't remember Stephen. I think he died when I was quite young. Either that, or Stephen left after a fight with Dad and never came back. It was never clear to me, because I didn't pay enough attention to family matters in my younger days. I did get to know my mother's father. He died two years ago, but Mother's mother is still living. You'll meet her when we get home. She lives in Florida. Our wedding was too small and too hastily arranged for her to have been there."

"Will that fact upset her?"

"I think she'll handle it well. She's adaptable to any situation, and she's a character. You'll like her."

Micki pulled into a long driveway on the left side of the road. They followed the curved ribbon of pavement through a clump of trees. When they emerged they could see three buildings ahead of them, a barn, a brick farmhouse, and a cottage with walls constructed from varying size slabs of local fieldstone. The single level building had a protruding entryway and two small skylights in the roof. Micki parked in front of the cottage. Jeremy slowed the Mini and brought it to rest alongside the Rover.

They got out and looked around as they gathered with Micki.

Micki said, "This is home. I live in the cottage. The people who rent and work the farm live in the farmhouse."

Debbie asked, "You said that your surname is Banyon. Do you have a husband and children?"

Micki's expression changed, suggesting impatience and causing Debbie to wonder whether her question had been unwelcome.

"Bert Banyon died a long time ago, in 1994. I'm not even sure why I still keep the name. It's probably because there aren't any other Banyons around here, so I keep my privacy. Come on into the cottage, and we'll relax with tea and coffee while we chat."

They followed Micki inside. Per her instructions, Jeremy and Debbie entered the front sitting room, while Micki went to get refreshments. Debbie sat in an upholstered chair by a fireplace that still had a few glowing embers remaining from the fire Micki had lit earlier that day. As Debbie opened her notebook, she heard Micki preparing her offerings in the kitchen. Jeremy wandered through the front hall and living room, examining items on tables and shelves as though they were unearthed artifacts from the Hadley family archeological dig ... as, in a sense, they were.

Micki returned with a tray of assorted biscuits, along with a pot of tea, a carafe of coffee, and cups with saucers. "Help yourselves. Since you're family, you get the informal service. Then tell me about the American branch of the Hadley clan."

Debbie gestured for Jeremy to respond.

"We're pretty straightforward. My dad, Walter, is Stephen's son. He owns a bakery and catering business. My mother, Shirley, is a secretary in a United Methodist church. Debbie and I operate a private detective business, the Sandley Agency. We've been trying to learn more about the rest of the family, because my grandfather, Stephen Hadley, would not tell Dad anything about his parents or anyone else who came before him."

Micki looked amused. "Debbie, you appear to be the genealogy researcher. What have you learned about the rest of us so far?"

CHAPTER 69 – DEBBIE AND MICKI

Debbie focused on Micki's expression and especially her eyes. She didn't know the significance of Micki's piercing stare. Was she trying to determine the limitations of Debbie's family knowledge, or would Micki volunteer new relationship information to clarify what Debbie had already learned. She decided to play it straight but to reveal the cards in her hand slowly.

"As Jeremy said, his grandfather, Stephen Hadley, would not tell others in our side of the family anything about his parents. We have learned that Stephen was the son of Stephanie Hadley, nee Wright, and either Michael Farrell Hadley or Thomas Easley Hadley. We thought that Stephen's father was Michael, but then we found a second set of data that suggested Thomas was his father. Would you care to clarify these relationships, Micki?"

The older woman laughed. "I can see why you're getting confused. The name Hadley appears on both sides of just about every branch of the family."

"We have observed the tendency for Hadley to be the name of both the bride and the groom in family marriages."

"I think we'll have to blame Thomas for that."

"Was he the one who gave the stillborn child's name to Michael?"

"So, you know about that substitution. That's very good. I didn't learn about that until my mother, Alice, told me after my father died. I'll anticipate your next question. Michael never revealed his original family information to anyone, not even Alice."

"Do you think he had a reason for hiding his background?"

"No one will ever know, Debbie. As I said, Thomas selected the stillborn child's name for Michael. They were doing hush-hush work, and they needed to give their new recruit a complete set of credentials."

"They being Mr. Churchill and his associates?"

"You have been digging deeply into our family mysteries. I'll neither confirm nor deny that conjecture. I will admit that my father, Michael, had a talent for becoming different people when required during his career."

Jeremy interrupted. "Enough general chit-chat. For the sake of my sanity, please tell me whether Michael or Thomas was Stephen's father."

"Your great-grandfather was Michael, Jeremy."

Debbie wrote rapidly in her notebook. "Then you and Stephen were half siblings."

"That's correct; we had the same father but different mothers. That would make me your great-aunt, Jeremy. I'd be your father's aunt, but I've never had the pleasure of meeting him."

"We'll have to remedy that, at least via the telephone."

Debbie looked up from her writing. "How did Michael and Thomas both end up being married to Stephanie, and was bigamy involved?"

"That's a very good question. Thomas arranged the marriage of Michael to Stephanie as a mission tactic, but I think that Thomas had planned to end up with Stephanie all along. As I understand the manipulations performed by Thomas, he prepared a counterfeit marriage license for Michael and Stephanie. They were married in a church ceremony, but the state of Connecticut wouldn't have recognized it as valid because the marriage license had been forged. Once Michael's assignment took him from the United States back to Britain, Thomas arranged to take his place as Stephanie's husband, this time with a valid civil ceremony. It must have been confusing to Stephanie's parents, but it was legal. On later occasions when I tried to discuss the unusual marriage arrangements with Stephanie, she always changed the subject. My mum, Alice, wasn't interested in having that conversation either. She always feared that the Connecticut marriage would somehow invalidate her own in London."

Debbie said, "I'm not very good at figuring relationships, but I'll guess that you and Stephen were not only half siblings, but also third cousins, since I show Alice and Thomas as first cousins in my notes."

"Something like that; it gets confusing, because by bloodline Stephen is not a Hadley. Neither Stephanie nor Michael was born into the Hadley family. However, Thomas adopted Stephen, so he is a legal Hadley."

Jeremy said, "I hope my dad will be satisfied with that. He wasn't happy when we told him that he wasn't a true Hadley because Michael had taken the stillborn baby's place in the family tree."

Debbie said, "I'll take your comment as my cue to get away from that family tree. Tell us more about your parents, Michael and Alice. We know that Michael wrote editorials for the *New York Times* and later magazine stories aimed at encouraging Americans to support Britain's war efforts and to enter the war as Britain's ally. What was Alice doing, and how did their roles change after America entered the war? Also, when were you born, during or after the war?"

Micki smiled. "That's a whole bunch of questions. Help yourself to more drinks and snacks. I'll do my best to supply answers. First, I was born December 1, 1946. I wasn't quite a Christmas baby. Save your calculating; I'm sixty-nine years old at this point. Alice and Michael were the best parents possible. They loved each other, and they treasured me. They taught me to appreciate many things without feeling it was necessary to own them. Rationing continued for several years after the war, so I learned the values of a wartime economy without the dangers of it. I grew up appreciating the physical damage that our country had suffered plus the moral and patriotic strength of its citizens.

"As you indicated, Michael did his best to encourage the Americans to support Britain and fight alongside us. Once the US did come on board, he had a major role to play. He was named Director of Interalliance Coordination. As an American citizen, he was in a position to assist the two military establishments in working together. That was a job that gave him many headaches. Alice spent the whole war working at Bletchley Park."

Jeremy said, "She was a code-breaker. I read that the work at Bletchley Park probably reduced the length of the war by years."

"She was proud of the work she did there, but she didn't discuss it for many years after the war ended. Once you learn to live within a bubble of secrecy, it's very hard to change your ways and share what had once been hush-hush."

Debbie looked up from her notes. "Has this cottage and farm been in the family for a long time?"

"You're in England now, so you have to be careful when you say 'a long time'. Alice inherited it from her maternal grandfather, but he purchased it sometime around 1920. By English standards, that's not long. In America, if something happened just less than one hundred years ago, is that considered a long time?"

Jeremy said, "A century would definitely be significant for us. Our country is less than two and a half centuries old. Have you always lived here, Micki?"

"I lived here as a child, but we had a small cottage on the western coast of Scotland where we spent our summer holidays. We also had a home in western Massachusetts where we lived for several years as a family, and where I lived while I attended Williams College. Dad insisted that Mum and I become naturalized US citizens and hold dual citizenships as he did. I still own that house, but rent it out as an income property."

Debbie looked up from her note-taking. "What was your major field at Williams College, Micki?"

"You'll have to promise you won't laugh."

"We promise."

"I went to college in America to study English Literature."

CHAPTER 70 – CAREERS

They spent the rest of the afternoon touring the farm and getting a feeling for rural life in England. Micki amazed Jeremy and Debbie by showing them a display case full of artifacts that had been found in the farm's fields. There were ancient Roman coins, pieces of pottery from the Roman era, spear heads from the time of William the Conqueror, and two-hundred-year-old farm tools.

Jeremy was impressed by what they saw on the tour. "Micki, you're a product of this place, so it seems natural and appropriate to you, but we would never encounter such artifacts outside of a major museum. This place gives me a feeling of continuity with history. I can see and touch things that were in use more than a thousand years ago. The grains and vegetables raised here may have grown from seeds that had a multi-generational history. It's awesome."

"Don't get too impressed, Jeremy. The stones in your fields at home are just as old. Farmers and archeologists in the States dig up dinosaur and mammoth bones. The only difference here is that we know the history of our homeland for thousands of years, but you don't know yours. Try an archeological dig in your own back yard, and you may be surprised at what you'll find."

"I did once find a buried front door key that had been lost by a previous owner of our house."

"There you go; there are artifacts to be found everywhere. Where did you grow up, Debbie?"

"I spent my earliest years in a small town in Maine, East Parsonsfield, but we moved to several other locations. Dad was a doctor, while Mom was an air taxi pilot. I assisted on many medical missions in rural areas of the United States and in Caribbean countries. Those projects had us living in many temporary homes. Later, Dad retired from doctoring and started a plastic molding firm in Tallahassee, Florida. We lived there for quite a while. He sold that company last year and is now preparing to move to the Boston area. He wants to be back in New England again."

Jeremy listened intently. "That's more than I knew previously about your parents' work and home locations. Family background and past adventures are topics that deserve more discussion."

"Don't look now, Jeremy, but that's why we're here. Micki, what can you tell us about careers and occupations in the family? Americans tend to have an image of Brits living off capital set aside by prior generations, but we know that most people have to work, no matter where they live."

Micki laughed. "When I lived in the States, I ran into that same false image of the idle rich country squires. Many Brits emerged from the Second World War penniless, or close to it. There were few things available at that time for purchase even if we did have funds. Of course, I was born in 1946, so I wouldn't have had to worry about an occupation immediately after the war.

"This may turn into a lengthy conversation, so let me begin by removing any time pressures. Following our afternoon discussions we'll adjourn to my favorite local pub for a light meal. I'm fortunate enough to have a decent budget, so I long ago ceased doing any serious cooking. Then, you are invited to stay with me in the stone cottage for as long as you wish. You can have the room where Michael stayed when he first arrived and was posing as Alice's brother. Given that nugget of information, you know you'll have to stay awhile, in order to hear more of the family's stories.

"As I said earlier, once America joined in the war against Germany and the Axis Powers, Michael became Director of Interalliance Coordination. Prime Minister Churchill wanted to give that job to an American who would be loyal to him. Given all of Michael's writing efforts to prepare Americans for the war, he was the perfect candidate. In fact, Churchill may have had the Coordination post in mind when he first added Michael to his unofficial organization.

"During the early Anglo-American joint efforts, Michael served as a diplomat trying to get the two military forces to have the same agenda. Shortly after they arrived, the Americans wanted to attempt a landing on the continent and a direct attack on the Germans. The British Command knew that the Americans needed a lot more training and combat experience before they would be any match for Hitler's forces. They also would have to learn how to operate under a single meshed Allied Forces command structure that included the remaining French forces too. The British argued for an initial campaign in North Africa while the Americans obstinately insisted on direct landings and attacks in mainland Europe. Michael was hopelessly caught in the middle, between two command structures that wouldn't yield and that both wanted him out of the way. The turning point came when President Roosevelt, acting in his capacity as Commander-in-Chief, ordered the American forces to work with the British in North Africa. The joint effort became Operation Torch, with first amphibious landings in Algeria and Morocco on 8 November 1942. This delayed the landings in France until 1944, but led to taking control of North Africa and assured that when the eventual Normandy landings came, they would be executed by combat-ready troops operating within a single command structure.

"Once command unification had been achieved, Michael performed one secret spy mission in Switzerland

and France under a different name. He returned slightly wounded from that one. Hitler tried to completely isolate neutral Switzerland. That led to Michael having a skirmish with German soldiers on his way between there and a village in the French Alps. Following that adventure, his coordination responsibilities turned toward the unenviable task of easing tempers on both sides as the British population learned how to live with an ever-expanding foreign army living in their midst while those forces prepared for the much larger battles ahead."

Debbie said, "I've heard about some of those arguments. The British military and civilians used to grumble about the Americans as 'overpaid, oversexed, and over here.' It must have taken a lot of effort to straighten out all the conflict points."

"It certainly did. By the time of the D-Day operation on 6 June 1944, Michael's staff increased greatly in order to handle arguments throughout the country. After D-Day, things went more smoothly, both because so many soldiers were now on the European continent and because the military people based in Britain were less tense after having completed the seemingly endless waiting period prior to action.

"At the end of the war, Michael received many compliments and honors, but he knew his future would lie in something totally removed from government and military affairs. He faced an additional internal debate concerning his relative loyalties to America and Britain."

Jeremy said, "I never would have guessed that my great-grandfather played such an important role in the war. He was quite an impressive guy."

"My father was that and then some. After the war, he went into the toy business with a woman he met during one of his prewar assignments. Years later, when we moved to the USA, he started his own toy business there, making sand-cast metal reproductions of classic cars. I guess I should say that he manufactured those items for collectors rather than to be used as toys. They were higher-priced sculptures. He sold that business when he brought the family back here to the farm. After that point, he tried writing children's books. He had a close friend from the Ministry of Information days who published those books. That satisfied him until he completely retired."

Debbie raised her head at the mention of retirement. "During our earlier searches, we couldn't find Michael in the Social Security Death Index. We wondered why that would have been the case."

"He wouldn't have had a listing there because he never filed for benefits. He was back in the UK long before he was eligible for Social Security, and when he reached the key age, he decided he was doing quite well without government assistance, so he would leave the available funds for others who needed a subsidy more than he did. Michael lived to be ninety-four years old, and enjoyed a big celebration-of-life party we threw for him on his ninetieth birthday."

Debbie said, "Indeed, he did do some special things. I'll bet that your mother was equally special in her own way."

"If anything, Alice was more unique, Debbie. She was part of Churchill's unofficial hidden network before Michael was recruited. Alice initially mingled at politicians' social events and gleaned the latest confidential information from in-power politicians who would never have gossiped with a known confidant of Winston Churchill."

Jeremy said, "She was a spy for one political faction against the other. That was exceptional."

Debbie glared at him. "Your naiveté is showing, Jeremy. That goes on in all political circles in all countries even today. Throughout the election process, candidates are always trying to find confidential information on weaknesses that will embarrass their rivals."

"Whether it was unique or not, Alice had a talent for flattering government insiders into sharing confidences with her. She also excelled at cross-tabulating the indiscrete morsels she received and detecting trends hidden within an assortment of seemingly unrelated facts. That's why she fit so naturally into the Bletchley Park group once it was organized.

"After the war, Alice maintained her confidence-prompting ways. She and Michael had become centers of interest at political, social, and business events. They compared notes following every soiree, and used their combined intelligence to do quite well in financial transactions. Several times insiders of both major parties asked Alice whether she would be interested in running for a seat in Parliament, but she was far more interested in family matters and her rural lifestyle."

"What about Thomas and Stephanie, Micki? What did they do after the war?"

"Well, Debbie, the answer to that is not much of anything. Thomas had resettled the family here because he needed their wartime moral support. Stephanie did volunteer work during the war, after having sent Stephen to live in safety with upcountry friends. She became a social worker when peace came. Thomas developed many government connections during the war, and he used them to secure a postwar seat in Parliament. However, he lost interest in politics after a few years. He had substantial capital and income, so he really didn't need an occupation. He and Stephanie put Stephen into a boarding school and went off to travel the world. They became what Americans called jet-setters. They enjoyed that life for many years and then retired to a nursing home in Florida. Thomas died from an illness in 1989, and

Stephanie died in an automobile accident seven years later."

Jeremy stood looking out the window during most of Micki's comments, but he turned to her with a question as soon as she paused. "What happened to Stephen, my grandfather, did he claim his inheritance and move into Thomas's family home? He would have been only fifty-eight when his mother died. I think Dad said Stephen also died."

Micki paused before replying. "No, Jeremy; Stephen is still with us, but he is in an assisted living residence because he has the beginnings of dementia. He can still recognize people and carry on a conversation, but he forgets many things. Thomas and Stephanie ran through most of their capital during their travels and their stay at that nursing home in Florida. Everything remaining in Thomas Hadley's estate was sold to provide for Stephanie and, later, to pay for Stephen's residential and medical bills. I was the executrix for Stephanie when she died after inheriting the estate from Thomas. I can tell you that there are only a few stocks and bonds left to support Stephen in the future. He does receive state pension payments."

Debbie asked, "Would we be able to visit Stephen while we're here?"

"It might take a day to make the arrangements, but I see no problem with such a visit."

Jeremy said, "Hold off on making arrangements until I contact Dad and Mom. It's time for a much overdue family reunion."

CHAPTER 71 – INTERNATIONAL CALL

Shirley Hadley wondered whether there was some kind of emergency when the telephone rang as she was preparing breakfast. She turned off the stove burner, wiped her hands on a dish towel, and grabbed the phone.

"Hello?"

"Hi, Mom, it's Jeremy calling from England."

"Is anything wrong? Are you and Debbie alright?"

"There's no problem. I wanted to talk with you and Dad about something."

"Why are you calling so early? He hasn't even made it down to the kitchen yet."

"I'm sorry, Mom, I forgot about the difference in time zones. It's afternoon here. Now I understand why your voice sounded apprehensive when you answered."

Walter Hadley entered the kitchen and leaned against the counter as he tried to get the gist of the conversation from Shirley's half of it. Confused, he nudged her and whispered, "Has something happened?"

Jeremy heard his father's stage whisper and asked, "Mom, may I speak with Dad? I need some information that only he would have."

Walter took the telephone from Shirley. "What is it, Jeremy? Are you out of money? Should I wire you some more?"

Jeremy laughed. "Now that is the mark of a good father. Thanks for always supporting me, Dad. We're looking into family background matters while we're over here, and I have to ask you a question. When did you last see your father, Stephen?"

"That's a strange question. My dad moved back to the United Kingdom when you were about two years old. I never heard from him directly, but his mother, Stephanie later wrote from Florida that he had died in an automobile accident."

"Think carefully, Dad, are you sure that letter came from Stephanie."

"I don't exactly remember the details. It may have been written by someone else at Stephanie's request. I do recall that the wording of the letter appeared to have a Spanish accent. Anyway, I was so upset by the news of my father's death that I probably had tears all over that letter. Why do you ask?"

"If you're not already sitting down, grab a chair. The letter that we just discussed must have been written by someone with a less-than-perfect grasp of the English language. There was a car crash, but it occurred in Florida and not in England. Stephen didn't die in the crash; Stephanie did."

"What happened to my father?"

"Stephen is still alive, here in England. He's in a nursing home, getting assistance for the early stages of Alzheimer's disease. I'd like you and Mom to come over here so that we'll all be able to visit him together. Will you be able to come, and if so, how soon?"

"Give me a few seconds to absorb your news. I'm pretty sure I'll be able to get Irma Blake to take care of the bakery for me. She's done it before. Your mother and I talked about a vacation, so our passports are current. It looks as though our schedule for that trip has been moved up. Thanks so much for the news. We'll be there in two or three days. I'll email the final details of our arrangements. You can meet the plane or give us instructions for joining you. Goodbye for now, son."

Walter turned to Shirley. "I don't know how much of that conversation you understood from hearing only my end of it, but when Jeremy was still young, we made a tragic mistake. We received a letter and interpreted it to say that my father died in a car accident, when it was intended to say that his mother died in that crash. It was a Spanish accent letter with confusion between the names Stephen and Stephanie. My father is still alive in England, and we're going there to join Jeremy and Debbie in visiting him. You've always said you like spur-of-the-moment vacations. You're about to have a great one."

Shirley hugged Walter and then sat down. "Are you sure they won't mind our crashing their honeymoon?"

CHAPTER 72 – PILGRIMAGE

When Walter and Shirley Hadley arrived at Heathrow Airport, they found Jeremy and Debbie waiting for them, even though it was barely six o'clock in the morning local time. Walter and Shirley cleared customs and then they all stopped at one of the airport restaurants for a brief reunion party and breakfast snack.

Walter asked, "Do you have a car in the lot, Jeremy?"

"We won't need one, Dad. We'll take the London Underground from the tube station here to London's St. Pancras International Station and transfer there to a train for Corby, which is our destination."

"What's our objective up there?"

"Be patient, Dad. We may have a few surprises for you. You said that the flight was uneventful?"

Shirley said, "It was exactly the way I like to fly. We got on the plane in the late afternoon. Then we had a drink and some food before we slept our way across the Atlantic. Now, I can almost believe that it's early morning. We shouldn't take too long to get our biological clocks matched to the local time. They do say you shouldn't make any major decisions right after a big time zone shift, so I'll relax and let others do the deciding."

Debbie put her arm around her mother-in-law's shoulders. "We're heading for a rural area that you'll enjoy, Mom. Give me any questions or concerns you may have."

"Ooh, I like being called mom by my new daughter-in-law. Thank you, Debbie; I'm looking forward to this adventure."

After reaching the station at Corby, Jeremy gathered Walter and Shirley's luggage and led the group to the car park where Micki awaited them in her Land Rover. As they loaded the luggage with Micki's assistance, Jeremy introduced his parents to her.

"Micki Banyon, meet my parents, Shirley and Walter. Mom and Dad, Micki is Stephen Hadley's half sister. Michael Farrell Hadley was father to both of them, but they had different mothers. You'll get the full rundown later, and Debbie has it diagrammed on paper in case pictures will make the family relationships easier to understand."

Walter shook Micki's hand. "You're the one who told the kids that my father, Stephen, is still alive. Thank you so much. Due to a terrible communications mix-up, we thought he died many years ago. Thanks also for giving us this ride."

"Jeremy and Debbie showed up on the road to my place in a rented Mini. There was no way you would have all fit into that car along with your luggage. Besides, we'll all be staying at my cottage so that you'll appreciate the way some of the Hadleys live over here. It will be fun to exchange life stories and anecdotes anyway."

Shirley said, "If you don't mind my saying so, I love your boots and jeans. They make me feel as though I'm home where so many women wear them."

"People who live on farms dress pretty much the same way everywhere. If you don't have casual clothing for your stay, Shirley, I can lend you some. I think we're about the same size."

"Thank you so much, Micki. I feel very much at home already."

They drove to Micki's farm and cottage by an indirect route that allowed her to show them much of Corby and Upper Benefield, including Thomas Hadley's former home where he had lived with Stephanie and Stephen. Walter and Shirley enjoyed the meandering back road and the farm as they approached their final destination."

Shirley tried to focus on scenery on both sides of the road at the same time. "Micki, your farm is typical of places they feature in tourist guides. You should be very proud of it."

"I am that. This is the origin point for the saga of Michael and my mother, Alice. As far as I'm concerned, with Thomas's house sold, this farm is now Hadley Central. There is no other place more entwined with the history of our family."

Walter nodded his affirmation. "I'll add an Amen to that. Thank you so much for bringing us here. I have yet to go inside any of the buildings, but it feels like home to me already."

They parked and went inside the stone cottage where it all began. Jeremy showed his parents the back bedroom where they would be sleeping, he and Debbie having already moved their bedclothes to the sofa that converted to a bed in the sitting room. While Debbie and she were setting out drinks and snacks in the front room, Micki commented that the cottage would adapt itself to accommodating all of them.

Walter and Shirley joined them, sitting on the same sofa where Michael and Alice had once discussed the Hadley family structure. A few ales, teas, and coffees later, they began to exchange family stories and questions.

Walter started them off. "Micki, I've been told many times not to talk with a woman about her age, but I need a reference point. Who is older, you or my father, Stephen?"

"Stephen was born before World War II, and I was born after its conclusion, so he is definitely older. I was born in 1946, so that would make me one of the first so-called baby boomers. You really couldn't blame all those love-starved soldiers for celebrating the end of the war by having babies."

Debbie set her Old Speckled Hen ale on the table and wagged a cautionary finger at Jeremy. "Don't you stare at me like that every time someone mentions babies. We're still on our honeymoon."

Everyone laughed, and then Walter turned toward Jeremy and Debbie. "Shirley and I both want to thank you for sharing your special time with us, even though we knew you were going to check family genealogy during your honeymoon trip. Micki, your comments to the kids about Stephen still being alive will save us from eternal self-blame."

Walter recounted the story of the garbled letter that convinced them that Stephen had died when it had been intended to report Stephanie's fatal car accident.

Micki paused to finish her Guinness. "That story triggers memories of Stephen complaining that his parents treated him like a pawn in a chess match and that you folks, his American family, had forgotten him. At the time, I kept prodding him to contact you to see whether there was a problem, but he has always been a bit of a hermit."

Walter agreed. "I always had to approach him seeking attention while I was growing up. He rarely volunteered his time or made suggestions for us to do things together."

"He may have been preoccupied. He often tuned out everyone around him while he wrote songs and computer programs. He had more than a few of his songs played and recorded by local bands, and he grew up during the early days of computers when you wrote your own programs if you wanted to get anything useful done. Nowadays, you just use other people's software and don't even think of writing your own."

"I didn't realize Dad was that creative."

"Very few did. Stephen felt unappreciated, so he did innovative things without telling many people about them."

"How bad is Dad's dementia?"

"He's still in the early stages. He has better long term memory than short term. He complains about things that he remembers as abusive from his childhood days, but he can't remember a person's visit two days ago. He can read, write, and converse adequately, but he has problems understanding the rules of a game or a puzzle. Outside of those difficulties, he'll enjoy your visit. Speaking of that, I've told the care facility manager that we'll be coming as a group to see Stephen tomorrow morning. I hope that timing is acceptable."

Shirley said, "Speaking for the newcomers, I'll agree to that schedule. I'm not as disoriented by the time change as I expected to be. I do have one question. What happened to Stephen's wife, Walter's mother?"

Walter said, "I told you, Shirley; Dad and Mother got divorced when I was just a boy. Dad said the problem was that they hadn't really considered how much work and responsibility it takes to raise a child. Mother left, but he stood by me because he didn't want me to feel unloved. That's the way he felt during his childhood."

Shirley patted Walter on his knee. "I appreciate anyone who takes the raising of a child so seriously. I'm looking forward to meeting Stephen tomorrow."

CHAPTER 73 – STEPHEN

The drive to the September Assisted Living facility took about thirty minutes. The building exterior was a modern version of a traditional brick industrial mill structure, but the interior layout included ten apartments for individuals or couples plus common rooms for gathering and special purpose use. Stephen's apartment was located above the dining room. His windows looked out upon the grassy area sheltered within the two wings of the ell-shaped building.

In accordance with facility rules, everyone signed the visitor book, and then the group followed the assigned guide to Stephen's flat. The guide, a medium-height dark-haired woman, opened the flat's door with a passkey and waited to see that Stephen was sufficiently alert to interact with visitors before she admitted the group and departed.

Micki introduced Stephen to Jeremy and Debbie and reminded him of his relationships to everyone. Stephen sat quietly during this process and then turned first to Walter. "How have you been son? It has been a while since you last visited."

This remark was greeted by prolonged silence, following which Walter said, "It's good to see you too, Dad. We saw each other last time in a different place. We've just now learned that you're living here. Do you like this facility and the other people who live here?"

"I do, Walter, especially because some of the people here have trouble remembering things. I can tell my old jokes to them over and over again. They're friendly, though."

"Do you remember my wife, Shirley, and your grandson, Jeremy?"

Richard Davidson

"I definitely remember Shirley. At your wedding I told her she was too good for you. I told her she should marry me instead. Jeremy is a different matter. He was a young child when I last saw him, so you could tell me anyone was Jeremy, and I'd have to take your word for it. I'd better shut up. Your wife wants to talk."

Shirley said, "Don't you believe him, Walter. He's trying to start trouble. He never said those things to me at our wedding. I think he had so much to drink there that he's remembering his fantasies."

Stephen laughed. "I like a woman with spunk. You don't really expect me to remember what I said at your wedding, do you? It's enough that I remember having been there. I keep finding that people who visit or interview me get excited when I remember things, so I keep them happy by supplying memories, some of which I invent as I go along. For instance, I remember seeing Debbie at her wedding too. She gave me a piece of wedding cake and kissed me on the cheek."

"This is the first time I ever met you, Grandpa Stephen. I'm beginning to think you're pretending to be sick so that you can have your own flat and people to take care of you. Even so, let's make your memory real." She walked over to Stephen and kissed him on the cheek.

Jeremy grabbed her arm. "Be gentle with him, Debbie. He may not know what he's saying."

Stephen said, "And you shouldn't talk about me as if I'm not in the room with you. Debbie's closer to the truth than you are. I know what I'm saying, but I sometimes poke fun at people who walk on eggs when they're with me because they think I'm sick. I'm not sick. I just have some memory gaps. Someday I may have trouble communicating, but that day isn't today. That being said, tell me the truth about why you haven't written or visited me for so long, Walter."

"That's an embarrassing topic, but you deserve to have the whole story. We haven't written to you or visited you because we thought you were no longer living. Many years ago, when your mother, Stephanie, died in an automobile accident, someone sent us a letter to inform us, but it was poorly worded, and it convinced us that you were the one who died in that crash. Bad handwriting confused the names Stephen and Stephanie, and they weren't clear about the location of the accident. We only learned that you were alive this week, when Jeremy and Debbie heard that news from Micki. We came as soon as we learned you were here. I hope you'll understand, Dad."

"I'll agree that thinking someone is dead qualifies as a good reason for not contacting him. I'll add my own regrets. You didn't contact me, so I was stubborn and pig-headed about not reaching out to you first. It doesn't take much to fracture a relationship. Anyway, you're here now, and we can all be friends again. Don't get mad if you have to remind me of all our family connections when you visit the next time. I can still read, even though they say I'll lose that skill someday, so be sure to send letters right away after you return home."

Jeremy said, "Grandpa, it has been great to finally meet you. I thought I never would. Dad told us that you were never willing to talk to him about your parents. Have you changed your mind about that topic? Why wouldn't you talk about them?"

"I suppose I'll have to say something, since you came all the way from America to visit. Besides, that chatterbox, Micki, may have given you a slew of wrong information. I wouldn't talk about my parents because in my mind, I disowned them. My father, Michael, left home soon after my birth and never regretted his departure decision. I was the product of a marriage of convenience during a so-called assignment for him. My stepfather, Thomas, supported me, but never had any emotional attachment to me. He was cold and manipulative in everything he did. Mother was the closest to being a true parent, but she was willing to put me into a boarding school so that she and Thomas could travel and party all the time. I was the child that no one really wanted. They weren't interested in talking about me, so I wouldn't talk about them. If I had, I probably would have shown my anger toward them. Instead, I was more charitable by not saying anything at all."

Shirley said, "Now that they've all died, do you feel any differently toward them?"

"Not really; they had their opportunities to be close to me, and they chose to serve country over family. Now it's my turn to neglect remembering them. Soon, I won't even have a choice. My memories of them are fading, both by choice and by the circumstances of my health. So be it."

Micki said, "You are a bundle of laughs today, Stephen. I think it's time for me to take your family away for some sightseeing. I'll be sure to let them visit you again before they go home. In the meantime, see what you can remember about your younger years and write it down. You have a good tale to tell about your own accomplishments. Your parental relationships are not your whole story."

"They won't want to hear everything."

"Write down the parts that you care to tell; that will suffice."

"Yes, ma'am, I'll get right onto it. In the meantime, everyone go enjoy jolly old England. Micki is a good tour guide, and she has that monster Land Rover to carry you around. You'll feel as though you're on an African safari."

CHAPTER 74 – MICKI

The three women, Micki, Shirley, and Debbie, sat on a bench near the barn discussing the operation of a farm when Jeremy walked up and put his hands on Debbie's shoulders. He waited for the next break in the conversation and then changed the subject.

"Micki, I was thinking about our session the other day when you filled us in on the careers of different members of the family. As I did that, I discovered an omission. You told us about your college studies, but you never mentioned your work after college. Would you mind touching on that subject now?

"I'll do that if Debbie and Shirley feel they know enough about farming. They were the first to request my lecture services."

Shirley said, "Since he was a little boy, Jeremy always wanted prompt attention and top priority for his desires. I'll vote to yield to his new subject. Will you go along with that, Debbie?"

"Given that tidbit about the spoiled little boy wanting attention, how could I do anything other than yield? Jeremy will, however, have to realize that I'll use his history of demanding priority against him in the future."

"Women always gang up on a man, but I'll accept your terms in order to learn about Micki's career."

"We'll start with the information you already know. I majored in English Literature at Williams College. They taught that subject primarily from the viewpoint of the reader. During the course of my studies, I decided that I enjoyed reading the works of some authors, while I found others to be boring or even distasteful. By the time I was graduated, I had a significant list of authors I didn't like. I decided that I could write material that would be more entertaining and informative than theirs and started to set my thoughts down on paper. By the time I returned to England, I had created first drafts of several novels.

"I dutifully revised my manuscripts until I deemed them worthy of publication. Then I submitted them to several publishers, both large and small. That's when I began to understand that the older novelists were famous, in part, because they had relatively little competition for a publisher's attention. Nowadays, there are many more books written each year and fewer publishers looking for the works of new authors."

Jeremy asked, "Were your manuscripts rejected?"

"They were indeed rejected on many occasions, and usually without the benefit of a personal comment. What bothered me most was that my parents, both Michael and Alice, had publishing connections that I could have used to get my manuscripts to the top of several firms' submissions piles. I was too stubborn to take advantage of my parents' links to publishers. I decided that I would do it on my own, or I would not publish at all."

"So, how did you finally break through the resistance of publishers?"

"I didn't. Instead of going over the blocking wall, I went around it. I wrote a series of short guide books highlighting some of the oldest UK farms that had been run continuously by a single family, and I set up my own publishing house to distribute them, Deep Roots Press. Those guide books sold fairly well to historians, antique collectors, and tourists. I followed the first set of books with others that discussed looking for archeological artifacts in different parts of the country. My research for the second series of books simply consisted of contacting the old farms that I'd previously featured and asked them about the artifacts they had each found. I then flagged their locations on a map, and I soon had a summary book covering likely locations around the country for finding different categories of antiquities. These books also earned a following, so I considered myself an established press and proceeded to issue my novels that the Old Boys Club of publishers had rejected. I didn't set the world on fire with my book sales, but I sold enough copies to satisfy my goal of achieving success on my own."

Debbie asked, "Did you stick with your writing over the years?"

"I filled the orders that came in, but I was ready to tackle a new challenge. Because of my knowledge of all the farms in this and other areas, I obtained an appointment as a Special Constable. Read the word special as meaning unpaid. Whenever there were local crimes, or crimes on farms, they would call me in to work with the professional police. Read the word professional as meaning paid. After a few years, I grew to like police work, and they apparently judged me to be good at it. The result was that I became a Detective Constable or DC working in the Criminal Investigation Department or CID."

Jeremy said, "I'm impressed. Are you still a DC, Micki?"

"Technically, I am, but I'm scheduled to retire within a few months, so they haven't assigned me to a case lately."

"Would that be because crime in this area is rare?"

"I wish that were so, Debbie, but crime is a fact of life almost everywhere. There's more emphasis on being on the alert for terrorism than in the past, and as in your country, there are always young rebels unhappy about a system that makes it difficult for them to achieve their dreams."

"Some of them are unhappy because the economy doesn't keep up with population growth."

"That's a factor, but here, as in America, many people are not as patient or as readily satisfied as once was the case. If they can't quickly obtain their own rewards, they decide that someone else has too many assets and that he or she should share the wealth with them."

"The increasing density of urban population has to be a factor also."

"Right you are, Jeremy. I can see that you and Debbie are thoughtful and experienced private detectives."

"Do you have a favorite case that you investigated?"

"It would be difficult to isolate a favorite, but of course I would choose to remember ones that we successfully solved. One of those that might interest the three of you I call *the Case of the Visitor's Revenge.*"

Shirley and Debbie both voiced their interest and approval. "Tell us about that one." They leaned back on the bench and each assumed a comfortable position.

"This matter involved Mrs. Rose Harnish and her husband Robert. She operated a confectionary shop in Corby, while he was a producer of documentary films. About two years ago, Robert decided to produce a film about the descendants of the Scottish laborers who once worked at the Stewarts & Lloyds steel tube works in Corby. That industrial complex disappeared after first being nationalized into British Steel, and then being abandoned in favor of establishing steel tube manufacturing plants in other parts of the country.

"Robert found Flora Firth, the granddaughter of one of the early supervisors, Angus McGregor. Flora had become a Carlisle, England local radio personality. Carlisle is near the Scottish border. Flora had her grandfather's diary covering the ten years he worked at Stewarts & Lloyds, including each and every one of his work assignments in the plant. Robert Harnish planned to show still photographs of each appropriate location in the plant, while Flora read the matching section from the diary. Robert was sure that he could edit the clips into an entertaining and educational finished documentary, using tricks and techniques pioneered in America by Ken Burns.

"Because Robert had a limited budget and because Flora would be so far from home during the shooting of the film, he announced to his wife, Rose, that Flora would live with them until he completed the project. Rose observed Flora and Robert working closely together and decided that she would have to take action to separate them.

"When Flora was scheduled to take a fortnight back home for her Christmas holiday, Rose presented her with a two-layer box of candy from her shop. Flora didn't know that the top layer was normal, but curled up in the bottom layer was a pearl necklace that Rose had nicked from me during a recent visit to my farm. "Rose had seen how much Flora enjoyed chocolates, so she was certain that Flora would be halfway through the top layer of her assortment before her train arrived back home in Carlisle. She waited until one hour after the train departed and then called me with the news that she had seen Flora hide my necklace in her candy box.

"I followed Rose's script and arranged for the police in Carlisle to meet the train when it arrived and search Flora's belongings for my necklace. That's when Rose's plan fell apart. It seems that on the train, Flora sat next to a nutrition advocate who spent the entire trip telling Flora about great new diets she should follow in order to lose a few pounds. With this woman giving her a continuous lecture about food values and diets, Flora didn't dare to open the tempting box of chocolates she carried. She felt obliged to say that it would be a Christmas present for a friend.

"The Carlisle Police stopped Flora upon her stepping off of the train and asked to inspect her box of candy. When they did, they found the box still wrapped in clear plastic and sealed by the store and the necklace hidden in the second layer of candies. The result was that we arrested Rose Harnish for stealing my necklace and for conspiring to blame Flora Firth for that crime. Rose went to prison, and Robert Harnish, her husband who hadn't been involved with Flora, felt so contrite about his wife's crimes that he showered Flora with attention and eventually became her lover."

Debbie said, "The moral of that story is that sometimes it's best to leave future developments to fate instead of trying to force them toward a desired goal. I enjoyed that story, Micki. I have one that resembles it that I'll tell you sometime."

CHAPTER 75 – NO PLACE LIKE HOME

Arthur and Irma Blake invited Penny and Joe Gonzalez to join them for dinner at their favorite Chinese restaurant, House of Ming in Parkville. Irma had triggered the event by commenting to Arthur that the worst aspect of their move to Amboy, Illinois had been that they no longer visited their friend Tony Fleming at his House of Ming restaurant. Arthur responded by setting up the current meeting with the added goal of learning more from Penny and Joe about investigative matters that had transpired during the Blakes' vacation in Florida.

Arriving first, Arthur and Irma visited Tony in his office and invited him to join them at the bar for a cocktail, their treat. Tony, in the midst of wrestling with tax forms, was happy to take a break and comply.

After their drinks arrived, Tony said, "No reflection on you, Irma, but I really appreciated those pre-marriage years when Arthur would eat here frequently and also recommend us to his flock at Parkville United Methodist Church. He directly and indirectly generated a significant percentage of our business."

"I still recommend House of Ming, Tony. I just don't talk with as many people now that I'm on leave of absence."

"Will you be pastor of a church again, or is your career headed in a different direction?"

"It looks as though Bishop Chandler and I have agreed that I'm more interested in investigating crimes and unusual events than in supervising the day-to-day activities of a church, although an unforeseen emergency may change his mind."

Irma said, "I have a proposal for increasing your business, Tony. How about opening a branch of House of Ming in Amboy? Then we could enjoy your food more frequently and recommend it to a new batch of friends and associates too."

"A branch somewhere would be a possibility. I'll check out the market in Amboy, along with a few other places. I see Penny and Joe Gonzalez arriving. I suspect they're here to meet you. Would you like your favorite large booth in the back corner?"

"That will be perfect, Tony, and I was serious about considering an Amboy branch."

"I'll have your booth set up in two minutes. Thanks for my cocktail."

Joe led Penny to the bar. "Greetings, folks; sorry we're a few minutes late."

Arthur said, "We're being informal today, so timing doesn't count. We enjoyed a brief chat and drink with Tony while we waited. Irma may have convinced him to open a branch of this place in Amboy, near our new home. She's a great salesperson."

Joe said, "I see Tony signaling that our booth is ready. Let's head over there."

They settled into their seats and gave the waitress their orders. Then Joe asked, "Are we here tonight so that you can tell us about a new investigation that you're about to tackle, or are you going to quiz us about Jeremy and Debbie's case and continuing adventures?"

Irma said, "We're curious about Jeremy and Debbie, both with regard to their genealogical investigation and concerning how well they work together as a separate team from the rest of us. Any comments on the team aspect, Penny?"

"We worked well with them on the initial stages of their project, but their current honeymoon trip may yield the best indication of how well they work as a stand-alone team. They were going to continue their family tree investigation as part of their honeymoon. I suspect they'll learn quite a bit by being on the scene where some of the Hadleys live or lived. You get a different level of intelligence when you have agents on the ground."

Joe said, "Don't take my contribution as being a reflection on Jeremy's style, but I have been impressed by the way Debbie analyzes the same data as the rest of us, but she comes up with a different interpretation of it that makes a lot of sense. I would not want to have the assignment of pulling a scam on her."

Penny agreed. "Debbie works well as part of a team, but she also functions well as a solo operative. It may be due to her background as a college library researcher. She'll defer to Jeremy when he voices a strong opinion, but she'll be ready with her own interpretation of the evidence should his not be sufficiently convincing."

Arthur refilled his coffee from the pot that Tony always provided for him along with the traditional Chinese tea. "We're interested in the capabilities of Jeremy and Debbie as a separate team because some cases will require investigators who can blend into a younger population. Do we know anything about their self-defense and weapons capabilities?"

Irma gestured for attention. "When they started the Sandley Agency with Wally Sanborn, Wally arranged for martial arts and marksmanship training with some of his Army buddies. I don't know whether they've received additional training since that time. Don't forget that some investigations won't require self-defense and weapons skills. They're working on a case right now that hasn't involved any type of violence."

Joe said, "I'm getting the feeling that Arthur has a specific investigation in mind for our young friends. Am I correct, and if so, would you like to share your thinking with us?"

"I don't have a specific case at my fingertips, Joe, but the trend, especially among younger populations, is toward violence and terrorism. We'll have to be prepared."

Irma clapped her hands. "That's it. It's applause time. Pastor Arthur Blake just jumped off that fence he's been straddling for a long, long time. He came down on the side of investigations rather than spiritual inspiration as his primary future concentration."

Penny and Joe also contributed a short burst of applause, causing the waitress to visit their booth to see whether additional service was required.

CHAPTER 76 – ONCE UPON A TIME

The Illinois Hadleys; Walter, Shirley, Jeremy, and Debbie; took a day away from Micki's farm to play tourists and visit Shakespeare's Stratford-upon-Avon. They felt quite satisfied and cultured-up during their return trip in the rented Mini, having unanimously agreed that a vacation in England required exposure to the Bard's iambic pentameter.

Shirley expressed her satisfaction with the trip up to this point. "You know, Illinois is fine, but I get such a sense of history here. The buildings, Shakespeare, artifacts found in farm fields, they all positively reek of history. It feels so different to me here."

Debbie said, "Illinois has its history too. Micki made a very good point when she suggested that the rocks in Illinois are just as old as the rocks in England. Our history is not as obvious because Native Americans from past centuries didn't write lots of books and plays about their lives and lifestyles. You've been quiet Jeremy. Would you care to voice your opinion on the subject?"

"I'm glorying in our family history. I met my grandfather for the first time, and that was almost a resurrection, because we had thought him dead for many years. I also met a great-aunt that I didn't know anything about. Dad, how good was it for you to see your father again? Stephen apparently has or had many talents that I knew nothing about."

"You're right, son; seeing Dad again was a special experience. I'll also contribute the fact that some of the talents Micki attributed to my father were news to me too. A parent is regarded by his or her child as a source of

Richard Davidson

security and love and taken at face value. Very few children critique their parents in the same way they analyze strangers, at least not objectively."

"What was your relationship with Grandpa like, Dad? That name sounded strange to me when I said it. Because we thought Stephen died when I was quite young, I never needed to decide what I would call my grandfather. I think I like the informality of Grandpa."

"It's interesting that you phrased your comment that way, Jeremy, because my father was anything but informal. He was socially stiff with me, and he studied my behavior, almost as though I was a lab rat in an experiment he was conducting. He did have some background in chemistry, but I don't think he ever used that training in a job situation. By the time I reached the eighth grade, he became bored with the idea of hands-on parenting, so he sent me off to a private boarding college prep school instead of a public high school. I smiled to myself because of that when he talked about feeling abandoned at his boarding school."

Debbie said, "I'm not a parent yet, but I can understand a first-time parent studying his or her child. From what I've heard from relatives with children, it's absolutely amazing when you observe your youngster absorbing information and skills at a very rapid rate."

Shirley said, "I'll agree with that. When Jeremy was learning to talk, he would add any new word he heard twice to his spoken vocabulary. Walter had recently returned from his enlistment in the Navy, and I cautioned him continually not to swear in front of Jeremy, who was soaking up new words like a sponge."

"I hardly ever swore. You should have heard some of the other guys in my unit."

Debbie asked, "Dad, do you remember much about your mother?"

"I'm afraid I remember very little. I was quite young when she gave up on parenting and left Dad. I must have been a difficult child to cause that split."

Shirley patted him on his thigh. "Don't feel guilty about your parents separating, Walter. They may have used you as an excuse, but your mother's departure was probably due to incompatibility. It would have happened sooner or later, even without you being there."

"Well, I have Debbie to thank for giving me back my father. If she hadn't tackled her genealogy project, we never would have discovered that he's still alive."

They reached the junction with the unpaved road to the farm. Jeremy took the turn at a speed that was slightly high. As they cornered everyone shifted to the right. When they approached the stone cottage, they saw that the Land Rover was missing, and that a sheet of paper was tacked to the front door.

CHAPTER 77 – POLICE BUSINESS

The note read, "Duty calls - Report of possible terrorist activity in Milton Keynes – All hands on deck - Food in fridge – Will contact later – Micki"

Jeremy read the note aloud and commented to no one in particular, "I guess the terrorist concern is universal. Here they scramble more than just the local cops when there's a problem."

Shirley said, "Let's go inside and get comfortable. I've been strictly a passenger on our tourist outing. It's time for me to get to work and generate a light supper for us. If you don't mind a sexist allocation of resources, you can give me a hand, Debbie."

"That sounds fine to me, Mom. We'll have to get used to working together at family functions anyway."

"I have to get used to your being new to the group, Debbie. I keep feeling that you've been in the family for years."

"Jeremy and I were together for a while before our wedding, but I know what you mean. You marry the family as well as the spouse, and in this case it has been a completely natural fit."

After the women went into the kitchen, Walter and Jeremy sat across from each other in the sitting room. Walter studied his son's expression.

"You tensed up when you read that note on the door. Has your private detective business involved you in terrorism?"

"Not yet, Dad, but I'm sure it will. We faced some related situations when I was a member of the ABC Consultants team with Arthur and Irma."

"Are you ready for a violent confrontation?"

"I've received some training from Wally Sanborn's Army friends, and I expect that I'll have more of the same. You need to be ready for anything that comes along."

"Well, I just want you to know I'm proud of the way you're prepared for danger."

"Don't get things wrong, Dad. I'm prepared, but I don't expect a steady diet of violence. Most cases won't require anything more than studying the facts and gathering evidence. A private detective gets to choose his or her cases, unlike a member of law enforcement."

They were interrupted by Shirley arriving with a platter of sandwiches and fruit, which she placed on the coffee table. Debbie followed with tea and coffee.

Debbie said, "I heard someone mention private detectives. If there were a case requiring our participation over here, we'd be completely unofficial. We're not licensed in the UK, or even outside of Illinois."

"Relax, Debbie; Dad and I were simply comparing official law enforcement people with private detectives. There's no case here for us to handle."

Debbie smiled and headed back to the kitchen to get silverware. As she walked away, Jeremy thought he heard her mumble, "Little does he realize."

They finished eating and were clearing the sitting room of dishes and leftovers when the Land Rover arrived and parked outside. Shirley quickly arranged the remaining food on a clean dish and sent Debbie to the kitchen to brew fresh tea. When Micki entered, she found a plate of food and tea set up for her on the coffee table and the others sitting away from the sofa so that she would have room to eat.

"It appears that you've already eaten, but that you saved a bit for me. Thank you very much. These call-outs make one hungry."

Jeremy asked, "Did you have a terrorist situation?"

"It was a potential problem, so they brought us out in force. It turned out to be a protest by a large crowd of young people at the Bletchley Park heritage attraction in Milton Keynes. They were protesting government monitoring of telephone traffic and other communications. There's always a conflict between privacy rights and anti-terrorist monitoring. This time, the crowd was relatively peaceful. They shouted hateful slurs about police and government that we ignored. As is usual, they dispersed as soon as the television news crews departed."

Walter said, "That doesn't sound very different from what goes on in the US."

"Causes and protests are quite similar everywhere."

Debbie said, "I have a protest, Micki."

"What's on your mind?"

"It has to do with you and the Hadley family tree."

"I've just returned from an assignment. Can we hold that discussion until later this evening?"

"We can have it any time you're ready."

Micki stood and left the room. Shirley and Walter stared at their new daughter-in-law.

Jeremy said, "I don't know what you have in mind, but that exchange with Micki sounded impolite."

"It was meant to sound that way."

CHAPTER 78 – WORDS AND DEEDS

Later that evening, Shirley and Walter entered the sitting room and found Debbie and Jeremy sitting quietly across the room from Micki. After his parents took seats, Jeremy stood and faced Micki.

"Debbie hasn't told me what she had in mind to discuss tonight, but I want to apologize for her abrupt tone this afternoon. You've been a great host to us, and we should be more respectful."

Micki gestured for Jeremy to sit down. "Debbie's behavior was not out of line. She knew that we would need to have this conversation sooner or later, and she simply instigated an acceleration of the schedule. I was stalling, and she countered that action. Debbie, go ahead with your comments and questions."

"Let's start with Bert Banyon. My guess is that he never existed. Would you like to respond to that suggestion, Micki?"

"As I said earlier, I've kept Banyon as my surname because it gives me a shield of anonymity. There is no one else with that name in the area. The exploits of my parents, Michael and Alice, before, during, and after World War II attracted too much attention, and visitors kept showing up wanting to talk about them. That's why, on our initial meeting, I asked why you wanted to know about Alice before I admitted a connection to her."

"You were a bit too Dickensian in selecting that name. Charles Dickens loved to name a character to show his or her characteristics. The name Oliver Twist told that lad's story as *all of a twist*, and Banyon suggests *ban yon visitors*."

"I agree. What else would you like to discuss?"

"Calling him Bert was a little suggestive.... Walter, or I should say Dad, where were you born?"

"It was a small town in Massachusetts. I've never even been back there."

"Do you remember that town's name?"

"I think it was North Adams."

"There's a very interesting fact about North Adams, Massachusetts, Dad."

"What's that?"

"It's the next town east of Williamstown, the home of Williams College."

"I think I recall that college coming up in conversation recently. What was the connection, Shirley?"

Shirley looked at Micki. "I remember Micki saying she went to that school. Ordinarily, I'd say that was a coincidence, but I believe that Debbie is connecting some dots for us. Please continue, Debbie."

"Dad, when you were born, your Aunt Micki, here, would have been twenty-five years old, several years out of Williams College but still living in western Massachusetts. Micki, would you like to add anything about where you were when Walter was born in 1971?"

"You're both perceptive and persuasive, Debbie. Welcome again to the family."

Jeremy said, "I'm just a bit confused. Where is this going, Debbie?"

Micki held up her hand in a traffic policeman's stop gesture. "I'd better take control of the conversation at this point. Continuing with answers to Debbie's probing, I was living in Pittsfield, the larger town south of North Adams, and when Walter was born, I was as close to him as I could be. It's time to drop the veil.... Jeremy, I'm your grandmother. Walter, I'm your mother. I haven't been a good mother to you, but I did what I felt was necessary for you to grow up in a normal way." She stood and faced him.

Walter hurried across the room and hugged Micki. "I did sense something familiar about you. I remembered certain hints of your style and tone even though I was so young when you left. Now I understand why Stephen kept studying me all the time."

Jeremy approached Micki. "You're serious about this? My newest friend is also my grandmother? You're too young to be my grandma, but I'll take a hug."

After they separated, Micki said, "Every woman likes to hear that too young to be a grandma line. Yes, it's really true."

Shirley walked over to join in the hugging. "I may have just gained a mother-in-law, but I don't understand how they let you and Stephen marry. He's your half-brother."

Micki said, "Everyone sit down, and I'll tell you the story – everyone except Debbie. She's the detective who cracked this case and the only one I haven't hugged. Come over here granddaughter-in-law."

Debbie reported as ordered for her hug plus a kiss. Then everyone sat to hear Micki's story.

"In response to Shirley's question, a half-brother cannot marry his half-sister in either of our countries. However, when Stephen Hadley walked into North Adams Regional Hospital with Michelle Hadley, who was full-term pregnant and going into labor, they just assumed we were married."

Debbie laughed. "There's that coupling of two Hadleys again!"

"Naturally, we were nervous because there was a twenty-five percent chance that the baby would have genetic weaknesses because we were too closely related. As you suggested, Walter, that's why Stephen monitored your health closely as you grew older. We couldn't be certain your birth health would continue. When it came time to fill out the birth papers, I used my middle name, Celia."

Debbie said, "That was another one of my clues. Early in our study of the family tree, Jeremy said his grandmother's name was Celia. Only after we arrived in this country and checked the records, did I learn that Great-grandfather Michael had married Alice Hadley. I quickly realized that Celia is an anagram for Alice. Michelle Celia Hadley had been named after both of her parents. Also, Micki's mythical husband, Bert Banyon, took his first name from Stephen's middle name, Albert."

Micki became serious. "I have to give a heartfelt apology especially to Walter, but also to the rest of you, for disappearing out of my son's life. I didn't want Walter to grow up regarded as a freak because he was the product of the love between two half-siblings. That would have been a tremendous stigma for him to carry all these years. Instead, I became an immature mother who couldn't handle the responsibility of raising her child. It's a much more socially acceptable story."

Walter walked over to the sofa, hugged Micki, and sat next to her. "It may take a while to get used to newly discovered relationships but, Mother, I think I could have taken the flak at school and from others."

"You say that now, but children can be quite cruel, as can neighbors and even relatives. We knew that we had crossed society's line in the sand when it came to having you. We loved each other enough to disregard taboos, but we didn't want you to bear the burden of our sins. All that close monitoring of your health and behavior by Stephen prepared him for creating letters and reports to me. I still have drawers full of those documents, and you're welcome to read them. I want you to know that I didn't abandon you, but rather physically distanced myself, keeping in contact with the events in your life through your father. Several of the presents Stephen gave you along the way actually came from me, for instance that huge Teddy bear you had when you were young, the Shetland wool sweaters, and the deerstalker hat you wore in that high school play when you were Sherlock Holmes."

"I remember those things. At the time, I wondered when Dad bought them. He didn't go to shopping centers very often."

Jeremy asked, "What did the rest of the family think about you two having a baby together?"

"They didn't think anything, because they didn't know about it. Stephen left home at the age of sixteen because he felt that he had been a convenient accessory to a false family. Once he learned that Stephanie married Michael to enhance his background for the *New York Times* editorial position, Stephen decided that he didn't have a family that actually wanted him. Couple that situation with Thomas moving in to take over Stephanie's marriage without even consulting Michael, and you can see why Stephen wanted no part of the Hadley clan."

Walter nodded in affirmation. "That explains why he wouldn't tell me anything about his parents or the rest of the family."

"He wouldn't tell you because of his anger and because you were our secret, kept hidden from the rest of the family. Stephen stayed in America to raise you, while I went back to England and continued with clan Hadley as though nothing had happened between Stephen and me. I didn't tell you the whole truth earlier, Walter. I returned home so that you would be able to live a normal life, but I also hid you from the rest of the Hadleys so that my life would be normal too. I was partly motivated by selfishness, which I regret."

Debbie said, "Stephen felt no such concern, Micki, because he had essentially disowned the British branch of the Hadley family. He had become the patriarch of the American Hadleys."

"That's true, Debbie, except that even now I don't understand Stephen's relationship with Stephanie. She was a native-born American and she stood by Stephen through two versions of her marriage. Despite that, it's clear that she was much closer to Thomas than to her son Stephen."

Shirley said, "I'm looking at the family tree from the greatest distance, because I'm in the family by marriage, and I haven't been delving into relationships as Debbie has. My perspective from this point of relative distance is that Stephanie looked on her time with Michael as a premarital affair, even though it spawned Stephen. In her eyes, her true marriage would have been the one with Thomas."

Micki nodded. "I agree with you, Shirley. Once the war ended, Thomas and Stephanie became a true couple, being completely satisfied with each other. That's why both of them were quite willing to send Stephen to boarding school. They wanted someone else to finish raising him. They needed only each other, and they didn't want any child to distract them.

"I think I've now laid all of my hidden cards on the table. Does anyone have any remaining questions? If not, I need a Guinness after all of that talking. I will say that you've opened Pandora's Box, and now you're stuck with me as mother, grandmother, and all of the other convoluted relationships of this Hadley family for the rest of my life, and I'm planning on that being a very long time."

Jeremy said, "One final comment before I grab a bottle of ale from Grandma's supply ... Dad, you no longer have to worry about not having Hadley blood in your veins because of Michael being an impostor. Alice was pure Hadley, and you are her grandson."

CHAPTER 79 – STEPHEN AND MICKI

The next morning, the whole group again went to visit Stephen at the September Assisted Living residence. Stephen had barely returned from breakfast when he heard a knock on his door. He opened the door to see a bunch of smiling faces gathered behind the staff guide.

"What's going on, people? Didn't you get enough of me the other day? Micki, are you up to one of your pranks?"

"It's time to let the whole family in, literally and figuratively. I confessed everything last evening, so welcome your son and your grandson plus their wives."

"You are all most welcome. Come on in. I find it hard to believe that this taciturn farmer and detective actually bared her soul." Stephen walked over to Micki and kissed her in a decidedly non-brotherly way.

Micki disengaged herself from Stephen's embrace. "I had no choice. Our granddaughter-in-law, Debbie figured it all out. She put me in a position where I could either admit the truth or turn my life into one big lie. I feel relieved to have everything out in the open and to have a complete family again."

Stephen said, "Micki, you always had me, even if you did mislabel our relationship. Walter, and all the rest of you, let's make with some hugs. Pardon me if I'm slow on keeping the names straight, but I'll get it right eventually. You're all important to me."

Many hugs and kisses later, Walter said, "You know, Mother and Dad, you're welcome to come and live near us now that we've reassembled the family. At the minimum, come for a long visit."

Micki said, "Long visits are a fine idea. We're too blended into the English countryside to consider a permanent shift at our age. We'll have to take turns. You've visited us and changed our outlooks. Next year, we'll try to get back to our other country. We do both have dual citizenship, and we need periodic injections of the American spirit. However, before we end this gathering, we should remember that this trip was supposed to be a honeymoon for Jeremy and Debbie. To be sure that they're not cheated out of that, we'll put the two of them on a train later today bound for our cottage in Ballantrae, Scotland. Jeremy and Debbie, stay there as long as you like, and bill your expenses to my accounts with the local shops. Call it a wedding present from your grandparents. While you're gone, Stephen and I will spend quality time with Walter and Shirley. This family has a lot of catching up to do."

Jeremy and Debbie looked at each other and nodded. They chorused, "Thank you Grandma!" Then the kisses and hugs started all over again.

CHAPTER 80 – HOMECOMING

When Walter, Shirley, Jeremy, and Debbie Hadley exited the customs area at Chicago O'Hare Terminal 5, they encountered a reception committee. Irma and Arthur Blake held one end of a long banner stretched between two poles, while Penny and Joe Gonzalez anchored the other end. The banner read, *Welcome Home, Hadleys,* in dark blue letters on a white background. When the Hadleys approached the sign-bearers, Irma let Arthur take sole possession of their sign pole and moved forward to greet them.

"Welcome home; we were afraid you'd decide to reside in England."

Walter said, "That would have been tempting, but we're loyal Americans. I also was afraid I'd lose you as a friend if I left you managing the bakery much longer."

"Don't worry about that. I've enjoyed the retail experience. The rest of our group has appreciated having day-old pastries delivered to them. I told them they'd have to work off the extra calories by carrying signs and luggage. Did you have a good flight?"

Shirley said, "We did, and now that I've crossed the Atlantic both ways, I feel very cosmopolitan. I won't spring any surprises now, but you're going to be amazed at the results and events of our trip."

Walter said, "Thanks so much for coming to collect us. If we had parked in the lot for this length of time, we would have to remortgage our house to pay the charges."

"Did the honeymooners get any time off by themselves?"

"They did indeed, some of it in a quite romantic way, but that's part of our dog and pony show that we'll present for you once our biological clocks match local time. Let's schedule our trip summary session to be at our house tomorrow evening at seven o'clock."

The following evening, when the Blakes and the Gonzalezes arrived at Walter and Shirley's house, they found the living room rearranged to face a chalkboard on a stand. Small tables in the front hallway bore desserts and drinks. Jeremy took their coats and put them out of the way in the guest room.

As usual, Arthur Blake filled a mug with black coffee before heading for the living room. The others decided to wait until there was a pause in the presentation before taking drinks or goodies.

Once everyone found a comfortable seat, Shirley Hadley went forward to act as master of ceremonies for the evening.

"Welcome to you all, and thank you for the many assistances you gave our Sandley Agency detectives and us to bring us to this point. Most of you are here to learn about our travels and the revised version of the Hadley family tree. We will talk about those things, but first, Walter will pass out glasses of champagne so that we may offer toasts to our honeymooners, Jeremy and Debbie.... I'll start by saying that I've always loved you, Jeremy, but it's great to have a beautiful and talented daughter too. Welcome to our family, Debbie. Everyone will soon know how much you've added to our clan already."

Walter raised his glass toward the young couple. "I'll second Shirley's enthusiasm, and I'll highlight my pride in you both. You're resourceful, prepared for any challenge, and you look good together too."

Penny said, "I'll speak for the Gonzalez clan ..."

Joe interrupted. "She usually does."

Everyone laughed and then Penny continued, "We had some minor experiences working with Jeremy in the past, but the challenges of researching the impostor in the Hadley family tree brought us into a closer working relationship with Jeremy and a deep appreciation of Debbie's talents. Your Sandley Agency is an outstanding success, and we look forward to working with you again."

Irma raised her glass on behalf of the Blakes. "We enjoyed working with Jeremy within the context of our old ABC Consultants company, and we saw your capabilities during our investigation of events at the Parkville Rehabilitation Home. Now you have successfully soloed in pursuing an investigation on two continents while we were away on vacation. I'm sure that Arthur will join me in wishing you continued success and in promising to go off for another vacation whenever you wish to solo again. Congratulations to both of you."

Debbie and Jeremy walked to the front of the room, gave slight bows, and applauded their audience.

Jeremy said, "We're very impressed and honored by your enthusiasm for us and our marriage. We'll remind you of it in the future when we run into problems during an investigation. However, our family tree investigation has been successful beyond any reasonable expectation. Most of the credit belongs to Debbie, our research ace with great assistance from Penny and Joe Gonzalez. I'll yield the floor to my wife and our newest Hadley, Debbie."

"Thank you all for coming. When I first studied the Hadley family tree and discovered that a 1914 baby who lived only one day had been replaced by someone else, I had little hope of learning much about that person. Today, I stand before you barely believing how much we have learned. We started out assuming the impostor would have been someone evil and fraudulent. Today, we know a great deal about him and regard him with pride in his contributions to the family and to Western Democracy."

Debbie proceeded to chronicle the events of Michael's life, all the way from pretending to have Oxford credentials in order to impress a girl at a party, through his playing a major role in convincing the American public to support entry of the US into World War II, his activities during the war, and his marriages, first to Stephanie Wright and then to Alice Hadley. She did her best to underscore the romance between Michael and Alice and to describe the family tree complications introduced by Thomas Hadley.

"We had limitations to the facts we could learn from documents and statistical records, so we decided to move up the date of our marriage and combine our honeymoon with research on location in England. In case you hadn't realized it, I was quite happy to take Jeremy as my husband as soon as possible, so I heartily endorsed this approach. Once we arrived in England, we quickly confirmed the old adage that the best intelligence is achieved when you have humans on-site. We walked in the shoes of Michael Farrell Hadley, so-to-speak, and learned through an individual calling herself Micki Banyon that Walter's father, Stephen, long thought to have died, was alive and in an assisted living facility. That's when we called home and asked Walter and Shirley to fly over to join us. The reunion with Stephen was perfect for all of us. The biggest surprise ..."

Walter said, "If you don't mind, Debbie, I'll take it from here."

Debbie nodded and sat down.

"Our new daughter-in-law amazes me sometimes. One afternoon she spoke abruptly and rudely to our host, Micki Banyon, and Micki didn't mind it at all. We had a follow-up session where Debbie accused Micki of not being the person she appeared to be, and after some give-and-take on both sides, Micki dropped her mask. I want everyone to understand that this trip was special and very meaningful for me. I found my father whom I thought had died long ago, and in Micki, I found my mother too. Debbie will use the chalkboard to draw up all of the tangles in our family tree, but the crux of it is that my father, Stephen Hadley, and my mother, Michelle Celia Hadley are half-siblings who fell in love with each other. I'm the product of that love, and now my aunt is also my mother, while my father is also my uncle; Jeremy's great-aunt is his grandmother, while his grandfather is also his great-uncle; and I have Hadley blood in my veins even though my grandfather was an impostor who took the place of a stillborn infant. That last fact is true because Michael Farrell Hadley married Alice Hadley who gave birth to my newly rediscovered mother, Michelle Hadley. Our family tree is really a bramble bush, and I'll tell you right now, I've never been prouder of anything than to be a part of it."

CHAPTER 81 – ARTHUR AND JOE

The two men sat on the porch of the old Queen Anne style house enjoying the warm March sunshine. Irma and Penny had taken advantage of the mild weather to go on a major shopping outing, leaving their husbands to pass the time doing whatever men do when their wives aren't there to pep up the conversation. The serious nature of the two men's conversation contrasted with their continuous passing back and forth of a soft orange foam football while they talked.

Arthur stretched toward his right to grab Joe's slightly errant projectile. "I've been meaning to ask you what you thought about that celebration at Walter and Shirley's house after the Hadleys returned from England."

"They were all enthusiastic about finding missing members of their family alive and, for the most part, well. Why do you ask? I thought it was one of the better gatherings I've attended. I enjoy seeing people celebrate."

"Do you think they learned the whole story concerning Michael Farrell Hadley?"

"They may have failed to learn a few facts, but they found enough material to make that gentleman a major legend in their family history. They'll be telling children about him for several additional generations."

"Debbie appears to be a very thorough researcher. Do you think she covered all the bases during her efforts?"

"I think I see where you're going. You think she found some additional information but edited it out of the material she shared with the rest of the family. Do you think she found it herself, or did she get the missing nugget from Micki Hadley?"

"Based on your telling me about Debbie's early linking of Michael to Winston Churchill, I'll bet she found it on her own."

"Arthur, you do realize we're talking circles around each other, like two boxers feinting punches as they try to determine the opponent's strengths and weaknesses. Tell me where you see hidden aspects of Michael's life."

"I think you know, but I'll get to the point. Debbie neglected or skimmed over some passport usage."

"Maybe she skipped it because she had no knowledge of what happened."

"You're having fun countering my observations, aren't you, Joe?"

"Call it a combination of having fun and being cautious about discussing something that should remain unmentioned."

"Fair enough; I can be oblique rather than direct in my approach to it. Do you happen to remember the dates covered by Michael Farrell Hadley's passport usage on his trip to Argentina?"

"Off the top of my head, I'd speculate that he went there sometime in 1953."

"Do you know when during that year he traveled there?"

"It may have been April, for a spring vacation."

"Joe, you either have some knowledge or you're quite good at speculating. Any suggestions as to whether Michael would have gone alone or with others?"

"I wouldn't know, but I'd guess that he met a few other travelers there, along with some local folks."

"You just happen to remember that specific timing and the possible involvement of other people? I won't comment on the vacation speculation. I find that travel record interesting because it meshes with something I found online, on *Wikipedia*." Arthur removed a piece of paper from his shirt pocket and read it aloud. "*On 15 April*

1953, a terrorist group (never identified) detonated two bombs in a public rally at Plaza de Mayo, killing 7 and injuring 95. The article went on to say that Juan Peron told the crowd to take revenge on the group he suspected to be behind the bombing. During the resulting chaos, buildings were burned and many additional civilians were killed. I've done some snooping through several of my sources, and I discovered something interesting. Peron opened Argentina's borders after the war to thousands of Nazis who wanted to avoid prosecution or reprisals."

"That's common knowledge."

"What's not common knowledge is that nine key Nazis hiding in Argentina just happened to have died that day during the rioting that followed the political rally explosions. There was never any proof that their deaths were anything other than coincidental."

"They must have been interested in the speakers at that rally, Arthur."

"You're probably right; we should let them rest in whatever chamber of Hell they occupy. I thought I'd mention these miscellaneous facts confidentially in order to avoid anyone thinking our collective group missed something."

"That's fine, so long as we don't spread unproven rumors to anyone, especially the Hadleys. Their legend of Michael Farrell Hadley should remain unblemished. It's the old adage about the three monkeys: See no evil. Hear no evil. Speak no evil."

"Your comments and reaction confirm my other speculation about Michael and his trip to Argentina."

"What do they confirm?"

"There was a reason for his using his American passport, rather than his British version."

- END –

ACKNOWLEDGEMENTS

Many thanks to Brenda Rossini for reviewing the sections set in England and/or involving British natives for use of wording appropriate to the UK version of the English language. I originally planned to vary my spellings to alternately match American and British locations and speakers, but I decided that would be unsettling for my readers and settled for American English spellings throughout the novel.

Thanks to Dwight Jon Zimmerman and the Defense Media Network for drawing my attention to Edna St. Vincent Millay's poem, excerpts of which I quoted herein: *There Are No Islands, Any More*
Lines Written in Passion and in Deep Concern for England, France and My Own Country.

I drew upon many sources, printed and internet, for the factoids that populate the historical background information in this book. I believe them all to be accurate, but should you find a background event not quite factual, please remember that this is a work of fiction, created for your entertainment, but with the hope that it will have educational value as well.

I suggest that you discuss genealogical quirks in your own family history with friends and relatives. You may encounter surprises.

Richard Davidson

ABOUT THE AUTHOR

Richard Davidson is the author of the self-help guidebook: *DECISION TIME! Better Decisions for a Better Life*. He has written the five-novel Lord's Prayer Mystery Series: *Lead Us Not into Temptation*, *Give Us this Day our Daily Bread*, *Forgive Us Our Trespasses*, *Thy Will Be Done*, and *Deliver Us from Evil*. He has edited an anthology, *Overcoming: An Anthology by the Writers of* OCWW. His latest three novels, *Implications*, *Impulses*, and *Impostor*, from his new series, the Imp Mysteries, continue to chronicle the exploits of Arthur Blake and the investigative associates who aided him in the earlier mystery series, taking their interests in new directions. Mr. Davidson is Past President of Off-Campus Writers' Workshop, the oldest ongoing group of its kind in the U.S. and is the founder of the ReadWorthy Books Book Review Blog. He is the founder of the Independent Mystery Publishing Society (IMPS). Mr. Davidson is a Certified Lay Servant Speaker and a former Lay Leader in the United Methodist Church. He is also an aeronautical & astronautical engineer and a businessman.

WORKS BY THIS AUTHOR
NONFICTION:

DECISION TIME! Better Decisions for a Better Life,

VBW Publishing, Inc.

ISBN 978-1-60264-063-4 (paperback)

ISBN 978-1-60264-064-1 (hard cover)

RADMAR Publishing

ISBN 978-0-9829160-7-0 (2nd edition paperback)

ISBN 978-1-4581-8395-8 (Smashwords eBook)

ASIN B0052GOZEO (Kindle Edition eBook)

Where you are in life today is the result of all of the past decisions you have made or which have been made for you in response to the various situations and events that have impacted your life. The decisions that you will make from this point forward will determine the degree to which your future will be positive or negative. *DECISION TIME!* gives you insight into the subjective decision-making process as applied to both small and large choices you will face. It includes dynamic aspects, cultural effects, and morality as applied to decision-making for individuals, teams, corporations, and societies. *DECISION TIME!* prepares you to face the continuous impacts of decision situations confidently and without hesitation.

Richard Davidson

FICTION:

Lead Us Not into Temptation (The Lord's Prayer Mystery Series, Volume I),

VBW Publishing, Inc.

ISBN 978-1-60264-407-6 (paperback)

RADMAR Publishing

ISBN 978-0-9976381-0-3 (2nd edition paperback)

ISBN 978-1-4581-7381-2 (Smashwords eBook)

ASIN B0052MGI6Q (Kindle Edition eBook)

Arthur Blake, former NASA engineer turned minister, receives an emergency appointment to be pastor of the United Methodist Church in Parkville, a distant suburb of Chicago, following the bizarre sudden death of the church's unusual former pastor. Pastor Blake's attempts to unravel the mystery that shrouds his predecessor become involved with tracking the child of a possibly bigamous soldier in World War II England, art and jewelry treasures plundered by the Nazis and their sympathizers, and the eventual results of childhood sibling conflicts in combined families. Arthur's allies in his investigation include Parkville Police Chief Bobby Andrews, County Medical Examiner Irma Custis, and the married team of Penny and Joe Gonzalez who work for a clandestine government agency. During the course of *Lead Us Not into*

Impostor

Temptation, the reader discovers how seemingly minor historical events lead to major present-day dislocations in church, village, and family relationships.

Richard Davidson

Give Us this Day Our Daily Bread (The Lord's Prayer Mystery Series, Volume II)

RADMAR Publishing

ISBN 978-0-9829160-0-1 (paperback)

ISBN 978-0-9829160-5-6 (2nd edition paperback)

ISBN 978-1-4580-6717-3 (Smashwords eBook)

ASIN B0052MQI66 (Kindle Edition eBook)

Arthur Blake, Pastor of Parkville United Methodist Church, has to deal with the aftereffects of a traumatic communion incident. He works to assist the authorities in investigating the cause while doing his best to convince members of his congregation that it is safe to return to church. Working with the police and federal agencies, he discovers that the terror of the initial event is minor compared with the potential chaotic impact of future disasters being planned by the perpetrator. The investigation is interwoven with several relationship situations that affect the final outcome.

Impostor

Forgive Us Our Trespasses (The Lord's Prayer Mystery Series, Volume III)

RADMAR Publishing

ISBN 978-0-9829160-1-8 (paperback)

ISBN 978-1-4657-3739-7 (Smashwords eBook)

ASIN B005SULQ6Y (Kindle Edition eBook)

Arthur Blake, Pastor of Parkville United Methodist Church, tries to assist his father to resolve his trauma after learning that his best friend, recently killed in a car accident, may have been an imposter with a heinous background. The investigation reveals that the presumed accident was but one link in a chain of murders. Blake works to determine the true identity of his father's friend, while also discovering the man's past activities and affiliations. Arthur works to solve the murders in conjunction with his colleagues at ABC Consultants. He also draws on assistance from associates at a covert government agency with which he has worked before. The coordinated effort to solve the puzzle examines incidents that span the period between World War II and the present in order to defuse the personal, national, and international dangers resulting from them.

Richard Davidson

Thy Will Be Done (The Lord's Prayer Mystery Series, Volume IV)

RADMAR Publishing

ISBN 978-0-9829160-2-5 (paperback)

ISBN 978-1-3013-4293-8 (Smashwords eBook)

ASIN B009JU6EZM (Kindle Edition eBook)

The sudden death of a young woman attending Parkville United Methodist Church infuriates her brother and leads to congregational outrage over his outburst and subsequent murder. The investigation of that slaying by Pastor Arthur Blake and his associates leads to revelations of a previously undetected criminal organization operating in the area. Unraveling the mystery and scope of this group entangles Arthur and his associated investigators in a web of conspiracies extending from Illinois to both U.S. coasts and through Mexico to Guatemala.

Impostor

Deliver Us from Evil (The Lord's Prayer Mystery Series, Volume V)

RADMAR Publishing

ISBN 978-0-9829160-3-2 (paperback)

ASIN B00EBDUXFY (Kindle Edition eBook)

Arthur and Irma's wedding day has finally arrived, but an unexpected interruption leads to their need to investigate a possible murder committed by someone close to them. With the aid of friends and federal agents Penny and Joe Gonzalez, they follow a series of clues, crisscrossing the United States to learn more about the murder, related subsequent events, and the significance of a rare object brought home by a veteran of the Iraq War. A second murder close to Pastor Arthur Blake's church involves them in a new investigation, assisting Parkville Police Chief Bobby Andrews. Are these murders and the tracking of that strange object connected? Will marriage deteriorate or improve the relationship between Arthur and Irma? Character flaws in many relationships color the outcome.

Richard Davidson

Overcoming: An Anthology by the Writers of OCWW

Edited and with an Introduction by Richard Davidson

RADMAR Publishing

ISBN 978-9829160-4-9 (paperback)

ASIN B00E80NN4I (Kindle Edition eBook)

This anthology covers many aspects of overcoming life's problems, obstacles, and challenging developments. The contributing writers have used fiction, non-fiction, memoir, poetry, historical chronicle, and drama to highlight our continuing need to overcome our problems, rather than dwell on them. The reader will learn from many talented writers the skills needed to respond constructively, energetically, and sometimes humorously to whatever obstacle bars one's path. Apply their lessons to your own needs and to those of others you cherish.

Impostor

Implications: An Arthur Blake Mystery Novel (Imp Mysteries, Volume 1)

RADMAR Publishing

ISBN 978-0-9829160-6-3 (paperback)

ASIN B00LY9IBWK (Kindle Edition eBook)

Bishop Howard Chandler has assigned Pastor Arthur Blake to investigate the burning of a church in the small city of Amboy, Illinois. He learns from that church's pastor that she had to overcome past improprieties by former members. During the investigation of the fire's cause, Arthur and the other state fire investigators uncover disturbing aspects of the ninety-year-old church's design and history. Arthur calls on his federal associates for assistance, as the investigation of a local church fire expands to seeking solutions to related crimes occurring from the present to recent years and back to the Prohibition Era. Progress in the investigation intertwines with new developments in Arthur's family life.

Richard Davidson

Impulses: An Arthur Blake Mystery Novel (Imp Mysteries, Volume 2)

RADMAR Publishing

ISBN 978-0-9829160-8-7 (paperback)

ASIN B012LFQXYI (Kindle Edition eBook)

Several disturbing dreams cause Arthur Blake to wonder whether he is trying to do too much for the many people who seek his services. These qualms are complicated by Bishop Howard Chandler's suggestion that Arthur temporarily set aside his official duties and take an extended sabbatical leave. His resulting internal debates about career moves are set aside when the pastor who replaced him at the Parkville church dies in an apparent suicide possibly linked to several deaths at the Parkville Rehabilitation Home. The bishop assigns Arthur to determine the circumstances behind the new pastor's death, while Arthur and Irma, his wife and constant investigative partner, also study a mysterious shipment at his father's antiques shop. The sudden disappearance of a young associate provides another mystery and leads to questions of life after death and reincarnation. Events that initially appear simple become increasingly complex as the true natures of many people come into question.

Impostor

Impostor: A Genealogical Mystery (Imp Mysteries, Volume 3)

RADMAR Publishing

ISBN 978-0-9829160-9-4

When Debbie Danforth discovers a flaw in the genealogy of her live-in boyfriend, Jeremy Hadley, he and his family try to discredit her findings, but eventually admit they must be true. Jeremy and Debbie run a private detective business, the Sandley Agency and commit their skills and resources to learning about the impostor Debbie has discovered in the Hadley ancestry. They are assisted in this effort by Penny and Joe Gonzalez, principals in a covert federal agency, with whom Jeremy has previously worked as a consultant. Their joint investigation uncovers both unique details concerning the mysterious Hadley impostor and little-known facts about events leading up to World War II in both Britain and the United States. Was the person who masqueraded as a Hadley a villain or a hero? Did other Hadleys know he was a fraudulent member of their family? Did his actions assist or impede the British and the Americans as they faced the growing menace in prewar Europe?

Richard Davidson

Learn more about the writings, humor, and random thoughts of Richard Davidson at: radmarinc.com davidsonbookshelf.com betterlifedecisions.blogspot.com and at the Independent Mystery Publishing Society (IMPS) https://www.mysteryimps.com

Richard Davidson's author page on Amazon is located at https://www.amazon.com/author/richarddavidson Follow and *Like* Richard Davidson, Author on Facebook at https://www.facebook.com/richarddavidsonauthor?ref=hl Follow him on Twitter @mysteryimp